FITZ OF RAGE

ANDREW NANCE
AND SCOTT ABRAMS

Fitz of Rage
Red Adept Publishing, LLC
104 Bugenfield Court
Garner, NC 27529
https://RedAdeptPublishing.com/

---

1.   http://StreetlightGraphics.com

Scott would like to dedicate this book to Tara, for facing what rages within us all.

Andrew would like to dedicate this book to Grimm, for your talent, humor, and especially for all the wild adventures of creativity we've undertaken.

Chapter 1

He threw a mean punch. He always could, and now he was kneeling over me, all blond and manly and with skin sun-baked as brown as a palmetto bug. Knees on either side of my chest, he pulled back an arm to launch another fist missile. Even so, I couldn't stop laughing. I always cracked up when Rick's emotions took over. I'd seen it plenty of times when we were friends, though rarely aimed my way. However, these past few years since our friendship ended, I was a frequent target. What had once been a brotherly bond had been replaced with fierce loathing, at least on his part. As for me, Rick was still one of my favorite people, even if he was about to lower the boom again. Before that could happen, two arms in a long-sleeved white shirt whipped under his armpits, locked him in a full nelson, and pulled him off. The crowd encircling us groaned in disappointment.

"You two should be embarrassed. You're both in your forties, but here you are, fighting like a couple of hormonal teenagers," the man holding Rick said.

I pushed up into a sitting position on the dock. "Hey there, Eddie. What brings you here?"

"Shut up, Fitz. I'm saving your ass," Eddie said. The tall Black man turned his attention to my assailant. "Calm down, Rick."

Rick struggled against the tall detective's grasp, but as strong as he was, Eddie was stronger.

In basso tones, Eddie said softly, "You know better than this. Fitz isn't worth it."

"I don't need your help," I told Eddie. "I had it under control." That would've sounded more convincing if everyone gathered around hadn't laughed. "But the cop is right, Rick. I'm not worth it."

Rick Forester was captain and owner of a forty-three-foot Chesapeake-style charter boat, *Titanic II*. His grandfather had named it, reasoning that the odds were long that two ships with that name would sink. Rick and I had been best friends ever since we were kids. Back then, Rick's dad called us Tweedle Dumb and Tweedle Dumbass. The cause of our friendship's demise was well-known. Let's just say that when it came to a good-looking woman, I was about as trustworthy as a pickpocket in a pants factory.

"Say it again, you bastard, and I'll kill you!" Rick shouted.

"Come on, buddy." I picked up my sunglasses, grateful they were still in one piece. I stood and slipped them on. "The cops are here. The fight's over. Besides"—I touched my tender chin—"you got a good one in."

I bent down to pick up a notebook that had fallen from one of the pockets of my cargo shorts. It contained all the words for the wedding service I'd just conducted as a Universal Life Church minister. Not forty-five minutes earlier, down by the water, I'd proclaimed fifty-one-year-old wealthy widow Wynona Hightower and her thirty-three-year-old heartthrob, Matt Byers, cougar and cub. It had been a beautiful ceremony on the banks of the Intracoastal Waterway. Rick, still touchy on the subject of marriages, had shown up shortly after.

"That's right," Eddie said, "it's all finished."

Rick stopped struggling, breathing like a bear. The onlookers started to walk away.

"You done, Rick?" Eddie asked.

Rick nodded and looked down. "I'm done."

"You sure?" Eddie asked.

"I'm done."

"Okay," Eddie said and released him.

I grinned at Rick and held out a hand to shake. Rick's fist shot out and connected to my head above my left ear, which sent my sunglasses skittering down the dock. He'd hit me in a sturdy part of the skull, and I had a hard head, but the impact rang my bell. Seriously, I heard a bell. The onlookers cheered and rushed back. I weaved one way and then another, my left eye winking involuntarily.

"You guys hear the birdies?" I asked.

Rick got set for another swing, but Eddie planted a foot on Rick's ass and shoved him off the dock. The spectators broke into laughter as Rick splashed near the bow of his own boat. He resurfaced a few seconds later, sputtering and indignant. A couple of guys helped drag him up onto the dock. The rest of the bystanders headed back to the bar for more booze, offering me high fives as they passed. It didn't matter who'd won the fight as long as it was entertaining.

Though wet, Rick didn't look much calmer. Eddie turned, showing where handcuffs hung from his belt. Rick made a face, spat on the dock, and climbed onto his boat.

I felt the side of my head gingerly. "You could have imposed your authority a little earlier."

"Be glad I don't run you in for what I'm sure you started. What'd you do this time?"

"A couple of days ago, I heard Rick got himself in some trouble, and I offered my assistance."

"That's what started the fight?"

"No, that happened when I told him I was dying to meet his new girlfriend."

"Makes sense," Eddie said. "Seeing as you married his last girlfriend, and that only lasted a hot second."

"Yeah." I took a few steps to retrieve my sunglasses.

"Carrying on your fine tradition of pissing off everyone."

"Yeah, well, friends are overrated." I put on my sunglasses and picked up my vestments from a picnic table. When I first became a minister with the Universal Life Church at an online cost of thirty-nine dollars and ninety-nine cents for the deluxe package, Ivy, my second wife and Rick's old girlfriend, took a bunch of my old Hawaiian shirts and sewed them into a colorful patchwork minister's robe. Believe me—I outshone every bride.

We started up the docks toward Doone's. In the morning, Doone's Fish Camp was a place where fisherman gathered to buy their bait, gear, and beer before heading out in their boats to catch the big ones. By early afternoon, Doone's turned into a popular bar on the river, serving up fish tacos, steamed shrimp, and platters of oysters, along with countless brands of beer and liquor. The clientele was mixed, with students from San Marco University rubbing shoulders with blue-collar and white-collar workers, surfers, fishermen, retirees, and tourists. Doone's had started out as a small shack, but additions of wood and sheet metal were added over the years, as well as several decks shaded by palm trees and gargantuan live oaks, their limbs draped with Spanish moss. The back of Doone's and the decks all faced two docks that could accommodate more than two dozen boats.

"So, what's up?" I asked.

Eddie said, "I'm here on business."

I turned and looked past Rick's boat to where the sun glinted off the Intracoastal Waterway. The river widened, and the current nearly stalled out in the shadow of the Carroll Street Drawbridge, providing a lazy current for the carefree happy-hour traffic jam of pontoons, bass boats, kayaks, canoes, and even inner tubes.

"This business have to do with me?"

"Yeah." Eddie looked me over. "You look like crap."

I glanced down at my faded blue T-shirt, khaki cargo shorts, and sandals. "What's wrong with how I look?"

"Give up shaving?" he asked.

I rubbed the whiskers on one cheek. I'd been pondering a beard. My hair was somewhere between brown and red, and my beard, which I grew on occasion, looked good. "Chicks dig the stubbled look."

"Uh-huh."

A petite tan brunette poured into a tight Doone's T-shirt and cutoff denim shorts met us at the end of the dock, holding a serving tray with a short glass of dark liquid and an open can of Diet Coke beside it.

I handed her a crumpled bill and said, "Thank you, Seri. After that," I motioned with my thumb toward where the fight took place, "I'll take my rum straight." I picked up the glass and took a swallow. "Mmm, buttery."

Seri stepped closer, pressing one of her breasts against my arm. "Anything else you need buttered?"

I smiled. "Is he watching?"

"Like a hawk," Seri whispered, a sexy grin on her lips. "Go ahead and do it."

She turned from me, and I slapped her ass. She giggled as she made her way up to the nearest deck, hips swaying.

Eddie cocked an eyebrow.

"What?" I asked. Eddie shook his head and looked away.

"She's young enough to be your daughter."

"But she's not," I said. "Besides, she's not really into me."

"Looked like it from here."

"Not that it's any of your business, but she asked if she and I could overtly flirt whenever her ex-boyfriend-slash-almost-stalker was here."

I nodded toward a deck filled with a college-age crowd. A tan surfer with long sun-bleached hair was glaring down at me.

"It's working," Eddie said, looking at the surfer. "That is definitely a glower."

Up on the deck, we passed the angry surfer, cut through all the bodies, and went into the bar as the jukebox shifted from Bob Marley's "Get Up, Stand Up" to Merle Haggard's "Okie from Muskogee." Though the back wall of the shack was open, the wood-paneled neon-lit room was gloomy compared to the outside blaze of afternoon sun, and my eyes needed a few moments to adjust. We found an unoccupied high-top table in a corner, and I draped my colorful robe over the back of the stool.

When I sat, Eddie informed me, "We brought in Mack Thorpe this morning, and he's asking for you."

I snorted a laugh and joked, "Who'd he kill?"

Eddie stared at me a moment before answering, "The senator."

I blinked a couple of times. "Really?" I could feel my smile fall by degrees. "That hothead finally killed someone, huh? And the senator too. Wow." Absentmindedly, I used my fingers to comb my hair and winced as I brushed against the tender flesh over my ear. "Back in a sec." I stood, drank the rest of my rum, grabbed my vestments, and made my way through the crowd to the bar. I waved at Skipper Ricci, a retired navy man. Sporting his trademark crew cut–Hawaiian shirt combo, he looked like a drill sergeant on shore leave as he went about his bartender duties.

"Whatcha need, Fitz?" Skipper called, his voice raspy from years of barking orders aboard naval vessels. He owned Doone's and seemed content as happy hour was its usual wall-to-wall party even though summer tourist season had just ended.

"Can you keep this somewhere safe?" I asked, handing him my robe.

"Sure thing." He balled it up and shoved it into the lost-and-found box he kept under the bar.

"I'd also like what the doctor ordered," I said.

He poured me a shot of rum, which I downed with a toss of my head. When I turned, I found myself facing Seri. She stood on tip-toes, grabbed my head, and kissed me like she was drawing venom from a snake bite. She broke the lip-lock with a wet smack, handed me a slip of paper, and vanished into the bustle.

When I got back to the table, Eddie said, "That was some flirt."

"That was the beginning of trouble." I showed Eddie a hastily scribbled phone number. I took another moment to shake off the effect of that kiss. "Let's go see what Mack has to say."

Chapter 2

We'd have left sooner had Eddie not been concerned with my sobriety.

"I'm fine. I can drive," I stated for the third or fourth time.

And for the third or fourth time, he said, "You get behind the wheel of your truck and I'll pull you over and give you a field sobriety test."

I fixed him with a steely gaze as I got in the passenger seat of his sedan. Eddie backed out of his parking space, where a white panel van sat on one side with a chromed-out red Harley-Davidson on the other. As the dark-gray Crown Vic jostled toward the exit, I took in the eclectic collection of vehicles sprawled out from the front porch of Doone's: beat-up pickups, more motorcycles, a couple of restored muscle cars, sports cars, high end, low end, and the inevitable number of Corollas, Camrys, and Civics.

Eddie pulled out onto A1A and accelerated.

Being in the police car took me back, and I admitted, "It's like the good ol' days."

"Not really," Eddie said. "You weren't a belligerent pain in the ass back then."

Surprisingly, his barb stung.

Glancing at me, Eddie seemed to pick up on that and quickly added, "And you never let me drive."

"That was an alpha-partner kinda thing. That and the fact you drove like an old lady." I glanced at the speedometer. "Which you still do."

When Eddie moved from uniform to detective, I had been his senior partner, though we were almost the same age. I taught him countless valuable lessons that helped shape him into an effective detective with the San Marco Police Department. I wouldn't admit it out loud, but he was a damn good detective. Still, I was better. Up until I quit, I had the record for closing the most cases. It was a sad day when yours truly, Detective Awesome First-Class Geronimo Fitzgerald, retired.

"Tell me about Mack offing the senator."

Eddie slowed and made a left turn. "The coach is just a suspect right now."

"Any sign of uncontrollable anger during the commission of the crime?"

"And then some."

"Then Coach Thorpe is guilty."

Eddie said, "It's one thing to know it…"

"And another to prove it," I finished, fighting to keep a smile from my lips.

Eddie looked over and said, "Just one of many wise things you used to throw at me."

I put a foot on the dashboard, claiming my turf like a dog peeing on a hydrant. "So, how'd McGovern die?"

Eddie sighed and said, "He was bound, gagged, and beaten. We won't know what specifically killed him until the coroner is finished."

"Where'd it happen?"

"At his home."

"In Flagler Plantations?"

"No, his beach place."

I snorted. "I read a story in the paper where he called it his beach bungalow. The thing's—what? Six thousand square feet, at least."

"That is a bungalow compared to the McGovern mansion."

"Still, he seemed a decent guy."

"I thought so too," Eddie said.

"How does Mack connect?" I asked.

"A couple of nights ago, there was a fundraising soiree for the senator's big homeless initiative at the San Marco Four Seasons."

"Yeah, I heard about that."

The party had been played up in the news weeks before the event, and the *San Marco Ledger* had been trumpeting the initiative for months. Though I could be dense about a lot, I thought the homeless thing sounded pretty good. Basically, Senator McGovern was trying to lure businesses to his legislative district with promises of huge tax breaks as long as those businesses hired and trained a certain percentage of homeless people. His plan was an expensive undertaking that involved temporary housing, counseling, and training.

Eddie went on, "Congress has been on recess, and the fundraiser was McGovern's last public event before heading back to DC next week. The San Marco gossip hotline was all fired up because a bunch of people saw the coach and senator exchange heated words."

"*Heated words.*" I gazed out the window. "That's a funny term when you think about it."

"Apparently, things were more heated on Mack's side because they say the coach threatened bodily injury, but his wife dragged him out before he started swinging."

"Always knew that temper of his would get him in trouble. And he can hold a grudge."

"Anyway, the senator's body was found this morning. First person we interviewed brought up the fight at the fundraiser, so Lou and I drove over to our old alma mater, San Marco High."

Just to be annoying, I broke into song. "San Marco High, how we love thee. Fore'er the crimson and gold shall fly."

"The school colors are green and orange."

"Really? So, how'd it go in the hallowed halls?"

"Mack smelled like a distillery, and his knuckles were busted up. He says he got in a bar fight at Drew's Northside Hideaway."

"It's a dive," I said. "Go there and you're liable to get in a brawl."

"Says the guy I just pulled from one at Doone's."

"That wasn't a fight. I was just helping Rick blow off steam."

"Right. Anyway, Lou suggested Mack come down to the station and we continue our interview there. He lost his temper, shoved Lou, and tried to storm off."

"Lou didn't like that, did she?" I asked.

Eddie's partner, Lou, was Louise Peters.

"Had cuffs on him in an instant."

"Where is Lou? I'd rather be in her company."

Eddie turned narrowed eyes my way before continuing. "We brought him in on assaulting a police officer and resisting arrest. Funny thing is he doesn't want a lawyer."

"He never was the sharpest bulb in the tool bag."

Eddie looked at me.

"What?" I asked, struggling to keep a smile from my lips. I liked to mix up those sayings, idioms or metaphors or whatever, just to mess with Eddie. I'd misquoted one by mistake years earlier when we were partners, and I saw how it got on his nerves.

"It's just like the old days—you're mixing your..." Eddie stopped and shook his head. "Never mind. All Coach Thorpe is saying is that he didn't kill the senator and he'll only talk to you." Eddie glanced sideways at me. "How well do you know Mack?"

I took off my sunglasses and wiped them with my T-shirt while thinking about it. "About a year and a half ago, I did a job for him."

"Security?"

"Nah. What nine out of ten clients want to know: is my spouse cheating on me?"

Eddie said, "Lots of gossip about Ronnie. Any truth to it?"

"Let's just say that Veronica Thorpe has a healthy sex life."

"Yeah? Who was the guy?"

"A fitness trainer from St. Augustine. I got photos at a sleazy motel, and the pictures showed quite a limber twosome."

Eddie turned off of US 1 onto Constabulary Boulevard, which led into the San Marco Police Department complex. "How'd Mack take it?"

"Like you'd expect. I gave him my report, and by the time I got to the photos, his face had turned purple. Later, I heard that he kicked Ronnie out of the house and was working on a divorce. He caught up with Romeo a couple of weeks later and put him in the hospital."

"I saw he had an assault conviction on his record," Eddie said. "But he didn't do time."

"He's a damn good coach with a winning high school team. That garners some friends in high places."

"They won't help him this time." Eddie parked and looked at me. "None of that explains why he wants to see you."

I got out, Eddie a moment later. Over the car's roof, I said, "As for that, I don't have a clue."

Chapter 3

I would be the first to admit that I wasn't tall, but I felt like a Munchkin extra on the set of *The Wizard of Oz* next to Eddie Schmitt. He'd played basketball in high school and college. I remember one guy we arrested who said he'd considered running but knew he wouldn't be able to outrun a giant. I knew what he meant. I had to work to keep up with his long-legged strides as we weaved through the squad cars filling out the cramped lot behind the ugly gray hulk of a building. Glancing up toward the rear entrance, I spotted a copper mane and a tight skirt. I've always been a sucker when it came to redheads. She had her back to us as she talked to a uniformed officer.

"Who's that?" I asked, pointing.

Eddie looked at her then back at me and smiled. "If you're attracted to her, I think you should introduce yourself, ply her with some of your charm."

"Maybe I will."

Eddie took the wide steps up to the building two at a time. I was tired of trying to keep up with him and trailed at an unhurried pace, looking the woman up and down. She had long, strong calves, a straight back, and a Scarlett Johansson neckline, visible as a warm breeze blew her red hair. I risked a glance back down, shame on me, at what I judged a perfect posterior. When I got beside her, I shifted my gaze to what I was sure would be a face equal to Helen of Troy.

I put on my warmest smile, which quickly twisted into revulsion. "Mattie Castro?" I said in a stunned voice. "I've been ogling the devil's daughter."

"Knock it off, dumbass," the woman told me.

I turned to Eddie and saw him fighting not to laugh. I shook my head. "'Why don't you introduce yourself, ply her with your charm.'" I mimed laughing. "Ha, ha. Yuk it up, Eddie."

The redhead rolled her eyes then softened her tone. "Hi, Eddie. How's the family?"

"Doing good, Mattie. Little Ed is almost as big as me and playing football at San Marco Middle."

"Little Ed is in middle school?" I asked, amazed. "Last I saw him, he was crawling around in diapers."

"Yeah, well, time flies when you have a chip on your shoulder," Eddie said.

Instead of acknowledging what he said, I stepped close to Mattie and peered at her head. "What the hell are you doing, Fitz?" Eddie asked.

"I wanna see it when her hair turns into snakes."

"Fitz..." Eddie said.

"It's okay, Eddie. Let him go on. What more can you expect from a man who installs smoke detectors for a living?" Mattie said, looking at me from head to toe.

"Smoke detectors?" I crossed the personal-boundary border and got in her face. "Lady, I am a consultant for Buddy Reid Security Systems." I put up a hand and counted on my fingers. "And not only a consultant, but I'm also a wedding minister, a licensed private eye in the state of Florida, and if the consumption of good rum was an Olympic event, I'd proudly represent our great nation."

"Oh, I stand corrected," Mattie said. "What more can you expect from a drunken alarm-installing clergyman who pretends he's Sam Spade?"

Switching tactics, I took a jab at her employer, the *San Marco Ledger*. "My feelings would be hurt if those words weren't coming from the star reporter of the *Mullet Wrapper*."

"Why are you even here?" Mattie held up a finger and feigned discovery. "Oh, I know. You're here to renew your license to be a private dick..." She paused for two beats and ended with "...head."

The uniform she'd been talking to laughed.

"Hey"—I stepped up to the cop and poked him in the chest—"don't you have some policing to do?"

His smile fell, and he stepped close enough that I could smell Juicy Fruit on his breath.

"Or not."

The cop shook his head, bade farewell to Mattie, and walked into the station.

"Maybe you're here because the police department is installing a new fire alarm," Mattie said.

"It's not that kind of security company," I said, wishing I didn't sound like I was whining.

"Mack's waiting for you, Fitz," Eddie said.

Mattie's posture stiffened, and the blue in her eyes seemed to intensify as she focused on me.

"What? I got something in my teeth?" I asked.

"Why are you meeting with Coach Thorpe? Are you helping the police with the senator's murder?" She turned to Eddie. "Detective, do you have evidence that ties the coach to the crime? Was it a case of sadomasochism that got out of hand?" Turning back to me, she fired more questions. "Why are you here? Do you have information pertinent to this case?" A small voice recorder materialized, and Mattie held it close to my mouth.

"Whoa! Back off." I pushed the device away.

"Detective Schmitt," Mattie said, "I saw the crime scene. Do you know who the senator was involved with?"

She saw the what? "You were at the crime scene?"

Eddie sighed. "She was at the crime scene. I know—it's not exactly by the book."

"That's hitting the nail out of the ballpark."

"There you go, doing it again," Eddie said.

"Doing what?" I put on an innocent expression to match my tone.

"Those little sayings." He pointed at me. "You keep mixing those up."

"Eddie, I don't have a clue what you're talking about," I said then asked Mattie, "How the hell did you get into the crime scene?"

"I not only got into the crime scene, I found the body," Mattie said. "Talk about an exclusive first look."

Eddie's phone rang, and he checked the caller ID. "It's Lou." He stepped away to talk.

Mattie looked around conspiratorially, grabbed my arm, and pulled me farther from Eddie. She whispered, "If you're here to help the police, how about an exclusive?"

I yanked free and brushed my arm, hoping to dislodge her cooties. "How... Why... What were you doing at the crime scene?"

"We didn't know it was a crime scene."

"We?"

"I was there for the *San Marco Ledger*. Also there, representatives for the *St. Augustine Record*, the *Jacksonville Times Union*, the *Daytona Beach Journal*, and two TV crews. There were a couple of guys with a catering truck as well."

"And all of you found the senator's body?" I had a hard time grasping that. In my tenure as a homicide detective, I thought every murder victim was important, as was every violent-crime scene. I could only imagine how badly they'd contaminated that one. And while I firmly believed every victim and their families deserved justice, plenty of people would think Mitch McGovern deserved justice even more. Rich as hell, the senator's family had settled in San Marco during the eighteenth-century British period and had been major players ever since. "How did a group of reporters find the senator's body?"

"A press conference," Mattie said.

"Eddie said it happened at the senator's beach home," I said.

"Right. He invited us to breakfast to talk about his homeless initiative. No one answered the door, so we waited fifteen minutes, and then I tried the door, and we went in."

"The door was unlocked?"

"Yeah. The producer for *Good Morning San Marco* and I went upstairs and found the honorable senator all fifty shades of dead."

In finding the body, Mattie had learned something that Eddie had yet to fill me in on.

"Eddie said McGovern had been bound and gagged, but this wasn't your ordinary binding and gagging, was it?"

"There's an ordinary binding and gagging?" Mattie asked.

"You know what I mean," I said. When Mattie stepped back and grinned, I cursed myself for thinking how pretty that smile was. "Well, what'd you find?"

She shook her head and sang, "I know something you don't know."

"Come on, Mattie."

"I'd tell you, but it'd inflame your famously testosterone-fueled horniness, and I'd have to suffer your lame attempts at seduction."

"Mattie Castro, if I ever so much as laid a finger on you, I would cut that finger off in shame."

Eddie ended his call and returned in time to hear my last comment. "Good lord, Fitz. I save you from one fight, and here you are, trying to get your ass kicked again."

"By a girl," Mattie pointed out.

I started to reply but shook my head before saying to Eddie, "Tell me about the crime scene."

Though she wouldn't tell me before, Mattie launched in. "The master bedroom was upstairs, and he had a sex room on the other side of a hidden doorway, a built-in bookcase door."

"A sex room?" I asked.

"Oh yeah. With a big ol' California king four-poster bed and pornographic artwork on the walls. A giant flat-screen TV for his porn library. He had an oversized wardrobe filled with lingerie, leather wear, rubber costumes, restraining tools, phallic devices, and vibrating toys with enough batteries to fuel a Tesla."

I stared at her with wide eyes and open mouth.

"See, I told you this would turn you on. Should I talk slower... breathier?"

I shook the image of a sex room from my head. "What about the senator?"

"Tied to the four-poster bed, gagged, and wearing a black silk blindfold," Mattie said matter-of-factly.

I was trying to wrap my mind around it all. "Bound and blindfolded?"

"And beaten to death," Mattie said. "Shouldn't leave that part out."

Eddie jumped in. "We don't know the cause of death yet. But yeah, he'd had the stuffing beat out of him. Handcuffs at his wrists, scarves securing his ankles, and one of those S-and-M rubber balls in his mouth."

"You think he was playing with someone other than his wife?" I asked.

Eddie said, "From what little we know, she was at their estate all night. Her mother's visiting, and the senator was supposed to be at the beach house alone."

"Damn," I muttered. "And you think Mack Thorpe was involved?" That thought took me somewhere else, which led to another route that took me to a place I wished I hadn't gone. "Gross."

"Homophobic much?" Mattie asked.

"What? No. But when I think of the coach of the San Marco High Gallopin' Gopher Tortoises going all Marquis de Sade on the senator, it makes me want to take a scalding shower with a box of Brillo pads."

Eddie said, "Look, we don't know what part the coach played, if any. Go talk to him and we can find out."

"I'm ready," Mattie said.

Eddie looked at her a moment and shook his head. "I swear it's like being stuck with a couple of kids."

I stuck my tongue out at her.

"We'll be in touch, Mattie," Eddie said.

Mattie gave him a rueful smile and said, "Worth a try." She turned and waved over her shoulder as she sauntered through the parking lot. I cursed when she glanced back and caught me staring at the pendulum swing of her backside.

Chapter 4

I sat across from Coach Mack Thorpe in the interrogation room. The table between us was bolted to the floor. Eddie agreed that I should go in alone and Eddie would monitor our little chat via CCTV. Mack was slumped at the table. He looked like hell, and his knuckles were cracked and scabbing up. The cop who'd brought him had looked at me and pointed at the iron ring bolted to that side of the table. I subtly nodded, and the policeman ran Mack's handcuffs through it. Having worked for Mack before, I had witnessed his sudden bursts of temper. I thought it best he be restrained. Mack was a tall, pot-bellied, thinly muscled man going to bald. Dark hair ringed his head with only a few wisps on top. His cheeks were full and would obviously turn to jowls when he got old. Being held and not charged, Mack was still in his street clothes that had the rancid smell of a man who'd drunk a bottle of whiskey the night before then spent the day sweating it out.

I'd interviewed countless suspects and witnesses in the mottled green room, so it felt familiar and homey. I put my arms on the table and leaned forward. "Well, Mack, quite the pickle you're in."

Mack raised his head and gazed at me with bloodshot eyes. "I didn't kill the senator."

"Why don't you tell me what you did do last night?"

"I got my ass kicked."

"By who?"

"Jack Daniels."

I made a show of nodding, building camaraderie. "Yeah, ol' Jack's got a mean right."

"I was still drunk—and hungover, to boot—when Eddie and his dyke partner stopped by school and started giving me a bunch of crap, so I gave 'em crap back."

"Don't call Lou names, Mack. She's married with three kids. You're just pissed that she got the best of you."

"Whatever."

"Look, Mack, I was at Doone's happy hour having a lovely time"—I touched the places Rick had punched me—"and Eddie came to say you were locked up and wanted to see me. So what do you want?"

Mack pulled at his wrists and rattled his cuffs. "I want you to prove I'm innocent."

"Why me? Why don't you just talk to the cops?"

He looked up at the CCTV camera mounted in the corner. "I don't trust them."

"And you trust me?"

"I hired you before. You did a good job. I want to hire you again."

I stood and went to sit on a corner of the table closer to him. "You don't need me. You need a lawyer."

Mack's demeanor instantly changed, and he slammed his fists on the table. Though his cuffs gave him little slack, he hit the table hard enough to shake it. "I didn't kill McGovern, and I want you to prove it." He stared with eyes no longer bleary but ablaze.

I watched him silently until his anger deflated. I faked a yawn and said, "I'm not one of your football players, Mack. That kind of thing doesn't work on me." I waited to see what kind of reaction I'd get, but when Mack didn't respond, I told him, "I'll take your money. In fact, I'll start billing you from the moment Eddie pulled Rick Forester off of me at Doone's."

"I didn't kill the senator" was all Mack said.

I stood and started pacing. "Tell me all about last night."

Mack dropped his gaze to the tabletop and said, "Nothin' happened. We're playing St. Augustine High on Friday, so I held a special practice for the team, mostly going over film. After that, I went to Drew's for a few drinks."

"Drew's Northside Hideaway?"

"Yeah, and then I went home."

"Can anyone prove you were home?"

"Ask Ronnie."

I paused a moment and tapped my lips with a finger. "You said you were going to show Ronnie the door after the last time you hired me."

"She asked me to forgive her and promised not to screw around anymore." He shrugged. "I figured that was cheaper than a divorce, so I let her come back."

"Very magnanimous of you."

"I woke up in front of the TV in time to go to school. Then Eddie and his partner showed up. I was feeling like shit and didn't need any grief, and... well, here I am."

"It's understandable they brought you in. The senator was beat all to hell, and look at your knuckles."

Mack looked down and made two fists. "I pounded some loudmouth at Drew's."

"Why? What'd the loudmouth say?" I asked.

Mack didn't answer.

"So, why'd you fight?"

Mack grunted and looked up. "He pissed me off."

I put both hands on the table and leaned toward Mack. "You and Ronnie went to Senator McGovern's homeless initiative fundraiser. I heard you made a scene."

Mack licked his lips. "Can I get something to drink?"

"Water? Coffee? Coke?"

"Get me a Coke."

"Hang on," I said and went out the door.

Eddie met me in the hallway, gave a uniform a couple of bills, and sent him to the soda machine. He nodded in the direction of the interview room. "He's lying."

"Obviously. The question is how much. Could be one little part—could be everything he's saying." I took a moment to ponder how to proceed. "I'm going to piss him off, see what happens."

"It's your interview."

The uniform came back and handed me a cold can of Coke and a straw so that Mack could drink it with his hands cuffed. I went back in and opened the can, put it down in front of Mack, and stuck the straw in it. "Cheers."

Mack sucked up a mouthful and gave an appreciative "ahh."

After he took a couple more swallows, I said, "Ronnie's a beautiful woman."

Mack's head snapped up, and he stared at me. "So?"

"So, with someone like that, why mess around?"

"What are you talking about?"

"Well, McGovern's body was found in an... oh, let's say... embarrassing situation."

"Huh?"

"It looked as if he was killed while engaged in some sort of kinky sex play. I guess what I'm getting at, and believe me, I'm open-minded to any relationship between consenting adults, but if you and he were—"

"*What?*" Mack jumped to his feet, sending the Coke can flying. I was amazed that he didn't yank his shoulders out of their sockets when he pulled against the iron ring. Mack's face flushed red, the cords in his neck grew taut, and I stared in wonder at a vein visibly throbbing in his forehead. Mack opened his mouth and roared. I turned to the CCTV and gave the camera an are-you-seeing-this look. Mack yanked at the cuffs several times but finally stopped.

I rolled my eyes. "By your reaction, I can guess that you take offense at me wondering if you had a gay fling with McGovern."

Breathing hard, Mack said, "If I wasn't cuffed like this, I'd—"

I waved a hand dismissively. "No threats, Mack. If you want my help, you answer my questions. If you're going to throw a hissy fit at each question you don't like, I'll walk."

Mack glared.

I glanced at my wrist like I was checking an invisible watch. "You've got thirty seconds to make up your mind."

Mack took ten more seconds to get his breathing under control then sat. I glanced at the half a can of soda on the floor and decided Mack could die of thirst before I would get him another one.

"I'm going to give you two bits of advice," I said. "Anger management and Alcoholics Anonymous."

"I know I got a problem," Mack said, looking up at me.

"Well then, you're halfway to a cure. So, no hanky-panky between you and the senator?"

The red started to rise in his cheeks again, but he held it together and grumbled, "No."

"How did you end up at the fundraiser?" I asked.

"Ronnie's a board member of McGovern's homeless thing."

"What'd you and the senator fight about?"

"We didn't fight," Mack said.

"I stand corrected. What did you argue about?"

Mack sighed. "I'm still a little touchy about Ronnie and other guys. He was flirting, and I called him on it."

"Some of the witnesses said it got pretty heated."

"Look, I got pissed. McGovern stayed calm, like he's so much better than me, which pissed me off more. Finally, Ronnie dragged me out. That's it."

"Look at me," I said. We eyed one another. "I know you're lying about something, Mack." Mack started to say something, but I cut him off. "At some point, you will have to tell me the truth. Like I said, I'll take your case, but I'm telling you now, if I find out you're guilty, I will turn over everything I have to the cops, and I will still bill you. So let me ask again. You sure you want to hire me?"

"I didn't kill the senator."

"We'll see." I stood and left the room.

I found Eddie and Lou watching Mack over the CCTV.

"That guy's fuse is way too short," Eddie said.

"Guys like Coach always have their fuse lit," I said. "It's only a matter of time before they go boom."

Lou gazed at the monitor and watched a uniform escort Mack out of the interrogation room. "I checked with Drew Coughlin. Mack was telling the truth about getting in a bar fight last night. Drew said the other guy only got one swing in for the dozen or so Mack laid on him." An athletic woman with short hair, Lou was just tall enough to make the San Marco PD's height requirement. Though she was petite, violent offenders quickly learned not to piss her off. She'd earned a lot of trophies at mixed martial arts tournaments. Somehow, she still found the time to be a loving mother to a young girl and two boys, though having her husband work from home helped.

"If Mack was smarter, I'd say that intentionally getting in a bar fight would be a good cover for knuckles busted up in a murder," I said.

"But you don't think he's smart enough?" Lou asked.

I shrugged. "Facing a prison sentence might have raised his IQ."

Addressing Lou, Eddie said, "Let's see if the senator's staff can shed some light on what happened."

I checked my phone clock, which read a little after five-thirty. "Kinda late for office hours, isn't it?"

"Trust me. The senator's staff will be working late tonight," Eddie said.

"I'm coming with you," I said.

"No, you're not," Eddie said.

"Why not?"

"The captain would serve my head on a platter."

"Then we won't tell him." Lou looked at me with one eyebrow raised. "But you better behave."

"Yes, ma'am. I call shotgun."

Chapter 5

Trapped in the back seat, I waited patiently to be released from the cruiser parked in front of the five-story luxury Hotel Aviles. The hotel dated back to the late nineteenth century, and the style was both Spanish baroque and Moorish revival. Mitch McGovern's father, Arnold, purchased the building in the early nineties, but only the first four floors were used as a hotel. The top floor was where Arnold McGovern had his business offices. The senator's father passed away in 2002, and Mitch took over the building's fifth floor. In 2007, it became his campaign headquarters, and after his election to the United States Senate, it had been his San Marco offices when he wasn't up in Washington, DC.

Lou opened the back door for me. "Watch your head."

"I could get used to this chauffeuring," I said.

"Chauffeuring? You're the only person I know of who likes riding back there," Eddie said.

"Add a lack of a sense of humor to Eddie's numerous faults. How do you put up with this guy?" I asked Lou.

"Sudoku," she said.

We climbed the steps, went in, and strolled past a gift shop, an art gallery, and a little coffee shop.

"Swanky place," I said.

"They charge accordingly," Eddie said.

I winked at the girl behind the front desk, and we passed high-priced wall art on the way to the elevator. After a slow ride up, we got off on the fifth floor.

"Snazzy," Lou said.

I looked around the vestibule. "This... this is like God's waiting room."

A throwback to the grand days of the Hotel Aviles, the floor was draped with intricate rugs, underneath which were hand-painted tiles depicting a rural Spanish village. The walls were a combination of polished mahogany and hunter green, on which hung the nearly photographic realism of Victorian paintings in extravagant frames. The ceiling featured a heavenly mural populated with clouds, cherubs, and angels.

"Come on." Lou led us to a dark wooden desk whose every inch was carved like jungle flora.

A young receptionist was talking into a headset while she swiped at teary eyes with a tissue. "I'm sorry, the senator's chief of staff is busy. The office plans to release a statement later today." She paused and looked at us and held up a finger. "If you'd like to leave your number, I'll see that Mr. Croft gets it." She took a moment to scribble a message then disconnected the call. She pulled another tissue from somewhere behind the counter and blew her nose before asking, "Can I help you?"

"Tough day, huh?" I asked.

The receptionist nodded, wiped her eyes, and asked, "Who do you want to see?"

I asked, "Who else has an office on this floor besides the senator?"

She sniffed and said, "The chief of staff, legislative director, legislative assistant, press secretary, personal assistant, and a couple of others. The rest of the senator's staff stays in Washington."

Eddie showed her his badge and said, "We're from San Marco homicide."

She pushed a button hidden behind the counter and spoke into her headset. "Mr. Croft, the police are here."

A minute later, we were ushered into the office of Isaiah Croft, the senator's chief of staff. "Anything you need, anything at all, you let me know," Croft said after the introductions. In his early thirties, he was a handsome and fit brunette wearing a tailored suit.

His office was a smaller version of the fifth-floor foyer. Eddie sat in a chair before Croft's desk, while Lou and I took chairs against the wall under a painting of a nearly nude woman on horseback.

Croft went on to say, "The staff is available for you. We're obviously very busy with the transition and with helping the family plan a memorial service."

"When's the funeral?" Eddie asked.

"That's what we're working on with his widow, but it will probably be put off for a couple weeks just so everyone can make arrangements to attend."

"You're talking about his fellow senators?" Lou asked.

"Right. Senators, representatives, a lot of people from DC will be converging on San Marco. Word is either the president or vice president will also attend." Croft sucked in a lungful of air and blew it out. "Still hasn't sunk in. I keep waiting for the senator to walk through the door. Anyway, we're as eager to get to the bottom of this as you are. And we want to make sure the citizenry's memory of the senator is as fond as ours."

"Good luck with that," I said, enjoying the angry look I got from Eddie.

Croft narrowed his eyes at me then sighed and said, "You're right, of course, but even if these allegations of—you know—turn out well founded, the senator was still an exemplary leader."

"Exemplary? No offense, but you're wasting sound bites on us," I said. "Your boss was found dead in a sex room, with a ball gag in his mouth and tied up like a rodeo calf. Were you aware of the honorable McGovern's proclivities?"

Croft's face reddened. "No, I did not—"

"*Proclivities*," I said, "that's an even better word than *exemplary*. Speaking of which, your cooperation is exemplary. So how about telling us where you were last night."

Croft frowned. "I don't like what you're insinuating."

Lou gripped my wrist and squeezed.

Eddie thought about it and said, "Insinuation or not, it is a viable question."

"*Viable?*" I repeated. "Is this Thesaurus Day, and nobody told me?"

Lou's grip turned into a vise.

"Ow! Damn, Lou, that's a hell of a grip."

"I wasn't needed until this morning's press conference, so I had dinner with my wife at a friend's home, and yes, they'll be more than happy to provide an alibi." The chief of staff looked from Eddie to me and back to Eddie. "By the time I got to the senator's beach bungalow for this morning's press conference, the police were there."

I yanked my wrist from Lou's grasp and asked, "Who climbs into the saddle now that the senator is dead?"

"In Florida, the governor appoints a replacement who will serve until the general election," Croft said.

I was hoping it was someone specific, because that someone would make an awesome suspect. "Any idea who?"

Croft shrugged.

"I imagine a man in McGovern's position had any number of enemies," Lou said.

"That's an understatement," Croft agreed. "Like the saying goes, *politics make strange bedfellows*. It makes even stranger enemies."

"Enough of an enemy to kill him?" Eddie asked.

Croft inhaled deeply. "We're in political waters here, and they can run pretty deep. You only have to look at all the assassinations and attempts to know that some people take it all very seriously. But if you're asking if there's someone who immediately comes to mind, well, no."

"Not even Glenn Golden?" I asked.

Croft gave a humorless laugh. "I can't see it."

Glenn Golden was a local big shot. His family went back to the founding of San Marco and had their fingers in city growth, politics, and influence throughout its history. A contractor and builder, Glenn had served on the county commission and did a term as state senator as well. His oldest son, Barry, was my age, and we'd gone to school together, though we pretty much detested each other. His younger siblings didn't think much of me either.

"Didn't Golden used to be a big supporter of McGovern?" Eddie asked.

"He was for years. Donated big bucks," Croft said. "They had a falling out a couple of years ago."

"About what?" I asked.

"Wetlands delineations."

"Which are?"

"Areas designated as Florida wetlands upon which it is illegal to build."

"Oh, I get it. Golden wanted to build on wetlands, and the senator wouldn't let him," I said.

"Basically. Golden's family owns land, a lot of land, including several hundred acres of wetlands on the west side of the Intracoastal Waterway. He wanted to build a subdivision of upscale Florida homes there, call it Bella Vista. He figured for all those years of support he gave Mitch, that Mitch should help him change the delineation so he could build."

"And Mitch said no," Eddie said.

"Mitch was well aware of the fragile Florida ecosystem and how much damage overgrowth in the state is causing. So yeah, he told Golden that not only would he not help him, but he would see to it that there was no way that specific wetlands delineation would change."

"Interesting," I said.

Croft looked at his watch and said, "Golden took it as a personal affront, called Mitch a backstabber, and announced his campaign to run against Mitch the following week. If you keep up with the news, you're probably well aware that his campaign has never reached double digits in the polls. As he was Mitch's only opponent, that was pretty much a death knell for his chance at taking Mitch's seat."

"That's a mighty fine motive for someone who has his heart set on becoming a United States senator," I said.

"Mighty fine and mighty obvious," Eddie pointed out.

"And worth looking into," Lou added.

"Can we speak with the other employees?" Eddie asked.

"Not everyone is in San Marco, but yes, whoever is here. I'll get someone to show you around." Croft called out, "Caroline!" When no one showed up, a look of annoyance crossed his face. "Excuse me." He stepped briskly through the door.

Lou smacked my arm.

"Ouch."

"What's with the hard-boiled act?"

"I was just trying to throw him off, see if he'd spill anything useful," I said, rubbing my arm.

"And did he?" she asked.

"Not really. But I'm just getting warmed up."

Lou lifted a finger. "I'll make you wait in the car."

I heard a hushed noise behind us and figured it was either a butterfly flapping its wings or a quiet throat clearing. We turned to find a young woman standing in the doorway. She was a tiny thing with enormous eyes.

"Have we met before?" I asked, standing.

"I don't think so," she answered quietly.

Then it hit me—she looked just like one of those big-eyed waifs painted by that artist, Margaret something or other. Of course, the waifs in the paintings weren't dressed in business attire or wearing a bejeweled wristwatch that I'd lay odds was a Cartier. Her black hair was styled with bangs and feathered to her shoulders. She had a delicate attractiveness about her.

Lou stood and said, "I'm Detective Peters, and this is Detective Schmitt." She indicated Eddie.

I stepped toward the young woman and held out my hand. "And I'm chopped liver."

The young woman stared at my hand then up at me, incomprehension evident, her eyes nearly swimming in stifled tears.

"I'm sorry. It's not the time to be making jokes. I'm Geronimo Fitzgerald, a private detective on the case."

She took my hand and sniffed. "Caroline Ortiz. I am—I was—the senator's personal assistant."

Lou took her hand. "We're sorry for your loss."

"Condolences," Eddie said.

"Thank you. Isaiah asked me to show you around, let you talk with the others."

The others who were available turned out to be a secretary, two interns, the press secretary, and the legislative assistant. No one knew of any enemies the senator may have had other than political adversaries like Glenn Golden, though most agreed that calling them enemies was a stretch. All knew about Coach Thorpe and the senator arguing at the fundraiser, but no one claimed to know the cause. I thought they were all lying through their teeth, maybe covering for their now-deceased boss. As for Coach Thorpe, no one thought of him as a murderer, though given his infamous temper, no one would be surprised if it turned out that he was the killer. Two of the women we spoke with cried openly, and a few other people came close, so I figured that my impression of McGovern as a decent guy was spot on—a shame he'd go down in history as the deviant senator from San Marco.

We asked to see the senator's office. Reticent, Caroline checked with Croft first, and he said it was fine. She let us in and stood by the door as we made our way around the room. The desk was made from the same polished mahogany as the walls.

I tapped the desk and asked Caroline, "Is this from the original Hotel Aviles?"

"Yes," Caroline replied. "It belonged to the man who built the hotel. The fifth floor was for VIPs and has been here since the hotel's inception."

I looked around the room, which I found reminiscent of a stuffy men's club. I turned my attention to the three photographs on the desk. One was a teenage girl, maybe a freshman or sophomore in high school. The other was a woman I'd seen before in newspaper stories or on TV. She had the same piercing eyes, elegant nose, full lips, and dirty-blond hair as the girl. The third framed photo was the senator with his arms over the shoulders of the woman and the girl.

"The senator's family?" I asked, holding up the photo of all three.

"Yes, that's Mrs. Combs-McGovern and their daughter, Jillian. She's in college now."

"We'd like to ask you some questions. Is this office okay?" Lou asked.

"Me?" Caroline said. "I don't know anything. I was just his personal assistant."

"Which means you were probably closer to him than a lot of people," I said.

"Not here. It wouldn't seem right. This is..." Caroline's voice trailed into a mumble.

Sacred ground? I wondered.

Caroline took us to a break room and got everyone a cup of coffee. We sat at a small table.

"Everyone thought kindly of the senator," I stated.

Caroline nodded. "Mitch was a good man."

Eddie asked, "Were you there when the reporters found the body?"

"No. But I should have been." She paused in thought then said, "I should've been there before the reporters. I could have spared the senator—"

I slurped my coffee loud enough to get everyone's attention and said, "I'm no expert, but it seems the senator would want you there before the press arrived to, I don't know, help prepare and all."

"Under normal circumstances, you're right. But since this was a breakfast press conference, the senator asked me to pick up bagels on the way."

Eddie consulted his notes. "I thought it was a catered event."

Caroline stared down at her coffee cup and said, "It was. But the senator loves the bagels and lox from Zayda's Deli. I had to wait until they opened."

At the mention of Zayda's, my mouth started to water. My opinion of McGovern rose another notch—he had good taste in taste. I pictured one of Zayda's ginormous bagels with slices of smoked salmon stacked on a generous helping of cream cheese, topped with capers and a couple of thinly sliced red onion rings. Shaking my head, I turned my attention back to the senator's personal assistant.

"...all the police cars and an ambulance. I thought the worst, but it was worse than the worst. I'm sorry, that doesn't make sense, does it?" Caroline's complexion, pale to begin with, turned ashen, and her large eyes welled up.

"Were you at the soiree Saturday night?" I asked, hoping this wasn't ground already covered while I'd been having my kosher fantasy.

She wiped at her eyes. "Yes, of course."

"At the Four Seasons, right?" I asked.

"Yes."

"How did the evening go?"

"Perfectly. Between the dinner, silent auction, and donations, a lot of money was raised."

"Good, good," I said. "Though it's odd you said the evening was perfect, considering there was a fight."

She glared at me through narrowed eyes. "There wasn't a fight."

"No? What would you call what happened between your boss and Mack Thorpe?"

"It wasn't a fight—more of an argument."

"What was the argument about?" Lou asked.

"I'm not sure," Caroline said.

I grinned at how badly she lied. "Come on. Everyone here claims not to know what they were arguing about, but I'm pretty sure they do—most of them, anyway. And you? You're the senator's right hand. If you didn't know what they were arguing about, you wouldn't be doing your job."

"Really, I don't know."

Back in my police days, I'd developed a technique that was excellent at throwing people off and getting to the truth. I put down my coffee, reached, and took Caroline's cup and placed it on the table as well. Taking both of her hands, I leaned toward her, and with a warm smile, I spoke quietly as if offering condolences, but my words went in another direction altogether. "The senator is dead. Half a dozen journalists saw his body hog-tied and gagged for a bondage lovefest. It's way too late to protect his reputation."

Caroline pulled her hands free and began to cry.

Lou glowered at me but didn't smack me again. "What Mr. Fitzgerald was trying to say is that right now, it's more important to find out who killed him than to protect his name. Caroline, we need the truth."

Caroline looked from Lou to me.

I nodded. "What she said."

Caroline turned her gaze down, and a tear fell to her lap. "It wasn't anything. I mean... it was, but it wasn't based on truth. Coach Thorpe thought that... He's very jealous that—"

"The senator and his wife were dancing the forbidden polka?" I asked.

"Yes." Caroline looked up and explained, "Mrs. Thorpe is on the board of the homeless initiative, and they meet when Congress is in recess and the senator is... was in town, but that's the whole board, and there are several people on it. Still, Coach Thorpe has it in his head that his wife and the senator were having an affair."

"Were they?" I asked.

"No, not at all. The senator was happily married. He wouldn't do anything like that," Caroline said. "He was loyal to those he loved."

I let that obvious fiction go.

"What do you think set off Coach Thorpe?" Eddie asked.

"I think it was his wife."

"What do you mean?" Lou asked.

Caroline looked around as if ready to bestow a secret. "Mrs. Thorpe is a flirt, and Mitch was handsome, rich, and powerful. That combination is like an aphrodisiac to some women."

"She flirted at the fundraiser?" Eddie asked.

"Uh-huh, and anytime she was around, which was whenever there was a meeting of the homeless initiative board."

"Did the senator flirt back?" I asked.

"No," Caroline said, sounding shocked that anyone would consider it. "If she said something or did something flirty, he'd pretend she was making a joke."

"Was she?" Lou said. "Making a joke?"

"I think she would have been happy if the senator was the kind of man who had affairs"—Caroline looked at them—"but he wasn't."

"Wow, denial ain't just a river in Egypt," I said.

She just stared at me with those big oversized orbs.

I cleared my throat and added, "Caroline, he was that kind of man."

Her expression changed in an instant, grief giving way to anger.

"Shoot your angry eyes at me all you want, Caroline, but it won't change the fact that the senator was found in a sex room, having engaged in some sort of fetish bondage thing with someone who was not his wife. So yes, he was that kind of man."

Caroline jumped to her feet. She turned, knocking her coffee cup onto the floor, where it exploded into pieces. "The senator was a good man!" she shouted. "If he was doing something like that, it was because someone made him."

"Made him?" Eddie asked.

Caroline started to cry. "Persuaded him, influenced him, kept pushing him. I don't know... I just don't—" Covering her face, she rushed from the room, pushing past a man in the doorway.

After a few seconds of uncomfortable silence, the man said, "Don't mind Caroline. She suffers from a bad case of hero worship."

"Fond of the senator, huh?" I said.

"Thought he walked on water." The man extended his hand to Eddie and said, "Roger Stansbury. I'm the office manager. I heard you were here and thought I'd save you the trouble of running me down if you had any questions. Caroline's a sweet kid, but she has daddy issues, and I think she saw Mitch as a father figure."

"Why the daddy issues?" Lou asked.

"You might recognize the name Reverend Ernesto Ortiz. He was her father."

"Rings a bell," I said.

"Goes back twenty years. He was the preacher at San Marco Bible Church."

"Oh yeah," I said. "It was something like Oral Roberts and Jim Bakker, but on a local level."

"Right," Stansbury said. "Let's just say that he'd spread his seed amongst his flock and got in trouble when he reaped what he sowed."

"You're saying he sowed an illegitimate child?" Lou asked.

"Two, with different women. Poor Caroline was probably six or seven at the time, but the scandal was big news. Her parents got divorced, and I don't know what happened to the good reverend after he got chased out of town."

I looked at the clock on the microwave oven. Zayda's closed soon, and if I was going to dine on one of their bagels, I was going to have to speed things along. "Mr. Stansbury, we know the senator and Coach Thorpe had words at the fundraiser on Saturday, and we've pretty much narrowed down the cause to jealousy."

"That's about it," Stansbury said.

"Was there just cause for the coach's jealousy?" I asked.

Stansbury stood a moment then stepped back into the hall and looked both ways. After stepping back in, he said, "Yeah, well, I was looking for the senator during the fundraiser. I went through a door that had an Employees Only sign, and though it was pretty dark, I saw him with Mrs. Thorpe under a staircase."

"Flirting?" I asked.

"I guess you could call it that."

I thought a moment and asked, "Was it the 'You have lovely eyes' kind of flirting or more along the lines of tongue-down-the-throat-dry-humping sort of flirting?"

"Uh, the second kind," Stansbury said.

"Aha, I thought so," I said and turned toward Eddie. "Can we swing by Zayda's on the way back?" Deciding to get two bagels on the way, one to eat there and one to take home, I rushed from the break room and out into the lobby. "Come on."

"What's your hurry?" Lou asked.

"All that talk about Zayda's, I'm having a bagel craving," I said.

"Ya know, that would hit the spot," Eddie said.

I pointed out, "We need to leave now. They close at seven."

The door to the vestibule opened, and a woman swept in with all the presence and drama of Scarlett O'Hara.

I recognized her from photos on the senator's desk. "Ah shit. My bagel's gone up in smoke," I said, looking at the late senator's widow.

Chapter 6

She was a gorgeous woman wearing a sleeveless blue blouse and skintight white slacks and was bedazzled with diamonds in her earrings, pendant, and bracelet. She looked like she worshipped frequently at the altar of Pilates or Zumba. She balanced like a tightrope walker on stiletto heels and had a bag over her shoulder that probably cost more than my entire wardrobe. In her right arm, she carried something white and furry with a wet nose. When it started to pant, I settled on dog. The one thing that seemed missing from her ensemble was tears. Hell, I'd have settled for red-rimmed eyes, but they were as clear, blue, and piercing as in her photo on her dead husband's desk.

The receptionist came out from around the mahogany counter and approached. "Oh, Mrs. Combs-McGovern, I'm so sorry. Everyone here is just sick with grief."

"Thank you, Beverly," Mrs. Combs-McGovern said.

I stepped forward. "Condolences. I'm Geronimo Fitzgerald, and this is Detective Schmitt and Detective Peters from the San Marco PD."

"And you, Mr. Fitzgerald. You are also with the San Marco police?"

"Call me Fitz, and no, I'd kind of hoped you'd overlook my omitting why I'm here."

"And why is that..." She paused a beat then added, "Fitz?"

I held out a business card.

The senator's widow took it and read out loud, "Geronimo 'Fitz' Fitzgerald, Private Detective/Security Consultant." She paused and raised an eyebrow as she read my final title, "Universal Life Church Minister?"

"Our motto: 'We take everyone, even atheists.' If you know any-one getting married, I'd be happy to conduct the services," I said. As she gazed at me uncomprehendingly, I added, "The thing is, Mrs. Combs-McGovern, my prime occupation is private detective, and I have been hired by Coach Thorpe."

Mrs. Combs-McGovern stared at me. "Let me get this straight. The man who is currently imprisoned on suspicion of murdering my husband has hired you?"

"Yes, ma'am."

"You already know that Coach Thorpe is in custody?" Lou asked.

"I have my resources, Detective," the senator's widow said, putting the business card in her purse. Looking back at me, she asked, "The coach hired you to do what?"

"He wants me to prove that he didn't kill your husband, ma'am."

"Good God, stop with the ma'ams. Call me Lucinda." She con-tinued to stare.

Feeling uncomfortable under her gaze, I cleared my throat and said, "I was over at Doone's, getting into some rum, when I heard about... which is why I'm dressed..." I shrugged.

"I like you, Fitz." She pushed past us and without turning around said, "Why don't the three of you join me in Mitch's office. I'm sure you have questions for me."

Back in the senator's office, Lucinda put her dog down and perched on the desk while Eddie, Lou, and I took chairs. The dog sniffed our legs then launched into my lap.

"Monty likes you, too, Fitz," Lucinda said.

"I'm more of a mutt kind of guy." I petted the dog. "Though Monty is a good mutt name."

Lucinda grinned and said, "Monty is short for Monarque Royale de Limoges."

I picked him up so that we were nose to nose. "Sorry, buddy. You've got too much lineage for my lap."

I put the dog on the floor. Monty chuffed and lay down at my feet.

"Monty is a good judge of character. I like you even more, Fitz."

"You're okay yourself, Lucinda, but can I point out one thing?" I asked.

"Fire away," she said.

"Everyone here is upset by the death of your husband..." I paused and watched her carefully. "And by the circumstances. No offense, Lucinda, but your eyes are dry as a cue ball."

I could sense Lou's restrained desire to punch my arm.

Lucinda, however, nodded and was silent for a moment. "This morning, as my mother and I were enjoying breakfast, one of your colleagues"—Lucinda indicated Eddie and Lou—"came to my door to inform me that my husband had been murdered last night. While he wouldn't give me details, I do have connections. After he left, I made a phone call and waited. While waiting, I cried, and my heart hammered so much that I thought I'd go into cardiac arrest. Twenty minutes later, I got a call that said Mitch was not only murdered but under circumstances that indicate sadomasochistic adultery. Since that moment, I have been numb—my brain, my heart, my everything is numb." She shifted on the desk and looked at me. "I've lived in San Marco a long time, Fitz. I know who you are. I know we have something in common and that you are in a good position to understand."

What she said hit home, and I had no comeback, so I nodded slowly.

Lou asked, "How about his argument with Coach Thorpe at the fundraiser?"

Lucinda sniffed and said, "It was a crude display of anger. When I asked Mitch about it, he assured me that Coach Thorpe was simply drunk and he thought that Mitch conversing with his wife constituted flirting."

Eddie started to ask, "Do you think that Mack Thorpe could—"

I raised my voice and said, "You must have known about the sex room, Lucinda."

Lucinda stared at me and cocked her head like she was trying to understand someone speaking a foreign language. A smile planted on her face, more of a smirk, and without looking away from me, she pulled a pack of cigarettes and a lighter from her purse. "Mitch would've killed me if he caught me smoking, especially here in his office. Doesn't really matter now, does it?" She lit one and inhaled deeply, and after exhaling, she said, "All today, I've considered what to say when someone inevitably asked about that damn room. I could probably get away with saying that Mitch told me it was a little man cave he had built and I'd never stepped inside." Another drag was followed by another exhalation of smoke. "But the truth is, yes, I was aware of the sex room because Mitch and I used it often some years ago, dwindling off to now and then these days." Leaning closer to me, she said, "Mitch had a healthy libido, and I do as well. It's one of the reasons we got along so well." She sat up straight and dumped an ash into the trash can.

"Here's something I wish I could purge from my mind," I said. "If it turns out that Mack killed your husband while he was, you know, all tied up. Could that mean that he and Mack were... you know... fooling around?"

Lucinda smiled and shook her head. "Mitch might have been twisted in his sexual life, but it was a straight twist."

"Excuse me?" Lou asked.

"Mitch was so straight they could have used him to calibrate rulers, yardsticks, and T-squares."

"The room had a lot of interesting devices," I said.

Lucinda shook her head and produced a tight smile. "Mitch and his toys."

"We're assuming those handcuffs were part of his collection," Lou said.

"He had a pair," Lucinda said. "I'm not much into bondage, so I think we only used them once, and that was a long time ago." She put on a false smile. "Any other personal questions you would like to subject me to?"

Eddie cleared his throat and said, "Thank you for taking time with us."

"Hold it," I said.

"Fitz," Lou warned.

"Did you and the senator have an open marriage?"

"Is that any of your business?" Lucinda asked coolly.

"Actually, it is. At least, it's their business," I said, pointing at Eddie and Lou. "A lot of his sex life will be the cops' business, considering how he was found. And for what it's worth, these two detectives will keep it as quiet as possible."

"And will you keep it quiet, Fitz?" Lucinda asked.

"Well, other than putting it on my blog, yes."

Lucinda's eyes widened, then she laughed, but it didn't last long. As she'd said, I knew what she was going through, and it was important to lift some of that numbness. A little laughter meant there was a little feeling.

"We did not have an open relationship. And not just because Mitch was a senator and of the publicity that could attract. He satisfied me, and I thought, until this morning, that I satisfied him." After taking a final pull from her cigarette, she extinguished it by grinding it out on the desktop. "Yesterday, if you'd have asked me if Mitch was fucking someone else, I'd have said no. Today, I can admit that I'm not really surprised." Getting off the desk, she said, "I want to go through some of Mitch's things, so if there's nothing else I can help you with..."

We stood and started for the door.

"Here's our card, if anything comes to you." Eddie handed it to the senator's widow.

"And if you come across anything to indicate who your husband was boinking, let us know," I said, earning another arm slap from Lou.

Caroline appeared at the doorway. "I heard you were here, Mrs. Combs-McGovern." She turned to the detectives. "And I want to apologize to the police for getting upset earlier."

Lucinda crossed to the door, took Caroline's hand, and said, "You're a mess, Caroline. In this line of work, you need to stay afloat in the worst of storms."

Caroline looked away from the senator's widow and quietly sobbed.

Lucinda pulled her hand away and shook her head. "This one is hopeless. Mitch was fond of her, however, and she was loyal to him."

"He was a good man, the best," Caroline said as she wiped at her eyes with a tissue.

"Show our guests out, Caroline," Lucinda said.

Chapter 7

Eddie checked the time on his phone as we exited the building. "Zayda's is closed by now. No bagel today."

"Now this crime has affected me on a deep and personal level." I shook my fist at the sky. In a voice that would impress Shakespeare, I proclaimed, "I vow to catch the culprit responsible even if it is my own damn client. This I do swear."

Lou watched my display and said, "You are such a pimp for justice."

"I know, right?"

"Let's go see what Mack's wife has to say," Lou said.

"I'm game," I said.

"Nope," Eddie said. "We let you come here, and you showed your ass, so I'm taking you back to Doone's."

"Fine," I said. Then I added, "Shotgun." But when we got to the car, I was once again placed in the back seat. "You guys have no respect for the rules of the road."

Ignoring me, Lou said, "Did you guys know that Lucinda and Ronnie are cousins?"

"No kidding?" I asked.

"No kidding. One of the things I found out while Eddie was fetching you was that Ronnie's mom and Lucinda's were siblings, and they grew up in Welaka. Ronnie and Lucinda moved here together after high school."

"How the hell did one marry Mitch McGovern and the other end up with Mack Thorpe?"

"A toss of the dice of love?" Lou asked.

"If that's not a country song, it should be," I said.

"We need to check out Lucinda," Eddie said. "With her husband's death, she's inherited quite a bit."

"A buttload of money." I thought about it. "And she's good-lookin' to boot."

"I don't think she'd consider you husband material," Lou said.

"I'd settle for cabana boy as long as she tips well."

Eddie adjusted the air conditioning and asked, "Anyone really think Glenn Golden could be behind it?"

"Nah," Lou said. "How about you, Fitz?"

"Not really. But maybe someone did it for him."

"Like he hired someone?" Lou asked.

"Not necessarily. Just someone who wanted to see him win," I said.

"You trying to pin it on his son, Barry?" Eddie asked. "Because you hate the guy does not mean he did it."

"His other son, Stuart, would be more likely. Is he still around?" I asked.

"Don't know," Lou said. "But didn't the two of you get close to the daughter in a murder case?"

"Yeah," I said then added, "My final closed case as a detective of the San Marco PD."

Eddie glanced back at me through the rearview. I thought he was concerned I'd go all maudlin.

"Kimberly Rice," I said, noting the sadness in my own voice. "Seventeen-year-old beauty and best friend of Glenn Golden's daughter, Ginny. Raped and murdered."

"Nothing pointed to a suspect," Eddie said.

"Until the infamous raid where I showed up drunk and ended my career," I admitted.

Eddie cast another look in the mirror and explained to Lou, "We were helping vice in a raid on the Cholos Boys gang."

"And I showed up under the influence and made so much noise it alerted the Cholos."

"They started shooting." Eddie hit his turn signal. "All three of them were killed."

"Thankfully, no cops were hurt, proving that God does indeed look out for drunks and fools. Anyway, in the living room, we found evidence that they were the ones who killed Kimberly."

Lou said, "I've heard various rumors about your exit from the department. Thanks for giving me the real story." Her cell phone rang. "What?" After listening, she ended the call and said, "Captain's secretary. They want us back at the station."

"Captain probably wants an update on the case," Eddie said.

"Want to bet he's holding a press conference in time to get on the eleven o'clock news?" Lou asked.

"At least he can say you guys have a person of interest in custody," I pointed out.

We rode the rest of the way to Doone's in silence. Eddie pulled into the parking lot and slammed the car into park.

Turning so that he could see me, he said, "I know how your mind works, Fitz. You're thinking about dropping in on Mack's wife, aren't you?"

"Maybe."

"Well, don't. I want to talk to her first."

"Uh-huh."

"I'm serious, Fitz. Got it?"

"Yeah, I got it."

Fifteen minutes later, I was piloting my truck in the direction of San Marco North, an older affordable neighborhood that had lots of rental homes, so that I could question Coach Mack's wife face-to-face. The trip took me by the city marina, where I pulled to the side of the road. Engine idling, I watched Rick at a distance as he piloted the *Titanic II* toward the dock after a day of taking fishermen out.

The boat had been constructed of oak and pine back in the late forties. It had seen its last paint job, royal blue, two decades earlier. Over time, the paint had faded unevenly. Rick had applied touch-up paint in spots, which made the vessel look like it had blue zits. The large letters spelling out the boat's name had once been a brilliant white but had turned a brownish yellow reminiscent of the teeth of a chain-smoking coffee addict. Between the appearance and the name, it was a wonder that Rick had any business at all.

Fuckin' Rick. I couldn't believe the guy was still mad at me. We'd been thick as thieves since we were students at Ponce Elementary. We'd been tight through middle school and high school, after which Rick went into business with his father and I went into San Marco Tech's police academy.

The *Titanic II* thumped against the dock, and one of Rick's young hands jumped from the boat and went about tying her off. I saw Rick exit the wheelhouse, smiling and saying something to his clientele.

Yeah, I'd screwed the pooch by stealing Ivy, his girlfriend of three years. One night at Doone's, when Rick was absent, Ivy and I walked down to the docks and ended up kissing. Rum was involved. From there, we made a mad dash to Fitz's Folly and did much more than kiss. The next day, Ivy broke up with Rick, and the following week, she and I got married. The marriage lasted all of five months. We both knew it was a mistake and picked up a do-it-yourself divorce kit from Staples. Rick forgave Ivy but still blamed me. And speaking of blame, I didn't blame him one bit.

Sighing, I put my truck in gear and pulled into traffic. My daily driver was also my business vehicle, a 1976 Ford F150. Some folks called it old. I said it was retro. The paint scheme was two-tone, white and rust, which matched well with the dents and dings. I had the radio tuned to a little AM country station that called itself San

Marco's Country Sunshine and included the slogan "Real Country, Old Country."

Putting on my best twang, I sang along with Buck Owens to "Act Naturally." While vocalizing, I thought back to the last time I'd worked for Mack Thorpe. I hoped his wife wouldn't connect me to being the private detective who'd snapped those photos of her and her lover.

I turned off of US 1 into the second entrance into the North neighborhood. I remembered where Mack lived from when I delivered the file to him. I followed North Shores Blvd., took a right on Dolphin Drive, and just when I got to where I could see a little of the Intracoastal Waterway reflecting the setting sun, turned into the driveway of a small two-story wood-and-brick house. My truck bounced as I drove over a section where live oak roots had cracked the driveway. The coach apparently had an aversion to lawn work. The grass was patchy and high, trees could've used a trimming, and leaves needed raking.

Humming the Buck Owens tune, I walked to the front door and rang the bell. After a minute, a curtain on a narrow window by the door shifted. The door opened, and a tall woman in cut-offs and a T-shirt stood there. I'd captured her long brown hair splayed across a motel pillow when I'd photographed her and the fitness trainer through the window of their room.

"Hi," I said, "my name is—"

"I know who you are. You're that two-bit private eye my husband hired back in the bad ol' days."

Crap. Ronnie might have been beautiful, but I'd seen that same look before in the eyes of a hungry cobra when a rat had been dropped into its cage at the San Marco Gatorland Zoo. I took a step back, putting a little distance between us. "Geronimo Fitzgerald," I said, holding out a card.

She snatched it, and standing in the screen door, she read it then let the card drop to the welcome mat.

"Um, yeah, well, your husband has hired me again. This time, to prove he didn't kill the senator."

"Yeah, well, Mack isn't too bright."

"Look, I know you might still be upset about what happened a couple of years ago, but I was just doing my job. What say we let bygones be bygones?"

Ronnie didn't respond.

"Or not." I cleared my throat. "Anyway, can I come in so we can talk about it?"

"No."

I looked around. "Yeah, you're right. It's a lovely evening—let's stay outside." Several long seconds of uncomfortable silence passed, in which I tried not to wither under Ronnie's glare. Finally, I said, "As we're both aware, your husband is in jail because—you are aware that Mack's in jail, right?"

"Yes."

"So, the thing is, the police started looking at him for the senator's murder because of what happened at the fundraiser. Mack says you're on the board for the senator's homeless initiative."

She sniffed like she smelled something bad and said, "I am. Several other people as well."

Her expression turned irate, and I followed her gaze to the screen door, where I was picking at a chunk of peeling paint. My hand dropped. "Sorry. You and Lucinda Combs-McGovern are cousins?"

"Yes."

"Have you spoken with her recently?"

"Not that it's any of your business, but yes. I called today to tell her how sorry I was and to assure her that Mack did not commit the murder, no matter what it looks like right now."

"What did the senator and Mack fight about Saturday night?"

Ronnie rolled her eyes. "They didn't fight. They argued."

"So everyone keeps insisting. What was it about?"

"Silly rumors," she said.

I smiled and said, "I heard it was because you and McGovern had a bad case of the gropes."

Ronnie stared at me, sighed, and stepped onto the porch. She sat on the stoop and said, "Look, ever since you stuck your nose in our marriage, Mack hasn't trusted me."

I sat next to her. "Really? That's how you see it? From my perspective, it's that ever since you got caught fooling around, your husband hasn't trusted you."

Although I was prepared to leap if the cobra eyes came back, Ronnie said, "Yeah, there's a lot of truth in that. Anyway, he saw me and the senator talking, laughing about something, and he turned into an idiot in front of all of San Marco's movers and shakers." She closed her eyes and shook her head at the memory. "So I got him out of there, and we came home."

"You said you told Lucinda that Mack did not commit the murder. How can you be so sure?"

"Because even though Mack can get madder than a hornet, he wouldn't kill anyone. He might beat the crap out of them but not do whatever happened to Mitch."

"Was Mack with you last night?"

She shook her head. "The team goes up against St. Augustine High on Friday. St. Augustine usually wins, and by a big margin, so Mack had a special practice yesterday evening."

"How about afterward? Mack said he came back here."

Ronnie stood and opened the screen door. "I went to bed early."

"He said he fell asleep in front of the TV."

Ronnie stepped inside fand gazed at me as the screen door started to swing closed. "I don't know. He might have. I went to bed before he got home and woke up after he left for school."

She shut the door.

As I drove off, I turned on the radio and laughed at the irony of Johnny Cash singing "Folsom Prison Blues."

Chapter 8

I nstead of heading home, I turned west off of US 1 onto County
Road 205. Outside the city limits, I slowed to find a paved drive
with a Private Road No Trespassing sign. There was no problem finding the road during the day, but it was tricky after dark, especially
with the lack of streetlights out in the boonies. I'd been there several
times six or seven years before, investigating a case. Glenn Golden
considered himself a gentleman farmer, and those one-hundred-plus
surrounding acres were his farm. He grew spuds, and a little farther
out on the county road, he had a big barn where he made and sold
Datil Dusted Chips, potato chips made from what he grew. Besides
salt, he seasoned them with dried, powdered datil peppers. Good
stuff, hot stuff, and they sold well—though I doubted Glenn made
much money off his farm and probably used it as a tax write-off. I
pulled up to his farmhouse, which was not an accurate term as it was
one of those Mediterranean-style McMansions with orange stucco
and red clay shingles. A circular driveway fronted the home with a
tacky mermaid fountain in the middle. I parked my ancient truck
next to what I thought was Glenn's work truck, which was forty-plus
years younger and sixty thousand dollars more expensive. Besides our
trucks, dozens more vehicles were parked around the circular drive.

The house was lit up, but music and voices were coming from
behind the home, where the swimming pool was located. Instead of
ringing the bell, I opened the front door and let myself in. Remembering when I was there last, I made my way down a wide, high-
ceilinged hallway floored with marble tile. I passed their restaurant-
quality kitchen to the left and saw a staff in white, preparing food. As

I got to the patio doors that opened onto the pool area, I heard my name.

"Fitzgerald."

I turned without slowing and saw my old high school nemesis, Barry Golden, at the end of the hall. I lifted a hand and waved with a big grin. "Barry, my man."

"What do you—" he started.

But I stepped out into the party and no longer heard him. The swimming pool area was surrounded by a ring of palm trees of varying heights and gardens that extended in three directions. The pool was large, with three diving boards, a slide, and a faux waterfall. No one was swimming, so it served more as décor than a functional pool. A couple of dozen tables with chairs were scattered around the pool, and the area was lit with tiki torches and paper lanterns. A small stage was set up at the far side of the pool, and a band I was familiar with, J. Everett Steele and the New Swamp Revival, was playing folksy country, much different than the gritty blues and rockabilly fare they played at Doone's Fish Camp. A few couples were dancing. I figured more than a hundred people were at the party. As the Florida night was warm, most were dressed appropriately. The men wore either guayabera shirts or flowery Hawaiian shirts and the kind of shorts somebody would wear on the golf course. Feet were clad in boat shoes or sandals, with a few in socks and shoes. The women, likewise, were dressed for the weather in thin-strapped summer dresses or slacks with sleeveless button-down blouses.

A long table, probably several covered with white tablecloths, extended a good twenty feet from side to side just outside the door. I stopped to nibble on a couple of local steamed shrimp and took in the buffet, which seemed a mixture of fine food, like escargot and Chilean sea bass, and Florida redneck cuisine, like chicken wings and little wieners in barbecue sauce. Exotic floral displays were placed every couple of feet, with an ice carving of a swan melting at the center of the table.

A hand grasped my arm. Chewing shrimp, I turned to smile at Barry Golden.

"What are you doing here, Fitzgerald?"

"Good to see you, too, Barry. Looks like your family is celebrating something." I paused to swallow. "Wouldn't be because a certain senator died, would it?"

"Don't be an ass. You don't throw together a party like this in one day."

I looked around. "Guess you're right. Though it adds to the levity, right?"

Barry, half a foot taller, gazed down at me, his lips twisted into a scowl. We'd never come close to being friends. In middle school, he was already turning into a boy worthy to be called Golden, with that kind of master-race look: tall, sharp-featured, and blond. He and his sycophant friends were classic bullies. When he learned Rick and I weren't the type to back down, his dislike grew. In high school, Barry and his brethren no longer beat on their victims but instead engaged in subtler forms of bullying. They'd disparage other students they considered not as superior as they, whether because of financial status, unattractiveness, dress, friend groups, vehicles driven, ineptitude in athletics, or local familial hierarchy. No reason was too shallow. In grand stereotypical fashion, Barry became the school's football hero.

I would give him this: he surpassed the dumb-jock stereotype because he was smart, shrewd, and perceptive. He went on to edit the school paper, the *San Marco High Clarion*, then he majored in journalism at FSU. After college, he got a job at the hometown newspaper and worked his way up to editor, which was why the *San Marco Ledger* embarrassed itself by endorsing Barry's dad in the senatorial race.

Over the years, I'd learned how to push Barry's buttons and decided to do so again. "You been gaining weight, Barry?"

"I'm not gaining weight," he said defensively and cast a quick glance at his belly. "Tell me what you want, or get out."

I walked away from the buffet table, Barry on my heels, and headed toward one of several small bars scattered around the party. "I want to talk to your dad."

"Why?"

I got to the bar and told the bartender, "Cuba libre, por favor."

"You can't order a—"

"It's about Senator McGovern's murder. I've been hired on to look into the case."

"Who hired you?"

By way of answering, I took my cocktail from the bartender, sipped it, and smiled at Barry.

Barry shook his head and said, "Follow me."

As we worked through the revelers, I nodded at some I vaguely knew and said a sociable howdy to those I knew better. We ended up at a table near the swimming pool waterfall. I thought it wasn't a great place to sit because the continuous splashing would have me up and running to the little boys' room much too often. But it was apparently considered a place of honor because that was where Glenn Golden sat. The other seats were filled, and several people stood around as he regaled them with an anecdote or joke or something.

"Excuse me, Dad," Barry said.

Glenn looked up, his smile faltering when he saw me.

"Geronimo Fitzgerald. What a surprise," he said. Like his sons and daughter, he'd been a blond in his youth. Presently, he had a full head of white hair. He'd kept in shape and looked like an extra in a Ricky Ricardo movie in his cream guayabera shirt and matching shorts.

"Mr. Golden, I'd like to ask you a few questions. Sorry I showed up now. I didn't know you were celebrating."

"It's an annual party I throw for friends and employees. And since I've been running for the senate seat, my supporters too."

I acted like I was digesting the info then asked, "Weren't you tempted to cancel the shindig when you heard about Senator Mc-Govern?"

A young man who looked like a banker vacationing in Hawaii jumped to his feet and asked, "What are you insinuating, Fitz?"

I looked at him carefully and realized it was Barry's younger brother. "Stuart. Dang, you've changed. Last time I saw you, your eyes were glazed, your hair was long, and I think you were wearing a Slipknot T-shirt."

Stuart said, "And you still look like—"

"Stuart," Glenn interrupted, "do not be rude to our guests, even the uninvited ones." He stood and said, "Fitz, let's take a walk, and you can ask me your questions."

"Dad?" Barry and Stuart said at the same time.

"It's all right, boys." Glenn picked up a mostly empty glass of piña colada and sipped through the straw until it made a sucking sound. "I got wind you were working for Coach Thorpe. Sounds like you're gainfully employed by the guilty party."

"That remains to be seen," I said then admitted, "but I wouldn't bet money against it."

Glenn smiled, placed his glass on the table, and led me away from the revelers. He didn't seem to mind when I stopped at a bar for a refill.

"How's Ginny doing?" I asked.

"She's good. She went through two years of therapy after that tragedy with Kimberly. Now, she's about to get engaged and is working as press secretary for my senatorial bid."

We took a pathway to the right that led into a garden of what looked like Florida natives: saw palmettos, dune sunflowers, confederate jasmine, maypop vines, Spanish bayonet, and more.

"Speaking of which, now that McGovern is dead, what happens next?" I asked.

"It's a complicated mess. You remember Paul Wellstone, don't you?"

"A senator. Didn't he die in a plane crash?"

"Back in 2002. He was running for reelection in Minnesota and died eleven days before the election. They replaced him with Walter Mondale. Wellstone would have won, but Mondale lost to Norm Coleman."

"So you'll be running against someone else?"

"Someone chosen by his party."

"You'll likely win, won't you?" I asked.

"I left my crystal ball in the house." He looked at me and added, "But yeah, history is on my side."

"Mack Thorpe hired me to prove his innocence."

"I hope you got paid up front," Glenn said.

"Damn, wish I'd thought of that," I admitted. "Though Mack and McGovern bumped heads at a party, it seems you have a much better motive."

"I'd be offended if it wasn't so true. On the other hand, isn't money the usual motive?"

"Usually."

"See who inherits his fortune. Perhaps their motive is greater than mine," he said.

"Thought I'd talk to you first. In your case, it also comes down to money."

Glenn sighed like he'd lost patience with a toddler. "What are you talking about, Fitz?"

I stopped walking. "You were a big supporter of Mitch McGovern for years, a personal friend, I'm guessing. You donated to his campaigns. And then when you needed his help to get some pesky little wetlands delineations changed, he wouldn't give it to you. Might be you're more concerned with... What were you calling your planned subdivision? Bella Vista?"

Glenn looked at me, eyes narrowed. He sucked at his lips and made a smack sound.

"If you were hoping that little bit of info would stay quiet, it won't. You may want to reconsider your confidence in winning the race."

"In the bag, Fitz—in the bag."

I shrugged, figuring he was right. Questionable politicos were elected all the time.

"I've already spoken with the police," Glenn said. "And I'm meeting with your old partner, Eddie, tomorrow."

"What will you give him for an alibi?"

"A pretty good one. Stuart, Ginny, and I were campaigning up in St. Johns County and spent the night at the Lodge and Club in Ponte Vedra. Lots of witnesses."

"Stuart's part of the campaign?"

"He's working as assistant for my campaign manager, Tom Mobley."

"Stuart's come a long way," I said.

"Mm-hmm."

"No offense, Glenn, but the last time I saw him, he'd do anything for a cheap high, and that included huffing glue and sniffing paint."

"I know. That's why I'm so proud of the kid. We finally sobered him up five years ago and discovered something about him."

"What's that?"

"Stuart is shrewdly intelligent, which is a great benefit in political campaigns."

We walked around a little more. I asked more questions, and Glenn gave me answers that didn't help my investigation.

We got back to the soiree, and I told him, "Thanks for letting me crash your party." I held out my hand.

Glenn took it, and we shook. "Believe me, Fitz, no one involved with my campaign had a thing to do with the senator's murder."

But I was already thinking I should look further into the alibis of all the Goldens. Ponte Vedra was only an hour or so away.

I walked around the side of the house under wind-twisted live oaks and found myself face-to-face with the third Golden.

"Hi, Ginny. Long time, no see."

"Barry told me you were here." It amazed me that she was the shorter of us but still managed to look down her nose at me.

"Have a lovely evening."

She glowered at me a few seconds, turned, and walked away. *Who says it can't get cold in Florida?*

Chapter 9

Heading back into town on 205, I considered returning to Doone's. But I was on the clock for the most quick-tempered client in the history of private eye–dom, and I wanted to chew on what I'd learned so far. I dug my cell phone out of my pocket, went through my contact list, and found a number I was surprised I hadn't deleted.

"Three things," I said when Eddie answered.

"Fitz? What do you want?"

"I talked to Ronnie Thorpe, and she admitted that she didn't see her husband after practice last night."

"What?" Eddie shouted. "You went... You talked to... I specifically told you to let us interview her first."

"Really?" I faked confusion. "I could have sworn you asked me to talk to her first."

"Why the hell would I...? Oh, never mind."

"What she specifically said was that she went to bed before Mack got home and woke up after he left for school, so even if he did go home, she still can't provide an alibi."

"Interesting."

"If I were you, I'd bring it up when you talk to her."

"Well, golly gee, thank you, Fitz. It wouldn't have crossed my mind. You said you had three things?"

"Seeing as how upset you got because I talked with Ronnie, I won't tell you I went out to speak with Glenn Golden."

Eddie groaned.

I said, "So I'll just jump to the third thing: can I see the crime scene tomorrow?" While he was silently strategizing arguments, I added, "You owe me."

"What? What the hell do I owe you for?"

"You're the reason I'm not a cop."

"You drunk again? You're the reason you're not a cop."

Neither of us said anything for what seemed like forever, then Eddie muttered something and followed it up with "A quick in and out. Can we make it midmorning?"

"That'll work. I have to see a client early. How's ten?" I asked.

"Ten will be good. The techs will be done by then, and no one else should be there. Not sure how much there'll be to see," Eddie said.

"Just want to get the vibe," I said.

"Vibe?" He laughed.

"What?"

"You'll see."

I drove toward the beach, crossed the Carroll Street Drawbridge onto the island, turned south on A1A, and honked as I passed Doone's. My elbow was resting on the open window frame, and I listened to the sound of waves crashing from two blocks away. I breathed deeply, relishing the smell of the salt air. Slowing, I turned west onto Dos Casas Lane. Though the sky was dark, I had enough time to stop at the first house on the two-house road. A two-story Florida cracker home, it was probably as old as its one resident. A multitude of colorful outdoor lighting illuminated the structure, its wood siding sun-bleached and the tin roof discolored with reddish patches. Heavy gray shutters hung at each side of each window, and a covered porch ran along three sides of the house. The porch held a smattering of old wooden rockers, a few small tables, and a couple of porch swings.

As I shut off the truck, the screen banged open, and my landlady charged onto the porch.

"*Buenos noches*, Feetz. Come, come, *rapido*." Consuela Morales Jenkins was a small, stick-thin woman. I had concerns that a strong coastal wind might carry her off someday. Her age was tough to pinpoint, though I estimated somewhere between seventy-five and a hundred seventy-five. Gray-haired, with more wrinkles than stars in the sky, she dressed like a Cuban peasant even though she'd left Cuba decades earlier. She spoke English peppered with Spanish and claimed to have slept with Che Guevara, but only once. She'd told me that his penis was *muy pequeño*, and she'd demonstrated by holding her thumb and index finger about a quarter of an inch apart.

I got out of my truck and said, "Buenos noches, Consuela. What brand of *loco* are you peddling tonight?" I pulled a roll of bills out of my pocket and handed it to the old woman. "September rent."

She stuffed it into an apron pocket without looking at it and grabbed my wrist. "Follow me—*aqui, aqui*." She pulled me into the house. We stepped around the stuffed eight-foot Cuban crocodile she kept by the door and went quickly down the hallway festooned with dozens of framed pieces of Cuban folk art. Her husband, Alonzo Jenkins, had been an eccentric artist who'd lived his whole life in San Marco, though he often took long sabbaticals in Caribbean nations. Consuela had been in her early twenties when he went to Cuba to study. They met and married two weeks later, and he brought her and a collection of Cuban art back with him.

We passed through the kitchen and its sixties-era appliances and pushed out the back screen door.

When I saw her destination was the backyard shed, I muttered, "Ah crap."

"*Alto*," Consuela barked, stopping me in front of the shed door. "Wait here." She opened the door and went in as I peeked in at her distillery. She came back out and handed me a green liter soda bottle filled with a liquid that I was sure had more to do with moonshine than Sprite. "*Esto es tuyo,*" she said as though making a great pronouncement.

"What's that?"

"Is for you." She patted the plastic bottle. "My best rum yet. *Muy bueno.* You try it."

Knowing from experience that refusing would be useless, I gave her a half-hearted smile and twisted open the cap. I loved good rum, rum that flew down the gullet potent yet smooth—preferably a dark rum with a beautiful clear amber tint made with the highest-quality ingredients and properly aged in a barrel. Consuela's rum was none of those. The fumes assaulted me, and my eyes watered. I held the bottle in front of a shed light and saw a cloudy concoction better suited to fuel a gasoline combustion engine than to introduce to the human body. I knew from past experience that the age of her rum could be counted in hours, not years. I brought the bottle up to my lips, planning to mimic a drink, but Consuela stepped forward and pushed the bottle up so that I got a full mouthful. I closed my eyes in resignation and swallowed. A second after the bomb went off in my stomach, a psychedelic light show began behind my eyelids. I could hear the blood rush through my body, and it sounded like ocean waves. Then I swore I could hear distant drums beating out a Latin rhythm while jungle birds squawked a melody. I opened my eyes, and the music stopped.

"Well?" Consuela asked.

I quickly screwed on the lid before she insisted I take another swallow. I smiled at her and said in a raspy voice, "*Abuela, que es la perfección.*"

She smiled maternally and patted my cheek. "You're a good boy, Feetz." She turned and went back into the shed before stopping a moment to say, "There is a woman at your house."

Thinking of a favor my second wife, now my ex-wife, had requested of me, I asked, "Is it Ivy?"

"No. Ivy is *bonita*, this señorita is *hermosa*," Consuela said and closed the door.

I took a couple of cleansing breaths as I tried to figure out if hermosa was preferable to bonita, decided it was, and started around the house, noting that my feet weren't cooperating so well. Normally, I'd be thrilled to know there was an hermosa woman at my house, but at the moment, my head was floating unsteadily.

I got to my truck and carefully situated the bottle of homemade rum in the bed so that it wouldn't roll around, slam against something, and explode.

I headed a hundred yards farther down Dos Casas Lane, rounded a thick stand of gigantic live oak and queen palm trees, and passed a rustic handmade sign that read Fitz's Folly. As I drove around a knoll of sea oats, sawgrass, and Spanish bayonet, I saw a car parked behind the second *casa* on Dos Casas Lane. I studied the vehicle, a nearly new black VW sedan, as I pulled alongside it and parked. I didn't have a clue as to whom it belonged to, but then, maybe Seri had dropped by for whatever kids call it these days. *A booty call? A hook up? A booty up hook call?* That would be a conundrum. On the one hand, even I had to admit that she was too young for me. On the other hand, her picture could be in the *Merriam Webster Lecher Dictionary* next to the term "smokin' hot." I got out, grabbed Consuela's concoction, and hoped my willpower was sturdy enough.

I'd retrieved numerous truckloads of bricks several years before from a demolished building and used them to create a brick walk from my parking spot at the back of my house around to the front door. I could have walked it in pitch darkness, but after a full slug of Consuela's rum, I was happy for the porch light. The night was quiet save for the lapping water from the Intracoastal Waterway, a mile-wide section of saltwater river that ran in front of my home and separated me and that stretch of A1A from the mainland. Rounding the corner of the house, I saw a lone feminine figure sitting in one of the chairs at my unlit firepit, gazing out at the Intracoastal.

I approached a few steps closer. "Uh, welcome to my humble house. Listen, we need to have a talk."

The figure stood and approached. The way she walked put my willpower into dire jeopardy.

Just as her face was illuminated by the porch light, Mattie Castro said, "Humble is right." She stopped a couple of feet from me. "You don't look so well."

"What the hell are you doing here, Castro? Come to do a follow-up hit piece?"

"I come bearing gifts," Mattie said, holding up a bottle.

My anger dissipated instantly. "I know that bottle. Pusser's Navy Rum?"

Mattie held it close to her face to read it in the near dark. "Aged fifteen years. Is that good?"

"Mattie Castro, you should visit more often," I said, leading her back to the chair at the firepit. "Give me a minute to get settled."

"Oh wait," Mattie said, seeing what I was carrying. "You have a bottle already. Do you want to drink that instead?"

"Perish the thought." I held up the liter bottle. "This is a combination of kerosene, turpentine, and nitroglycerin. What you're holding, Mattie, dear, is bottled nirvana. Let me get a fire going." I put some kindling and split logs in the firepit. Using a long barbecue lighter, I tried to get the kindling lit. After several attempts, I said, "The wood's damp." Looking at the liter of Consuela's rum, I grinned, unscrewed the top, and poured some of the homemade rum into the pit.

I let it soak in for a minute, clicked the lighter, and carefully put the flame against the wood. A fireball erupted, and I found myself sitting back on my ass.

Mattie jumped up and helped me to my feet. "Are you all right?"

"Damn. I knew that stuff was explosive. I just didn't know…" A coughing fit hit me.

Mattie stared at me, stifling a laugh.

When my coughs lessened, I managed to ask, "What?"

She pointed above my eyes. "Your brows—they're a little singed."

"What?" I brushed them with a finger, feeling their crispiness. "Damn."

Five minutes later, the narrow strip of land between my home and the Intracoastal Waterway was alight with a blaze in the firepit and dozens of strands of Christmas lights strung along my deck, throughout the trees, and around numerous pink flamingo lawn ornaments. I sat next to Mattie, and we each held short glasses with a couple of fingers of Pusser's Rum. Mattie wore tight jeans, sandals, and a white V-neck T-shirt. And since my powers of observation were staggering, I'd noticed early on that she was wearing no bra.

"I never drank rum straight before. This is pretty good," Mattie said.

"Very good. You chose well. Some rums make better paint removers," I said and looked toward where I'd dumped the rest of Consuela's rum onto the ground twenty feet away.

Mattie turned to take in my home. "Fitz's Folly, huh?"

"Has a nice ring to it, don't you think?"

"Sure, Fitz. Whatever."

"What do you think of the place?"

"The location is great, right on the Intracoastal. No neighbors in sight."

"The neighbors are there. That's why I like a lot of trees and scrub—keeps it private."

"And your house is…" She put a finger to her chin as she thought. "Antediluvian."

I took a moment to respond. "Thank you. I always thought of it more as a Caribbean-style bungalow."

Mattie held her glass close to her mouth, though I saw the smile behind it. "Oh, that would work as well."

I got up and shuffled around the firepit. "I moved out here after... Well, over five years ago. It'd been a one-room shack that my landlady's husband had used for storage. After he died, she had it cleaned out and repurposed as a little fishing hut she rented out to anglers for a night or two or three. I talked her into letting me rent it on a monthly basis, and as you can see, I've expanded on it." The center of the house had obviously been the shed. A wooden structure with an oversized door and steel roofing, it had one small window facing the river. I walked to the house, pointing toward a wooden addition on the north side. "My first building project was the kitchen. I like to cook, so I kept the fishing hut as my combination bedroom and living room and built the kitchen with all the necessary appliances. You can tell it's bigger, and that's because I've always wanted a big kitchen island."

Mattie got up and joined me as I approached the south-side addition. "Is that concrete?"

"No, but kinda sorta," I said, pausing for a sip and a second to relish it. "I went all historic on this expansion. The Spanish, when they were here centuries ago, built with, among other things, tabby—basically, a concrete mixture."

"There are seashells in here," she said, rubbing the wall.

I grabbed her wrist and pulled it from the wall. "Careful. Those are oyster shells and can be pretty sharp."

"And that room is?" Mattie asked.

"My bedroom. I usually sleep with that big picture window open. There's almost always a nice breeze to lull me to sleep. You can't see my third expansion—it's on the other side. For three years, I had the pleasure of using a chemical toilet and a shower about the size of a school locker. I put in a full bath complete with an antique claw-foot bathtub. Want to see the inside?"

Mattie pulled her hand free and said, "Maybe another time. I can't stay too late. My daughter is at a friend's, and I have to pick her up."

"A daughter? I didn't know you had a kid. How old is she?"

"She's four."

"You're married?"

Mattie looked away. "No. A little indiscretion with a very handsome moron." She looked back at me and grinned. "An indiscretion that led to the best thing that's ever happened in my life."

"Wow, Mattie Castro a mother. I'm assuming he was a male prostitute?"

She playfully pushed me. "Enough with the kidding. Let's go back to the fire. I have time for one more drink."

I beat her there. "You don't have to ask me twice," I said as I picked up the bottle and poured a couple of fingers into both glasses.

"You've been a busy man."

"I found it therapeutic. I've landscaped with Florida natives, so I don't have to take care of plants other than trim them back."

"Do you have a boat?" Mattie asked, pointing at the dock.

"Nah. Maybe someday." I looked at her. "So, what really brings you out here, Mattie?"

She smiled, though it looked counterfeit. "After our little confrontation at the police station, I felt bad."

"You? The iron lady of the San Marco press actually felt an emotion?"

"Yes, I did. We don't run into each other that much, but when we do, we always seem to butt heads."

I nodded. "Like a couple of angry goats."

"It doesn't have to be that way. I know we had that little problem in the past, and I just wanted to come over and give you this little peace offering," she said, picking up the bottle.

"Well, thank you, Mattie Castro. Damn neighborly of you. Anything else concerning tonight's visit?"

"Well, now that you bring it up, I also thought that on a case like the senator's murder, we're both basically working on the same side."

"We're the good guys," I said.

"Exactly. We want to root through the bullshit and get to the truth."

I smiled and stood. "You know, you're right. I want to get to the truth because I've been hired by a client to prove his innocence, and you want to get to the truth so you can report it to your readers."

Mattie stood and put her hand on my forearm. "Fitz, I think we should work together."

"What do you mean?"

"I think we should share the things that we each learn, help one another out."

I chewed on my bottom lip for a moment, creasing my brows in thought. "Interesting idea." I looked at her and smiled. "You first. What do you have to share?"

She said, "Sadly, I don't have anything to add to what I knew when I saw you at the police station. If I did, I'd tell you." She sighed and shrugged and went on. "How about you? Anything new?"

I wasn't about to tell her some of the things I'd learned. Instead, I said, "You know, Mattie, I have learned something interesting."

Mattie grinned and stepped close. "What?"

"I've learned that besides what I already knew about you, I can add 'condescending sneak' to the list."

"What?"

I locked eyes with her. "You said my home was antediluvian, thinking I'm too stupid to know what that means."

Mattie's face closed down, and I took pleasure in the anger brewing at herself for underestimating me.

I barked a humorless laugh. "I'm surprised you didn't demonstrate your superiority by further telling me my house is primordial."

"I was tempted," Mattie grumbled.

"You think you're the Mata Hari of reporters who's going to come weasel information out of... What'd you call me today? A drunk alarm installer pretending to be Sam Spade? And then you can claim credit for it so you can keep telling yourself you're some hot-shit journalist." Like the fire in the pit, my anger started to blaze. "The last thing you want to do is work with me."

"Why would I? You're a burned-out drunk. Give me my rum," she said, reaching for it.

I picked up the bottle, pushed the stopper into the top, and held it out of her reach. "To me, Mattie Castro, you'll always be a consummate lowlife, and if you were on fire, I wouldn't waste my piss to put you out."

"Well, aren't you holier than thou?" Mattie said, reaching again and missing the bottle. "First off, I only did my job, and if you'd been doing yours, I wouldn't have written those stories."

"I, too, was doing my job," I said. "And after your witch-hunt articles, I no longer had a job."

Mattie's eyes widened in disbelief. "You blame me, you blame Eddie, you blame the department, you blame the newspaper, you blame everybody but the one person responsible"—she pointed at me with her arm fully extended—"yourself." She took a breath. "I reported the truth of how you were conducting police operations while under the influence."

I shouted, "You used my wife's death to come after me!"

I threw the bottle of rum into the firepit. It exploded in a rum-fueled firestorm that reached toward the sky. The fireball illuminated

Mattie's open mouth and wide eyes. She held up her hands in an attempt to shield herself.

My voice dropped to a growl. "After what you wrote, I wanted to kill you."

Mattie stood still, hugging herself like she was cold. Finally, without turning her back on me, she moved to her chair and picked up her handbag. She walked hastily to the driveway, never taking her eyes from me for more than a second.

Opening her car door, she yelled, "It's been—what? Six years? Seven? And you're still a fucking mess, you know that?" She got in and drove off.

"Yeah, I know that," I mumbled and picked up my glass and drained it.

Chapter 10

On a stormy Florida night on a country backroad, headlights approached. I waved my arms, knowing that it was my car and my wife was driving it. Frantic, I ran toward her, shouting at her to stop. I knew that if she went around the curve behind me, she would die.

I woke shouting a garbled mass of words. After a few moments of staring up at the ceiling, I got my heartbeat under control.

"Son of a bitch," I mumbled. "That's a crappy way to start a day."

I checked the clock and saw it was early morning. After rolling out of bed, I stopped in the kitchen to get the java started then went to the bathroom to create some vacancy in my bladder for that coffee. I sat at the kitchen table and sipped my brew while researching the various employees from the senator's office on my laptop. Some had been in the political game for a long time, and others were so new at it that little was there to find, like Caroline Ortiz. I remembered what Roger Stansbury, the office manager, had said about Caroline, how her fondness for her boss was tied to daddy issues. I googled her father, Reverend Ernesto Ortiz, and found a plethora of information. I clicked on YouTube footage from a press conference at the height of Ortiz's trouble. He was standing at a podium, sweating heavily, eyes ablaze. I jumped ahead and watched as he ferociously defended himself by attacking the women he'd slept with, calling them sluts and whores then going all biblical and proclaiming they were harlots and strumpets. Veins stood out in his neck, and spittle flew. I thought about Caroline as a child going through all that. *Poor kid.* I shut my laptop, checked the time, and saw I needed to get on the road.

I spent an hour in Old City, San Marco's historic district. Ben Lightner gave me a tour of the British Colony, a three-acre outdoor museum of colonial history that highlighted Florida's brief twenty-one-year British period, which ran from 1763 to 1784. Lightner's problem was from a modern era: drunks climbing the fence after last call at surrounding pubs, clubs, and bars and partying on the property.

"Some mornings, I spend all my time picking up beer cans and bottles and cigarette butts and have to check for damage or graffiti." Lightner pointed up at the three-story watchtower with an expression of revulsion. "And I can't tell you how many times I've had to pick up used condoms from there."

"That's pretty damn gross," I told him.

I figured motion-activated surveillance cameras and spotlights would do the trick, and we walked the property once more as I figured out the best places to install them.

"How much we talking?" Lightner asked.

"Let me work up some figures," I told him. "We can do a straight-out rental, we can sell you everything you need, or we can do the Buddy Reid Security easy payment plan."

I got back in my truck and headed to the beach. While Senator McGovern's beach getaway house was in the same area code as the Folly, the median income of his neighborhood had a lot more digits than mine. Along the coast in southern San Marco County, Brisas del Mar featured rambling homes on one- and two-acre beachfront lots. Driving south on A1A, I remembered an article I'd once read in the *San Marco Ledger* about how beach property was considered nearly worthless in the early 1900s. The story included an old advertisement from 1903 listing citrus tree farmland west of San Marco, and if someone bought three or more acres, they could receive a free beachfront lot. These days, that beachfront in Brisas del Mar was a minimum seven figures just for the land.

The day was thinly overcast, the kind on which someone could go to the beach and get sunburned even without seeing the sun. Still, the sky was bright enough that I wore my aviator sunglasses. A1A through Brisas del Mar was hilly, a rising and falling road, which was a rarity in Florida. A patrol car was parked at the base of the senator's driveway by the open gate. I turned in, and the cop waved me on. I remembered him from my days on the force. His name was Deutch, and everyone called him Dutch.

The drive went up then down briefly then rose again, and I was at the house. The shingle-style three-story mansion looked too New England for Florida, but I wasn't an architect. Still, I knew enough to know those pointy parts on the roof were called gables, and the house had a lot of them, as well as chimneys, three that I could count, which seemed like overkill in Florida. What looked like a tower at one side of the house rose up to a flat part with a railing that I took to be a widow's walk, which Lucinda could now use literally. Funny that the senator called it his little getaway since ten or so Fitz Follies could be squeezed into it. On a humble note, the smaller version on the other side of the driveway, the garage with the guesthouse over it, was only three times the size of my house.

Eddie's unmarked was parked in front, along with a silver Toyota sedan. Eddie stood next to Caroline Ortiz by the steps up to one of the covered porches. Eddie grasped a manila envelope and was talking on his cell.

When he ended the call, he said, "You look like shit this morning."

"I'd hit you back with a witty zinger if I hadn't had a sleepless night." I looked at Caroline, who still looked like a waif even though she wore a name-brand pantsuit. "Morning, Ms. Ortiz."

"Call me Caroline, please."

"And I'm Fitz."

"Mrs. Combs-McGovern has meetings this morning, so Caroline was kind enough to come open the house for us," Eddie explained. Looking me over, he asked, "Went back to Doone's?"

"Give us a second," I told Caroline then pulled Eddie out of her hearing range. "I went home after talking with Ronnie and partying with the Goldens." I took off my sunglasses, folded them, and hung them from my T-shirt collar. "Mattie Castro showed up at my place."

"What? Where'd you bury her corpse?"

"Ha, ha. Very funny. I started to kick her tight little ass off of my property, but then she pulled out a bottle of fine rum."

"Which means you became the consummate host."

"My BFF for a while. She was trying to pump me for information."

"She's smart but naïve."

"Anyway, it got me to thinking about the past. There was a whole lot of tossin' and turnin' last night."

Eddie looked at me with grave seriousness. "I know you don't believe me, but if I could go back and do things differently, I would."

"So you've told me."

"You think I'm lying."

"I only know what happened."

"Sometimes, I wish that I'd tasered you and shut you in the trunk of our car until it was over." Eddie grinned a bit and added, "It would have saved everyone a whole lot of trouble."

I scratched a whiskered cheek. "You're probably right."

Eddie stared in silence and finally said, "Did I hear you correctly? Did you say I was probably right?"

"*Probably* is the key word, but yeah, that's a lot of what I thought about last night," I admitted.

"Well, gloriosky, if this isn't a red-letter day," Eddie said, more to himself than me.

Eddie and I weren't the touchy-feely kind of guys, but he knew it was my way of attempting to end six years of holding a grudge. "Now you'll know the proper thing to do next time I go off the deep end."

"How about no more deep ends?"

"You know me better than that." I looked up at the house then winked at Eddie. "Take me up to the sex room, you big hunk of man."

As we approached the front door, Eddie said, "Caroline."

She pulled a key chain from her bag and unlocked the front door. We entered, and she went to the security system and punched in a code.

I stood at her side. At first glance, I saw the security system was a piece of shit. At second glance, I saw the numbers she punched into the keypad. "That security system is junk." I took out my wallet and flipped through business cards, found one that touted only my work as a consultant for Buddy Reid Security, and handed it to Caroline. "I moonlight as a security consultant and can fix Mrs. Combs-Mc-Govern up with a good one."

"I'll let her know," Caroline said, depositing my card in her bag.

Taking in the grand foyer, I said, "This isn't even a real room, and it has more furniture than I have in my entire house."

"It's nice to be rich," Eddie said.

As we started down the hall, I noticed Caroline wasn't coming. "Where's our guide?"

Eddie whispered, "She told me she'd wait for us out front. Says she can't handle the crime scene."

I nodded, and we traversed past glorious rooms, beautiful paintings, and the finest furnishings. "The Folly just isn't going to seem as opulent after all this." As we started up the staircase, I pointed out, "Glenn Golden has a strong motive."

"I know. He'll probably take the senator's seat, something he couldn't have done if McGovern was alive."

"How strong do you think their alibis are? I'm talking the whole Golden clan."

"Glenn, Ginny, and Stuart stayed the night up in Ponte Vedra, that's for sure. On the other hand, any of them could have left late at night, driven down, killed the senator, and driven back up. We'll check with the staff at the place they were staying and review security footage, and the manager at the Lodge and Club said that their computer system makes a record of every time a key card is used at a room."

"How about Barry?"

"Home asleep. His wife confirms, but that's not a great alibi, is it?"

"Nope."

On the second floor, Eddie led me down to the master bedroom. Pointing farther down the hallway, Eddie said, "The sex room is on the other side of that long stretch of wall, but you have to go in here to get to it."

"How badly did Mattie and those other reporters contaminate the scene?" I asked.

"Not a bit."

I crossed my arms and gave him the side-eye. "Uh-huh."

"I know what you're thinking, but once Mattie saw the senator, she made sure no one stepped into the sex room. She said it was obvious he was dead and nothing could have been done to help him."

We went into the master bedroom, which featured blond wood furnishings and nearly pastel blues. The cool-colored walls were painted with a marble pattern. The window treatments on the big bay window overlooking the Atlantic Ocean matched the blue.

"The secret passage isn't so secret if they leave it open," I said, nodding at the open bookcase and the X across the entrance made by yellow crime scene tape. "I can't wait to see what a sex room looks like." I hurried across the room and ducked under the tape. "Hmm, kind of cheesy. And look at that." I pointed past a small chandelier hanging from the middle of the ceiling to the obligatory mirror mounted over the behemoth of a bed made of mahogany with four posts, a massive mattress, and box springs.

"The techies took the silk sheets and the pillows," Eddie said.

I strolled around, taking in the love seat and an oddly shaped chair that I figured offered all kinds of positional opportunities. I noticed something else and hopped up and down. "The floor's smooshy."

"It's some kind of matting, like a wrestling mat."

"Better than carpet burn."

The room was approximately thirty by thirty. Each wall was meant to hold seven large framed pictures that contained what looked like centuries-old etchings of sex acts. Some hung askew, and others had fallen to the floor.

"Did that. That one too," I said as I walked around the room, looking at each. "Had a girlfriend who wanted to try that, but I said no way. Checked that one off the list in high school. Did that with a gymnast, and it took me a month to recover."

I went to the open wardrobe, made of the same wood as the bed. Eight feet wide, it stood over seven feet tall and had a depth of four feet. The inner left-hand door had deep shelves that held a variety of dildos and vibrators, pointing up like missiles ready to launch. A chest of drawers was built into the right side of the wardrobe. One drawer was slightly open, and a couple of scarves dangled from it. I opened the next drawer down and saw all manner of restraining devices and bottles of lubricants. Curiosity had me reaching for the next drawer down, but I chickened out, fearful of what I might find. Instead, I riffled through what hung on clothes hangers—all kinds of outfits for role-play: nurses, French maids, cowboys, and burglars. All manner of lingerie and more hung in the wardrobe.

I pulled one hanger from the wardrobe and held it out for Eddie to see. "Look, a real gimp suit."

"And you're touching it."

"Point taken." I rehung it and wiped my hand on my pants. "I've been saving the best for last."

"I know," Eddie said.

I swept out a hand. "Why all the penis-shaped chalk marks on the floor?" Across the matted floor, from small to large, were random phallic shapes drawn carefully in chalk.

"That's a funny story," Eddie said. "Whoever killed the senator went on a rage, trashing the room and throwing stuff all around."

"Yeah, that's a real hoot."

"I haven't got to the funny part yet. Among the stuff scattered around were a bunch of sex toys."

"That's mildly amusing."

Eddie shook his head. "Remember the captain's nephew?"

"Always hanging out at the station when he was a teenager? Proof that a person can function with a single-digit IQ? Sure."

"That's him, Odean Hurley. Get this: the captain got it into his head to bring his nephew onto the force."

"No."

"He's enrolled in the program at San Marco Tech, and he's been interning with us." Eddie grinned. "The captain decided it was time he visit a real crime scene, and he came out yesterday with all the investigators and techies. Busby was in charge, and Odean kept bugging him, asking what he could do. Finally, Busby told him they needed chalk outlines around all the sex toys. He was just joking, but next thing he knew, Odean had actually done it."

Chuckling, I followed the chalk outlines around the corner of the bed and said, "Holy cow, is that one for real?"

Eddie looked at the huge penile tracing. "A real bruiser."

"Dildosaurus rex," I said with reverent awe. "I thought it was an urban legend."

"Here." Eddie handed me the manila envelope. "Crime scene photos."

I took the envelope and went to the funny-shaped chair and started to sit. I stopped when I thought about the purpose of the room and moved to sit on the very edge of the love seat.

"Good idea to limit contact," Eddie said. "They ran UV lights all over and said the room looked like the Milky Way."

I scooted even closer to the edge and opened the envelope. For the next five minutes, I carefully examined each of the photos then went through them again. I stood up and held a photo out to Eddie. "What's with the broken glass on his chest and the pillows?"

"The killer beat the senator with all kinds of things, not just fists. At some point, he grabbed a framed picture and drove it into the senator's face."

"Ouch." I placed the photos back in the envelope and handed it back to Eddie. "Let's get out of here." Looking around the room, I added, "I never thought something called a sex room would depress me."

Lou was waiting for us outside and talking with Caroline. Lou also wore a pantsuit, blue to Caroline's black. They were sitting on the front steps and stood when we came out.

"Took you boys long enough," Lou said. "Get some decorating tips?"

"It's like a pervert's Disneyland," I said then noticed Caroline's reaction—hands gripped into tight fists and her eyes cast down in anger or embarrassment or both. I told her "Sorry."

She nodded, though I doubt she forgave me.

Lou's finger danced over the screen of her cell until she found what she was looking for. She looked at Caroline then nodded to indicate we should step away. We went down the front steps, and Caroline went in to set the security system.

Lou said, "Some lab work is in. Only two types of blood were found at the scene, O positive and AB negative. The senator is O positive. Guess Coach Thorpe's blood type."

"AB negative," Eddie said.

"Bingo. We'll find out in a couple of days if it's definitely Mack's. The medical examiner says those big scratches on the senator's torso were caused by fingernails. We've confirmed the scrapings we got from under Mack's nails contained skin and blood, and we should find out soon if it's the senator's flesh."

"Not looking good for my client," I said.

Grinning, Lou said, "It gets worse for him. There were several sets of fingerprints in the room, including Mack's."

"Where were his prints found?" Eddie asked.

"All over. Even a couple of sex toys including something called the Sexterminator."

I held my hands over a foot apart and gave Lou a questioning look.

Lou rolled her eyes. "Yes, that one."

I leaned in and mock whispered, "We've christened it Dildosaurus rex." A thought came to me, and I shuddered. "There it is again, that mental image of Mack and McGovern."

Lou laughed. "Don't think about it too much. I'm guessing it's more a case of the coach interrupting some kinky coitus."

"Kinky coitus," I said. "That'd be a great band name."

Lou went on, "I'm guessing the reason Mack's prints were on the Dildosaurus was he was hitting the senator with it. The ME says some of the bruising matches the size and shape."

"Whoa. Death by dong. Can this case get any weirder?" I looked up at the house as I did some mental calculations. "So, the theory is shaping up that not only were the senator and Ronnie Thorpe up to some hanky-panky at the homeless initiative gala, they got to hanky-ing and pankying here, and the coach caught them."

"Which leads to something else pointing at Mack as the killer—he lied about a special practice for the team night before last."

"Really?"

Lou said, "I went to the high school and talked to an assistant coach and several of the players. They didn't know what I was talking about when I asked them about it."

"No practice, and the coach wasn't home."

Eddie said, "All that plus Mack's temper. He's the killer."

"Crap," I said. "Do you know how hard it is to collect a fee from someone on death row? Come on, I want another go at Mack."

I took another glance at the house and saw that Caroline was standing on the steps, listening to what we were saying.

"I hope that evil man gets the death penalty," she said through clenched teeth.

Chapter 11

Lou stayed out of sight and monitored the interview on CCTV. I paced the interrogation room as we waited for Mack.

"Chill," Eddie said. "You're making me nervous."

"No can do. I want to intimidate the coach, so I'm working myself up. And as I go over every lie he laid at my feet, it's not hard to build up a righteous anger."

When a uniform brought the coach in, I kept my back to him while he was cuffed to the table, and I stayed that way after the uniform left.

After a minute, Mack asked Eddie, "You guys learn anything?"

I spun around like Baryshnikov and brought my fist down on the table. "We learned you're a lying sack of shit!" I yelled it loud, and Mack shrank back as far as the handcuffs would allow. The fear on display proved that like most bullies, a little confrontation had him cowering. "All you've done is lie, and frankly, I don't like that. I hope they pin this on your sorry ass and send you to Starke. Hell, for snuffing a senator, they might pull Ol' Sparky out of mothballs."

Ol' Sparky was the electric chair Florida had used for decades, though they currently used lethal injection.

Mack strained to remain as far from me as possible. "I didn't lie or kill the senator."

"You lied about everything else."

"Easy, Fitz." Eddie put a hand on my arm and took the good-cop route. "Look, Coach, we've got your fingerprints and blood type all over the crime scene. You thought he was messing with your wife, which gives you motive, and since, as we've learned, you lied about a special practice Monday night, you had opportunity. All the evidence we've gathered points straight to you. If you've misconstrued anything—"

"Misconstrued?" I snorted. "He lied his ass off."

"Now's the time to tell the truth," Eddie said, "or we're charging you. And with what we have, you'll go down hard."

Mack sat there with wide eyes, not saying a thing.

I opened the door. "Come on, Eddie. I'm sick of wasting time on this guy."

Mack blinked, seeming close to tears. "Wait. I'll tell you the truth, everything."

I closed the door and approached the table, using a foot to snag a chair that was against the wall and pull it over next to Eddie's. "First hint of bullshit, and I'm walking."

The coach nodded and hung his head. He was silent for a long time, and just as I was about to say something, he said, "I didn't come up with the bullshit story about a special practice for an alibi. I came up with it so I could catch Ronnie in the act."

"You wanted to catch her and the senator?" Eddie asked.

"Yeah. Big-shot fucking senator. Lah-dee-dah. And it worked. I followed Ronnie over to McGovern's beach house."

"Now we're getting somewhere," I said.

"I wanted to scare the senator off, make him think twice before screwing another man's wife. So I waited until Ronnie left, which took two hours. What the fuck could they have been doing for two hours?"

I bit the inside of my cheek to keep from saying anything.

"I brought my gun just to put the fear of God in him. I couldn't believe it when I tried the door—it was unlocked. I went in, went through the first floor, didn't find shit. Up on the second floor, I began to hear, well, muffled grunts, what turned out to be the senator trying to yell with that thing in his mouth."

"Run us through what you saw," Eddie instructed him.

"Well, I went through his bedroom. A bookcase was swung away from the wall, and that was how you got in that room. I went in, just a step or two, and couldn't believe the shit I saw. The senator was buck-ass naked, tied to the bed—"

"Handcuffs," I said.

"One thing I liked was the fear in his eyes when he saw me. It was kind of funny because, even with the gag, he was trying to sound calm, saying who knows what. I kind of wandered around, and every now and then, I'd turn and point the gun at him like I was going to shoot him. Scared the hell out of him. And then as I'm looking around, I realized that my wife had been there in that room with him, and I started to get pissed. I looked at the dirty pictures, the dildos, the bottles of lubricants—who needs that much fucking lubrication?—and that fuckin' sex closet open with all that shit, and I just lost it."

"You lost it," Eddie repeated. "In what way?"

"I went apeshit crazy. I tore through that room, knocking shit over, throwing those sex toys all over the place, kicking things. The senator looked panicked, like he realized I might just kill his sorry ass."

"Is that what happened?" I asked.

"No, no. I mean, I just kept getting madder, and after I tore up the room, I looked at the senator, and the next thing I know, I'm slapping him, asking if it's worth fucking my wife. And I get even madder, and I start punching him, and yeah, I beat him pretty good." Mack looked past me and Eddie, like he was remembering something in particular, and smiled. "Then I got this huge dildo—I mean really big—and hit the senator with that five or six times." His attention turned back to us. "The thing was made from a rubbery kind of material, like those fake fishing worms, but it was big and heavy, and I liked the idea of Senator Mitch fuckin' McGovern going around a few weeks with dick-shaped bruises."

"There were scratches on the senator's torso," Eddie said. "Are you responsible for those too?"

"Yeah. I know it's the girls who do the scratching, and a guy is supposed to use his fists, but I was so fucking mad I swiped him a few times with my nails, and it felt good." Mack took a couple of deep breaths. "And after all that, I wasn't so mad anymore, and I left. And I swear the senator was alive."

"What time did you leave?" Eddie asked.

"I don't know. I wasn't looking at any clocks, ya know?"

"How long after Ronnie left?" I asked.

"With looking around downstairs and all, I left maybe twenty, thirty minutes after I saw Ronnie leave."

Eddie and I exchanged a glance, and I gave a subtle nod toward the door.

Eddie stood. "We're going to take a break. Can we get you something?"

"Can I get some coffee?" Mack asked.

"Sure," Eddie said.

Lou joined Eddie and me in the hall. "What do you think?" she asked.

"I think we're getting the truth this time," I said.

"Yeah, me too," Eddie added.

"Which means he beat up the senator but left him breathing," Lou said.

I scratched my chin while thinking and said, "Doesn't mean he didn't go back."

"I could see that," Eddie said. "Mack keeps drinking, the anger builds, and he goes back to finish the job."

Lou nodded. "And hell, if he drank enough, he might not even remember it."

"Ronnie can't alibi him because she doesn't know if he came home or not. I'm going to twist that a little bit and see how he reacts," I said.

Lou returned to the CCTV, I went back into the interrogation room, and Eddie joined us a couple of minutes later with a Styrofoam cup of coffee for Mack.

I let the coach enjoy a couple of hot sips before I said, "Ronnie says you didn't come home that night."

"She said that, huh?" He shook his head and took another swallow of coffee. Eddie and I looked at one another, noting Mack's lack of concern. "Yeah, I'd blown off steam at the senator's place, but I knew if I went home and looked at Ronnie, I'd remember she'd been in that fuckin' room, and I'd probably lose it again. I went to Drew's Hideaway, sat at the bar for a while, and tried to drink myself calm."

"That's when you got in a fight?" Eddie asked.

"Some punk I don't even know made the occasional comment about how crappy the team is this year. I was just going to ignore him, but then I looked down at my hands and saw how beat up my knuckles were after pounding on the senator. It seemed a bar fight might offer up a good reason for busted knuckles in case I got in trouble for kicking the senator's ass. The next time the fucker said something, I was all over him. Drew kicked me out of the bar, so I went and bought a bottle of Jack." He straightened up as a thought came to him. "Yeah, I got it at the ABC Store just up the street, paid with my credit card. You can check that, right?"

"You can bet we will," Eddie said.

"I ended up driving around and drinking," Mack said.

"When did you go back to McGovern's house?" I asked.

Mack looked surprised. "I didn't go back."

"You just drove around all night?"

"No. I was getting shit-faced and knew I'd probably end up with a DUI, so I headed over to the high school parking lot and sat there and drank until I passed out. I didn't wake up until school was underway, and then you guys showed up," he told Eddie, "and I've been here ever since."

I went around the table and sat on the corner, close to Mack. "What are the chances you drank so much that you blacked out and went back to the senator's place?"

Mack chewed on that for a moment. "Hypothetically, I suppose it's possible, but I didn't. I damn near finished that bottle before I passed out. And I can tell you that going back to the senator's place never once crossed my mind." Mack looked at us, trying to gauge our belief. "Senator Mitch McGovern was alive when I left him—beat up but breathing."

The door to the interrogation room opened, and Lou beckoned Eddie out to the hallway.

Speaking softly, Mack asked me, "How much trouble am I in?"

I sat in a chair and leaned back. "Hard to say. This whole thing is so screwy. But if what you're saying is true, you're probably looking at aggravated assault."

"Ah shit."

"Hey, that's better than murder, though leaving the senator tied up isn't going to work in your favor. Hell, the DA may want to try attempted murder."

"I didn't try to kill him."

"Right now, Mack, you want to do all within your power to clear yourself of murder, and then you can worry about the other charges. Time to call a lawyer."

"I'll think about it," Mack said.

Eddie came back in and sat in his chair, while Lou stood by the door with her arms crossed.

"Interesting turn of events, Coach," Eddie said. "Turns out Senator McGovern died of suffocation."

Mack looked at him blankly.

"He couldn't breathe," Lou said.

"I know what suffocation means," Mack snapped at her.

"Did you know you broke the senator's nose?" Lou asked.

"Yeah, so?"

I shook my head. "Come on, Mack, you're employed at an institute of learning. You may not have intended to kill him, but if you broke his nose and it swelled up so he couldn't breathe through it, and there was a ball gag preventing him from breathing through his mouth, then you're responsible for the senator's death."

Mack was led back to his cell in a daze.

I looked at Eddie and said, "He's up shit creek without a snowball's chance in hell." I noted Eddie's entire-body twitch, then I walked away, hiding a grin.

"Let's go visit Ronnie," Lou said.

Chapter 12

I gave Ronnie a big smile and said, "Happy to see me again?"

Ronnie stood at the open door to her house and glared.

Lou said, "Ms. Thorpe, I'm Detective Peters, and this is Detective Schmitt."

Ronnie stepped back. "Come on in."

She led us to the living room, and the furnishings were a stark difference to those in the McGoverns' beach house. All of it looked as though it had been bought years before at bargain furniture stores. Though all the curtains and blinds were wide open, the house was still dim, and I wondered if that was just a reflection of the overall atmosphere of the home. A brown recliner sat directly in front of the TV, the leather cracking in places, and I figured it for the coach's throne. Mack's glory wall was opposite the TV, featuring a number of framed photographs from high points in Mack's coaching career as well as when he was an athlete in school. A shelf held a number of trophies.

Eddie and Lou sat on a chenille sofa depicting a fox hunt. I sat on a gliding rocker, and Ronnie pulled over a ladder-back chair.

"When does my husband get to come home?" Ronnie asked.

"It's not looking good," Lou said.

Eddie added, "There's a lot of evidence pointing at your husband."

"He didn't kill the senator." She said it as if it were the silliest of notions.

"Maybe not intentionally," I said.

"What do you mean by that?" Ronnie asked.

Without answering her, Eddie asked, "Where were you the night Senator McGovern was killed?"

"Me? You think I had something to do with it?"

"Just answer the question," Eddie said.

"I was here, at home."

"Not all night," I said, wiggling my eyebrows.

"Yes, I was here all—"

Eddie interrupted her. "Detective Peters and I were coming to see you today, and Fitz told us he'd already talked to you. According to him, you don't know whether your husband came home Monday night or not."

"That's right. He had a special practice with the team, and then I assume he went out for a drink because he wasn't home by the time I went to bed. I didn't get up until after he usually leaves for work."

Lou asked, "Wouldn't he have woken you, getting into bed?"

Ronnie looked over at the recliner. "Sometimes, he falls asleep in front of the TV."

"Ronnie," I said.

"Mrs. Thorpe," she answered icily.

"Ronnie, your husband told us he didn't come home that night. He also admitted that there was no special practice."

Ronnie leaned forward, concern on her face. "What do you mean?"

Eddie started to answer, but I interrupted him. "He lied to you. He followed you to McGovern's beach place."

Normally a tan woman, Ronnie's face drained of color. Her mouth moved without making a sound, and finally, she mumbled, "I need some water."

Ronnie started to stand, but Lou got up and said, "You sit. I'll get it. Just point the way."

Without looking, Ronnie aimed her index finger in the general direction. Lou returned a minute later and handed Ronnie a glass.

Though she took a drink, Ronnie's voice was dry when she asked, "What else did Mack tell you?"

Lou, still standing, reached down to take Ronnie's hand. "He said that after you left, he went in and found the senator bound to the bed. He said he lost his temper and assaulted the senator."

Ronnie started to cry. "Mack, you stupid hothead."

I said, "Mack says he didn't intend to kill the senator. The medical examiner says McGovern died of suffocation, and since he had that ball gag in his mouth and Mack broke his nose, preventing him from breathing, your husband is in hot water."

Squeezing Ronnie's hand in sympathy, Lou said, "No more lies. We need the truth if we're going to help your husband." She handed Ronnie a tissue.

Ronnie sniffed. "Yeah, yeah, okay." She took a moment to wipe her nose. "The senator and I—ever since I've been on the homeless initiative board—he and I..."

"Have been canoodling," I finished for her.

She nodded.

"We don't need all the details, but we need to know all about that night," Eddie told her.

I jumped in. "Which was basically that you two did the bondage thing, and then you left."

"Yes."

"Why did you leave him handcuffed to the bed?" Eddie asked.

Confusion returned to her face. "I didn't. I mean, he shouldn't have been. He stayed in the cuffs and watched me dress, and then I left without freeing him... as a joke. But they weren't real cuffs. They're the kind you buy at the Marquis and Madame Adult Store. They have safety releases in case things get out of hand. I don't know why he didn't free himself."

Lou, Eddie, and I looked at one another.

I asked, "What do you mean he watched you dress?"

She shrugged. "Just what I said. I got dressed. He watched. It was a joke. And I left."

"Are you sure, Ronnie?" Lou asked.

"Yes, why?"

"Because he was found wearing a blindfold," Eddie said.

Chapter 13

I had ridden from the police station with Eddie and Lou, and after
we finished questioning Ronnie, I rode in the back seat on the return trip, going over what we'd learned.

As we approached Constabulary Boulevard and the police station, Lou said, "You're mighty quiet back there."

"Yeah, it's really nice," Eddie said. "It's a trait you should culti-
vate."

"Har-dee-har," I said. "You guys mind if I talk to Mack again?"

"Sure, I'll sit in with you," Eddie said.

"Nah, let's make this one of those private he's-my-client interviews."

"Those only carry weight if you're an attorney," Lou said.

"Don't make me go and get a law degree," I threatened.

"Fitz a lawyer..." Eddie said, turning to Lou. "Can you imagine
how annoying that'd be?"

She thought a second and said, "Yeah, sure, you go have a private
meeting with your client."

Eddie's phone rang. "Detective Schmitt," he answered. He listened and said, "Good job. Make sure I get a copy of your report." He
ended the call and told us, "They towed in Mack's car from the high
school and found a forty-four Magnum under the front seat."

It turned out that Mack had been moved to the county lockup.
Though still on the grounds of the police department complex, it was
operated by the county sheriff's department. Normally, once an in-
mate was processed, someone could only visit them via video visitation from a remote location. In San Marco, that locale was housed in

what used to be a convenience store five miles from the jail. Similar to Zoom, the video visitation all but ended contraband smuggled into the jail and allowed each visit to be videotaped. Of course, police interviewing inmates and lawyers visiting clients still met with them in person. As I was working on Mack's behalf, Eddie got me in for a face-to-face. I waited for Mack in an interview room with a Coke for him and a Diet Coke for myself. Mack showed up in a bright-orange jumpsuit, escorted by a deputy.

Mack sat, and I passed him the soda across a small plastic tabletop. "That color does not look good on you."

"I feel like a flippin' traffic cone," Mack grumbled and opened his Coke. "I got a lawyer. He says not to talk to anyone."

"How about me?"

"He said especially you."

"Who'd you get?"

"David Ross."

"He's a snake," I said and got up. "Which makes him a good lawyer. Well, if you're not going to talk to me, I won't waste your time or mine."

"Fuck Ross. What do you want to know?"

So I sat again. "I want you to walk me through that night again. Give me every detail as you remember it."

"Why?"

"I believed you when you said you didn't intend to kill the senator. I mean, you brought your gun to scare him, so if you'd planned to kill him, why not just shoot him? On the other hand, you broke his nose while his mouth was gagged, so you are unintentionally responsible for his death."

"What's the point of rehashing it?" Mack asked.

"There's something that bugs me."

"What?"

"That's what I want to find out."

Mack drained his soda, burped, and ran down everything again. He added a little more meat here and there but nothing that stood out as important.

Then the proverbial light bulb over my head went off. I asked, "When did you hit him with the framed picture?"

Mack blinked a few times. "What picture?"

I looked at him, judged his reaction sincere, and said, "That's a damn good question."

I left the county jail, and since it was a little past lunchtime, I hit one of my old haunts, Rhonda's. A chrome-sided diner near the police station, it had been feeding the men and women of law enforcement for years. Sitting on a cushioned stool at the lunch counter, I nodded at cops I used to work with and ordered what had been my favorite when I was a regular, Rhonda's Men in Blue Burger, a three-quarter-pound burger with melted bleu cheese, a slice of ham, and fried onion rings on top of that. I chowed down, pausing only to flirt with the waitress. I'd almost finished when my phone pinged. Eddie was texting that he wanted to see me. Five minutes later, I was sitting on Lou's desk as the detectives broke the news.

"The broken nose didn't swell enough to cut off the flow of oxygen," Eddie said.

"He didn't suffocate?"

"He did suffocate, but that wasn't the cause," Lou said.

"What was?"

"Don't know yet. Not only that, but Lou and I went to talk to some of the coach's players," Eddie said. "And guess what? He has an alibi."

"Really?"

Eddie said, "The coroner has put the time of death at somewhere between five and seven in the morning. Now, look at this." Eddie brought up a photo on his phone.

I took it and laughed. "Please, you have to send me a copy."

It showed Coach Thorpe passed out in the front seat of his car.

"Cooper Grant, one of the running backs, showed up before school to run the track. He found the coach like this and took a picture, which he shared on Instagram," Eddie said.

I texted the picture to my phone. "His team has as much regard for Mack as his wife does."

Eddie took his phone back. "Yeah, well, he took the photo right smack dab in the middle of the time of death, which gives Mack an alibi."

"What are you going to do with Mack now?"

"He'll still be charged with aggravated assault and who knows what else. But for now, we're going to release him," Lou said. "Want to go break the news with us?"

"Nah, I've had my fill of Mack Thorpe for the day. Tell him I'm off the case and will send him a bill." I hopped off the desk and headed for the exit.

Chapter 14

The sun started its descent and would soon turn the western sky bright pinks and oranges. I waited for sundown in a wooden Adirondack chair at the end of the small dock in front of my house and used a Zebco rod and reel to cast a line far out into the Intracoastal Waterway. Savoring the *ploop* sound every time the weight hit the water, I would then slowly reel it in. A whiskey glass and open bottle of rum sat on the dock next to me.

I thought of Senator McGovern's murder, and the Goldens nagged at me. If I really thought any one of them had anything to do with the senator's death, I would seriously consider investigating on my own dime. Not that I had anything against Glenn—he was a decent enough guy. However, he was a member of San Marco's good ol' boys club, which put a check in the negative column in my book. And yeah, there'd be a sadistic pleasure at seeing Barry behind bars. Though Ginny was a first-class bitch, I still felt sympathy for her from when her best friend was murdered, but Stuart was a surprise, his turnaround a revelation. If I'd had to put up money years before, I would've bet he would be dead already, either from an overdose or some drug-related violence. But it didn't really matter. I was off the case.

I cast my line back out into the water.

"Still fishing without bait?" someone behind me called.

"And without a hook," I said, not turning. "It's very Zen." A second later, a slim woman bent down and gave me a chaste kiss on the lips that made me smile. "How ya doing, Ivy?"

Wearing a half tank top and short cutoffs, Ivy kicked off her flip-flops and sat at the end of the dock, putting her feet in the water. "Busy with work." She owned a spa in town that offered hairstyling, massages, and mud wraps. "How about you?" Her brown hair was short and shaggy.

"I was knee-deep in a perplexing case, and now, I'm out of it."

"I heard. Senator McGovern's murder."

"Yeah, but my client has been cleared. I kind of wish I was still working it."

Ivy kicked at the water. "Also heard you were partnered with Eddie again. How was that?"

"Just between you and me, it was nice, you know? I mean, I was still pissed at him when we started, but Eddie's a good guy." I tried to better explain what I felt. "On the one hand, I know he did what he thought was right—hell, it was right—but on the other, he ratted out his partner, and that's not done."

"Quit being a drama queen, Fitz," Ivy said. "And since you're not currently working a case, you can do what you promised."

The previous week, I'd run into Ivy at Doone's and agreed to help Rick get out of a jam.

I started to respond but then got a good look at her. She looked like a pinup girl from an old calendar. I felt stirrings. "Shit," I said and reeled faster.

"Shit what?"

When the weight dangled from the tip of the rod, I put it on the dock. "I was thinking how nice you look, and the next thing I know, that ol' devil is dancin' in my loins."

Ivy held up a hand. "Uh-uh. We're never going there again. Look at the trouble we got in last time."

I chuckled. "I still put you in the 'good wife' category," I said.

Ivy stood and walked around the back of my chair and massaged my shoulders. "Fitz, you've only had one real wife. I knew there was no point in trying to compete with her."

Even with Ivy giving me one of her wonderful massages, a rush of melancholy pushed through me. "That's why you thought the divorce was a good idea?"

Ivy laughed. "Honey, that was just one of many reasons."

I patted one of her hands as she worked my shoulders. "We may not have been a good couple, but you're a hell of a friend."

"Speaking of friends, when are you going to help Rick?" Ivy asked.

Her hands moved up to my temples, and I leaned back and closed my eyes. After a long and appreciative moan, I said, "I tried a couple of days ago at Doone's. I told Rick I'd be more than happy to help him with the Bennett brothers. He said he didn't need my help."

But, of course, he did. The Bennetts would've been a joke if they weren't so damn dangerous. The best way to describe the whole clan was to compare them to—cue the banjo music—the hillbillies in the movie *Deliverance*.

"Those damn Bennett brothers should all be locked up," Ivy said.

In the past, when someone mentioned the Bennett brothers, they meant five, but two of them, Marlon and Jackie, were in prison. The remaining three were Tito, Jermaine, and Little Michael. Their mother was a serious Jackson 5 fan. And now, Rick was in bed with them.

"He wouldn't have gotten involved with them if his charter business wasn't struggling," Ivy said.

"I know."

Rick had run a couple of hundred pounds of pot on the *Titanic II* for the Bennett brothers. He thought it was a onetime deal. They thought otherwise.

"Now, they want him to run meth." Ivy shook her head.

The brothers had started to cook up the drug in Bennett Town, a name you wouldn't find on any map, though if it was, it would include a skull and crossbones. To get there, someone would need to take a boat through a maze of estuaries, interconnecting rivers, and creeks. A road also led in, but only the Bennetts knew the overland route. Rumor had it that the Bennetts had rigged the road with IEDs.

Ivy stopped her massage. There was a note of worry in her voice when she said, "They told Rick he has to do it or else."

Talking about this mess was getting me down, so I changed the subject. "I heard Rick has a new girlfriend."

Ivy stopped her massage. "Tell me you didn't go there."

"I went there."

She smacked the back of my head.

"Ouch. Why are women always hitting me?"

She came around and sat on the deck in front of me. "You should know better."

"You'd think. But I told him I couldn't wait to meet her. Next thing I know, we're rolling around on the dock. He got a couple of good shots in."

"You deserved it. He'll never trust you around a girlfriend again," Ivy said. "But that doesn't get you off the hook. He's in over his head. You need to help him whether he wants you to or not."

I wiggled my eyebrows Groucho Marx style. "I'm working on a plan."

"Fix this, and maybe he'll forgive you."

"I will, and he won't."

Ivy kissed my cheek, got her flip-flops, and headed back up the dock.

The sun hit the horizon, and the western sky turned orange. A mile across the Intracoastal, silhouettes of trees made up the skyline. I poured some rum into my glass and sat back, taking a moment to toast God for another beautiful sunset. I put the glass down and picked up my rod and reel.

Whizzzzzzzzzz–ploop.

Ivy was one in a million, but she'd been right when she said I'd had only one real wife. I saw Molly then in my mind, a memory from when we were going out somewhere and she asked how she looked. She wore a simple summer dress and turned this way and that as she waited for my opinion. God, she was beautiful.

"Fuck it!" I said it more loudly than intended. I repeated, "Fuck it," in a whisper. It sounded like a surrender.

Chapter 15

I woke with a head stuffed with barbed wire and a belly filled with acid—too much rum mixed with melancholy the night before. The only thing that would help would be more sleep, so I rolled over, hugged my pillow like a teddy bear, and tried to snooze. Instead, my subconscious settled in that place between wakefulness and sleep, the place where the mind runs toward whatever it chooses, like worries about the future, thoughts of what might have been, or in my case, events of the past. This time, my memory brought up the worst argument I'd ever had with my first wife.

Molly and I had been a young couple who, for eight years, had focused on our careers, hers as an executive assistant at the hospital and mine with the San Marco PD. We finally made the decision to start a family and celebrated with a trip to a little resort between Montego Bay and Ocho Rios in Jamaica. As we lay on those beautiful beaches, baking in the sun, an argument started about whether Molly was going right back to work after she had a baby. She wanted to. But I wanted her to be a stay-at-home mom until our progeny started school. She made the case that if I wanted a stay-at-home parent, I could take a leave of absence. I pointed out that mine was a real career—wrong thing to say. She stalked off one way on the beach and I the other.

I wandered until I admitted to myself that she was right and returned to our little beach hut. I apologized, we talked, and we realized that how we went about it was something we had plenty of time to work out. We made love that night in our tropical paradise. Afterward, we curled into each other like yin and yang.

"I don't want to leave," I whispered to her. "I want to stay here with you."

Candlelight reflected in her dark eyes as she smiled. "My paradise is wherever you are, Fitz."

"Molly," I whispered, nearly begging, "tell me we'll always be together."

Her hand caressed my cheek. "We'll be together forever and ever and ever." Sleep arrived with the memory of her comforting words echoing, "Ever and ever and ever…"

Then I heard someone singing out discordantly: "Rise and shine and give God your glory, glory…"

Two voices were there, one female and strong, the other also female but extremely high and hitting all the notes except the correct ones.

"Rise and shine and give God your glory, glory… Rise and shine and"—*bang-bang-bang* on the door, and I jumped—"give God your glory, glory, children of the Lord."

What the hell? Was this some horrible new tactic by the Seventh-day Adventists? I made it out of bed as the singer hit a high note that was perfectly out of tune. I flung the door open to find an unwelcome redhead standing on my welcome mat.

"Mattie fuckin' Castro."

"Actually, my middle name is Nora, and watch the language." She looked down at her side, where a little girl stood. Her hair was a lighter shade of Mattie's, bordering on blond.

The little girl held out a sad-looking bouquet of handpicked wildflowers and weeds. "Morning, sleepyhead," the little girl said.

Stunned, I blinked several times then took the flowers.

"You don't look like a drewscriver," the kid said.

"Excuse me?"

"Mom said you were a tool. You don't look like a drewscriver or a hammer or a—"

"That's enough, Sky," Mattie said.

"Sky?" I asked.

"Skylar."

Skylar was a cutie, with a tiny heart-shaped face and big blue eyes and her hair done up in pigtails with yellow ribbons. She wore purple overalls with Hello Kitty on the chest. I couldn't help but grin at her.

When I looked from Sky to her mother, my smile turned to a scowl. "What are you doing here?"

"A couple of things." Mattie turned serious. "The first being I want to apologize for trying to play you the other night."

"Mattie, go away."

Sky put her hands to either side of her mouth and whispered loudly, "You're right, Mom."

"Right about what?" I asked.

She turned to me, hands still up, and whispered, "You're a grouch."

Mattie held up her oversized leather bag. "I brought bagels."

My eyes widened. "Zayda's?"

"I'm not that sorry. Winn-Dixie."

"Fine. Come on in." I stood out of the way.

She looked me up and down as she entered. "Nice skivvies, but how about putting on some clothes?"

Sky laughed. "You're in your underwear."

"Kitchen's that way," I said and shuffled to my room. Ten minutes later, I was washed and dressed and stepped into the kitchen.

Mattie handed me a cup of coffee. "I'm guessing you take it black?"

"Like God intended."

My toaster popped up, and Mattie carefully pulled out two halves of a bagel and placed them on a plate. Sky was busy putting out butter, strawberry jam, and cream cheese. She'd also put out my bottle of ketchup, but I would pass on that.

As I started to prep a bagel, Mattie said, "The other reason I'm here is to see where you are in your investigation."

I looked at her as I spread cream cheese. "Mack got alibied. It's not my investigation anymore. You need to talk to Eddie and Lou." I brought the bagel up to my mouth.

"You're not going after the twenty-five grand?"

I stood there, mouth open, bagel inserted, then I took it out and put it on the table. Brushing crumbs from my hands, I asked, "Twenty-five what?"

Sky held half a bagel close to her face, her eyes squinched in concentration as she spread jelly on it. "Twenty-five grand."

Mattie said, "If you read the *San Marco Ledger* as much as you trashed it, you might be better informed." She fished around in her bag, pulled out a rolled newspaper, and handed it to me. "Open it."

I did and whistled when I read the headline. "Really? A twenty-five-thousand-dollar reward for the arrest and conviction of the senator's killer?"

"Back on the case?" Mattie asked.

Hot damn. On the inside, I was dancing a celebratory hokey-pokey. On the outside, I was playing it cool. "Maybe."

"Which brings me to my proposition. I told you the other night I'd never work with you, but that was before I heard about the reward. I think you and I should put our heads together, figure out who did it, and split the moolah."

I picked up the bagel, took a bite, and thought about the case as I chewed. I'd already learned a good deal, so it wouldn't be like I was starting at square one, though I would have to take a look at everything with a fresh eye.

"Well?" Mattie asked.

"Well?" Sky echoed while picking at something on the bottom of her shoe.

What I wanted was the whole reward, but on the very slim chance that Mattie got lucky and solved it, I'd settle for half. I'd just have to string her along for the time being.

"Let me think on it."

"Fine, but don't take too long."

"Don't take too long," Sky echoed and took a big bite of bagel.

"Have you learned anything since we last spoke?" I asked.

"You mean when you threw an expensive bottle of rum in the fire?"

"Don't remind me."

"No, nothing new. I thought maybe you and I could sit down and rehash everything," Mattie said.

"Maybe. I'll get back to you. And thanks for the bagels." I showed Mattie and Sky to the door.

"I feel like we're getting the bum's rush," Mattie said.

"Sorry. I have an appointment," I said and knelt in front of Sky. "You're welcome to visit anytime."

Half a bagel in one hand, she curtsied and said, "Thank you."

I stood and told Mattie, "You, however, need to call ahead for an appointment." I shut the door.

I went back to the newspaper and read the article, though nothing new was gleaned. Twenty-five thousand smackers would come in handy. I smiled then laughed like a mad scientist—time to break out the chalkboard. I loved my chalkboard, and with a passion. I had used it all the time as a homicide detective. Everyone else at the station hated it, thinking it was a prehistoric throwback to the days before computers. I'd picked it up for three dollars at a San Marco County surplus auction, figuring it had served for years in one of the local schools, which was fitting because I'd loved chalkboards as a kid in elementary school. I always volunteered to take the chalkboard erasers outside and clean them by beating them together, generating a fog of chalk dust. Rick and I used to drive Miss Tindal crazy in the fourth grade when we would occasionally sneak into class before school started and draw pictures of naked women on the board or leave witticisms like "I never finish anythi—"

In my days on the force, I would break it out on complicated cases, listing and tracking all the clues, the people involved, theories, motive, opportunity, and all the other stuff that goes into solving crimes. On really problematic cases, I would have to rewrite all I'd learned in smaller and smaller letters that covered the board and resembled complex scientific formulas from Einstein's laboratory. But it helped me think, to see everything I'd learned in one place like a puzzle that simply needed to be assembled correctly.

Feeling like I was about to meet up with a long-lost friend, I went to the shed behind the house, moved some of the clutter out of the way, and worked at bringing it out. A nearly full box of chalk sat on the tray under the board. Even though it was six feet long, four feet high, and sat in a free-standing wooden frame, it was light enough that I could carry it inside. Next, I wiped it clean with a wet cloth. While it dried, I printed a photo of Senator McGovern and taped it in the upper-left corner. Maybe I could get a picture of him dead and bound to the bed—that would look great next to his living picture. Underneath that, I wrote "murder by suffocation." I printed the picture of Mack passed out in his car and put it next to the senator's. Underneath it, I wrote, "Coach Mack Thorpe, suspect (cleared)." I spent the next thirty minutes carefully writing out the things I'd learned and listing them where they made the most sense. Next, I had to get out and learn more stuff to put on the blackboard. The best place to start would be where the whole thing had begun.

Less than an hour later, I was parked by the locked gate at the senator's beach house. Opening the diamond steel toolbox behind my truck cab revealed only a hammer, an axe, and a couple of screwdrivers. I removed the tools, looked up and down the road to make sure no one was in the immediate vicinity, and lifted the false bottom I'd made for the toolbox. That was where I kept the illegal tools of my trade: an unregistered handgun, a set of brass knuckles, a pill bottle with black beauties for all-night stakeouts, false identification, and more. I selected what looked like an oversized zippered leather billfold then put everything back in place. After waiting until a Cadillac SUV drove past, I scaled the gate and hopped over to the other side. I unhurriedly strolled to the front door, rang the bell, and waited. When no one answered, I examined the door lock and unzipped the leather wallet then took out a tension wrench, what looked like an Allen wrench, and a lockpick gun. Those were tools I'd acquired from my friend and sometime boss, Buddy Reid. First, I inserted the tension wrench then put in the pick gun. I clicked it three times, unlocking the door. I put the tools back in the leather case and pocketed it. The moment I opened the door, a beeping started, counting down the thirty seconds I had to disable the alarm before it tripped. I quickly crossed the foyer to the control panel. I put in the code I'd seen Caroline enter when I'd first visited and shut down the alarm.

There was no hurry, so I took my time wandering through the house. Not expecting to find much, I did hold out hope that I would discover one particular thing, and I did—when I went into the senator's home office. The furniture décor was chrome and black leather except for an antique desk that sat in the middle of the room. On the left-hand wall as one entered the room was a collection of framed photos, and I smiled when I saw one open spot amongst them all, where another would fit perfectly. That was where the picture used in the senator's assault had come from. The other photos featured the senator with celebrities, at events, and with people he worked with.

I didn't know what was in the picture, just that it had been broken in the assault. I'd figured it was something that had been grabbed randomly, but maybe that wasn't the case. *What if there was some significance to it?*

Chapter 16

Mattie had teased me that morning with Winn-Dixie bagels, so Zayda's Deli was my next stop, where I got three bagels all the way: lox, cream cheese, onion, and capers. I hotfooted the accelerator to the police station so that the bagels would still be warm for eating, and I rushed to Eddie's cubicle.

"Where's Lou?" I asked.

"She's taking the morning off. One of her kids has a play today," Eddie said.

"I brought Zayda's," I said, holding up the bag. "I brought a bagel for Lou as well. Put it somewhere safe."

"Yeah, sure, no problem," Eddie said in an odd tone while he kept his eyes averted.

"You're not going to keep it for her, are you?"

"Fitz, it's a Zayda's bagel."

I pulled up Lou's desk chair, and we dug in.

"So, why the bagels? Why the visit?" Eddie asked with a full mouth.

"A couple of things. First, the bagel is part apology."

"Hmm, looks like poppy seed to me."

"Come on, Eddie. This is hard enough as it is."

"Sorry. Go on."

"I was righteously pissed at you and at the department in general even though I knew it was all my fault. When I heard you tell Mattie the other day about Little Ed being in middle school, I realized I'd been nursing my resentment way too long. I'd like to put an end to it."

"Good." Eddie cleared his throat and said, "I always looked up to you, Fitz. I certainly appreciate everything you taught me, and it's been fun working with you again, even if you can be a bitch sometimes."

I started to respond to the bitch comment but then thought it would work against my second reason for stopping by. "I also want to ask a favor. I was hoping I could see the photograph that was in the frame. The one the killer broke over the senator's face."

Eddie took another bite and stared at me as he chewed. "Let me guess. You heard about the reward."

"And that's why you're such a successful detective. Your gut instinct is always dead on."

"You know what I don't like about rewards?" Eddie asked.

"All the bogus calls that come into the tip line?"

"Nah, lower men on the totem pole handle those. What bugs me is that, as a policeman, I'm not eligible to collect those rewards even if I solve the case single-handed."

"As a private investigator, I am eligible, so how about a little help?"

Eddie shook his head. "Fine. In the interest of putting past differences behind us, I'll get you a copy of that picture."

"Get me two copies of that picture."

"Two?"

"One I can take around. The other I can tape to the blackboard."

Eddie stopped in midchew and spoke with a mouthful. "The blackboard? You still have that old thing?"

"Haven't brought it out of storage since I left the force. But this case is blackboard worthy."

"You should have been a teacher," Eddie said and looked through a couple of files. He opened one, pulled out a black-and-white eight-by-ten photo, and stood.

"They use dry-erase boards these days. No wonder education is going down the toilet."

"Back in a flash." He went to the copier across the room while I thought a reward of twenty-five thousand dollars was a fine sum.

"Here you go," Eddie said, slid two copies in front of me, and sat.

I studied it and spoke nonchalantly. "As they say, 'a picture is worth a thousand eggs in one basket.'"

Eddie leaned toward me, raised his finger, and opened his mouth. He then closed it and shook his head.

"Interesting." I tapped the photograph. "The senator and a gaggle of gals. Both Lucinda and Ronnie Thorpe. Holy hell, Mattie Castro's in the picture too. Ooh, that's that jazz singer..."

"Dhalia Duchess Blackmoor," Eddie said.

Dhalia was a large woman with ebony skin and a beautiful face. In the photo, she was packed into an evening dress, something she might perform in, showing cleavage that would be visible to the astronauts on the International Space Station. A younger woman, probably in her early twenties, was also there, as well as an attractive slim woman and a woman well into her seventies.

"Why are they all in this photo?" I asked.

"I'm not going to solve this for you. Do some of your own sleuthing."

I snatched up the copies of the photo. "I'm telling Lou that you ate her Zayda's bagel."

I hopped in my truck and headed for the North. The radio was tuned to a classic rock station, and Santana came on. Making nice with Eddie had put me in a good mood, and I banged on my steering wheel like a drum. Hell, I even felt hopeful about the case. In fact, I would've been feeling on top of the world if I didn't have to figure out a way to get Rick out from under the Bennett brothers' grip.

Just thinking the Bennetts' name was a downer, and I stopped drumming. Jermaine was younger than me, Little Michael even more so. But Rick and I had gone to school with the rest of the brothers, Tito, Jackie, and Marlon. They were bullies to anyone other than a Bennett. The best thing about them was they were usually skipping school.

Rick and I had our share of run-ins with them. Later, as a cop, I arrested Jermaine twice and Little Michael once. Little Michael had the mental capacity of a preteen, which was why I'd first taken him for a soft-serve cone on the way to the police station to get booked.

I got to the north and navigated my way to the Thorpe house. Mack opened the door, looked at me, and turned to walk back into the house. Since he left the door open, I considered it an invitation and entered. I followed him into the living room, where he fell into a big chair in front of the TV. ESPN was on.

"Why aren't you at school?" I asked.

"Suspended. At least it's with pay. Asshole superintendent wants to meet with the school board before deciding what to do with me."

"What do you think will happen?"

"Nothing," Mack said. "They're too scared of the union. So, come to collect your pay?"

"No, I haven't even figured out what you owe me yet. You'll get a bill in the mail. I came to talk to your wife."

"What the hell for?"

"I'm back on the case, though for a different client." I didn't mention that I was my own client and I planned to pay myself twenty-five thousand dollars. "I have some questions for her."

"I thought I heard something annoying." Ronnie walked into the living room.

"Hey, Ronnie. Wondered if we could chat a few minutes." I turned to Mack and said, "Feel free to sit in if you want. Trust issues and all."

Mack shut off the TV with a remote and pushed himself up out of the chair. "Last thing I want is to listen to her slutty escapades." He went toward the kitchen, and a few seconds later, a door closed.

"Where's he going?" I asked.

"Some dive that hasn't banned him," Ronnie said.

"This time of day? It's not even two."

"It's five o'clock somewhere, right? He'll come back when he's good and drunk. Lucky me." She motioned for me to follow. "Let's go to the kitchen. I'll make some coffee."

We sat at the table and sipped from mugs. The one she gave me was chipped. I smiled to see that she used a Keurig machine, but I stopped smiling when I sipped some spiced concoction that tasted a lot like perfume smells. I took out a copy of the photograph from my pocket and unfolded it on the table.

"What's the significance of this?" I asked.

Ronnie barely gave it a glance. "It's a photo of the board members of Senator McGovern's homeless initiative."

"It's all women."

"Yeah, Mitch called us Mitchell's Angels."

"What was the purpose of this board? I mean, I know about the homeless initiative, but what did the board members do?"

"It depends. She pointed at the unknown attractive woman. That's Margaret Stone. She's married to the pastor at San Marco Baptist Church. She's in charge of getting all the churches behind the initiative." She tapped the image of Mattie. "Mattie Castro is a journalist and is in charge of marketing and publicity. That's the senator's daughter, Jillian," she pointed at the youngest of the women. "She's in college and works on getting support from college-age kids in the area."

I tapped the senator's widow. "What do you and your cousin do?"

"We're in charge of fundraising at the local level. We're the ones who put on Saturday's fundraising party. That's Dhalia Duchess Blackmoor, the jazz singer."

"Yeah, I recognized her."

"As a local celebrity, she brings a lot of attention to the initiative and helps line up entertainment at our various events. And finally, this woman is Elizabeth Melrose."

"She used to be a senator, too, right?"

"A representative. And her career included ambassador to both Thailand and Vietnam. She's doing high-level negotiations with businesses interested in relocating to San Marco." Ronnie looked from the photo to me. "How familiar are you with the homeless initiative?"

"From what I understand, tax breaks and some funding will be offered to companies that open facilities here as long as a percentage of the new hires are from our homeless population."

For the first time Ronnie smiled at me. "You're smarter than you look."

"Thanks... I think."

Ronnie tapped the image of Elizabeth Melrose. "She's very close to getting a Northrup Grumman plant built here, as well as a parts-manufacturing division for Hyundai."

I nodded, taking it all in.

"What's this picture got to do with anything?" Ronnie asked.

I didn't think the police were keeping it a secret. Besides, I was curious what Ronnie would say. "When the senator was assaulted, this framed photograph was smashed against his face. It wasn't in the senator's rumpus room but brought up from his home office, so I think it has significance. Mack says he didn't hit him with it, and I believe him. So that would mean the killer did it. Any reason you can think of?"

Ronnie shook her head while looking at the picture. "No, not really, though I suppose..."

"Suppose what?"

"No, it's stupid."

"That's the stage we're at, throwing out stupid possibilities and seeing if any stick," I said.

"I was going to say that if a man's wife found out about him and a lover, and the woman he was cheating with was in the picture, then maybe in the heat of the moment, the wife would hit her husband with it. But that's in general terms, not in this case. I grew up with Lucinda. I know her."

"So you're saying she wouldn't hit the senator with the picture frame if she caught him cheating?" I asked.

"No. Nor would she kill him."

"I'm curious. How pissed will she be when she finds out you and her husband were going at it?"

"She already knows. I told her, and she's angry." Ronnie looked out the kitchen window. "I'm not sure she'll ever forgive me."

I started to ask her if she was really surprised, but then I recalled how long Rick had held his grudge against me. I'd treated my best friend no better than she'd treated her cousin. "Okay. If Lucinda wouldn't do that, then it opens up a new scenario. Say McGovern wasn't fooling around only with you but with one of these other women in the picture as well." I paused when Ronnie started to scowl. "Hey, it's just hypothetical. What if that other woman thought she was his only—well—his only *other* woman. But she found out you and he were going at it, maybe even caught you two at it, though you were too busy to notice. She waits until you leave, but before she can do anything, Mack shows up and kicks the senator's ass. It's after he leaves that she hits him with the framed picture and then kills him." I paused then said, "Nah, that wouldn't account for the big gap in time between when Mack left and when the senator was killed. Maybe she showed up hours later—hell, he could have been expecting her—and with McGovern still cuffed to the bed, she figured out what was happening and lost it."

Ronnie grinned and sipped her coffee. "It would make a great made-for-TV movie, but no. Take it from me that Mitch was very up-front about his flings. If there were other women, which he alluded to, he told them the same. He was married to Lucinda but fooling around for fun and fuck's sake."

"Maybe. Do you think he was fooling around with any of the other women in this picture?"

"I honestly don't know, but I wouldn't be surprised."

"The preacher's wife?" Fitz asked.

"The forbidden fruit."

"Dhalia Duchess Blackmoor is a big woman."

"A big beautiful woman."

"Mattie Castro?"

"Almost certainly."

I wasn't expecting that. "Why almost certainly?"

"Not that I know anything for sure, but it's obvious that she's a woman with potent sexuality."

"Hmm. Up till recently, she always looked like a witch to me." As I gazed at the photo, I realized Ronnie was right. "Did you notice this photo in the room that night?"

"No."

"Okay. I want to revisit something. If those handcuffs had safety releases, what's your theory on why the senator didn't free himself?"

Ronnie stood and went to stand by the sink. "I've been thinking about that, and I really don't have a clue."

"How realistic are they?"

"I've never been arrested, so I can't say for sure, but to me, they were realistic. Supposedly, the only thing different between them and police handcuffs are little safety release switches down at the base of each cuff." She came and sat at the table again.

"Are you sure?"

"The last time we were together before that, I was the one in handcuffs. When we were done, he joked about leaving me cuffed in his bed forever. It didn't even take ten seconds to get out of them. That night, I told him turnabout was fair play. He kept them in a drawer in that wardrobe of his. I got them, put them on him, then went and got the scarves and tied his ankles."

"Any chance he had more than that one set?"

Ronnie smiled. "The senator loved his little toys." She turned serious again and said, "So maybe. Everything had its special place in the wardrobe. When you opened that drawer, the cuffs were set in a formfitting impression lined with black silk. They were the only cuffs there, and that was his binding drawer. I just assumed they were the same cuffs."

"Binding drawer."

"Handcuffs, leather cuffs, plastic ties, scarves—you know, restraints. The only thing I can figure is that he got a new pair, real handcuffs, and didn't realize we'd used those until after I left."

Out of questions, I bid her adieu and headed back to the Folly, calling Eddie on the way.

"Hello, Fitz."

"Those handcuffs used on McGovern—were they the kind with the quick-release buttons? And if so, why didn't they work?"

"I can tell you that," Eddie said then went quiet.

"Well?"

Eddie's voice turned into a whisper. "However, I'd like to hear a little gratitude and respect in your voice when I help you out."

"What are you talking about?" I nearly shouted.

"Look at it from my point of view. As a homicide detective, I have a stake in the game. Do I want a private investigator to solve a crime before me? No, I don't, and that is because of professional pride. Still, if it gets a killer off the streets sooner, I can swallow that pride. Will it make it better if the private investigator is my old partner? Yeah, a little. And if that partner says things like 'please' and 'thank you,' it will further take the sting out of it."

I was silent for a good thirty seconds. I had to make sure no trace of sarcasm was left in my voice. "Eddie, of course I respect you. I always have. So will you please tell me about those cuffs?"

"Was that so hard?"

"I would be ever so grateful." Try as I might, sarcasm reared its ugly head on that one.

Eddie seemed not to notice. "Ronnie told the truth. They were bogus handcuffs, sex toys with a safety release. You can pick up a pair at Madam and Marquis."

"Then why didn't the senator free himself?" I turned onto US 1 and drove past a public service billboard featuring a cell phone with a red circle around it and a red line through it. It read, Hang Up and Drive.

"Because someone put superglue in the safety release latches."

"Son of a bitch."

"Yeah."

Chapter 17

"**D**ammit," I grumbled, woken from a deep sleep by an early-morning phone call. I pawed for the phone and knocked it from the bedside table. "Shit." I nearly rolled out of bed reaching for it. Hitting the answer button, I growled, "Someone better be dead."

"Fitz, you gotta stop saying things like that." Eddie was on the phone. "Someone *is* dead."

The sky had just begun to lighten when I parked my truck by the curb two houses up from the Thorpe residence. There were three marked city PD cars, an unmarked that was probably Eddie and Lou's, an ambulance, two county sheriff's cars, and a fire truck, of all things. Two of the cop cars had their bars flashing blue and red lights.

Eddie walked out to the driveway and talked to a uniform, who let me by.

"Holy shit, Eddie. This is crazy."

Eddie motioned me to follow. "Yep. And once again, it's looking like your client."

"He's not my client anymore," I said.

"That's up to you, I suppose. But he's been asking for you. Same drill. Claims he didn't kill her and wants you to prove it. Higher-ups think this means we need to look at Mack for the senator again. The only way I see that is if he faked his drunkenness, killed the senator, and drove straight to the high school, where he pretended to pass out, all for an alibi."

"He's not that smart," I said.

"Everything points to Mack for this one. Look, he's asking for you. I want to see what you can get from him."

I cocked an eyebrow. "Fine, he's my client."

"The body is in situ. I'd like your take."

I was not eager to see what Mack had done to Ronnie.

We headed into the house, and I paused in the living room and looked around, noting a Jack Daniel's bottle with only an inch left in it. I peered down the hallway to the kitchen, where Mack sat at the kitchen table, looking miserable and sick while a couple of uniforms stood nearby.

"Come on," Eddie said, and we went up the stairs to the second floor.

Following a stained, off-white carpet, we paused at the door to the bedroom. Two gloved techs in protective booties were making their way around the room.

A third tech was closely examining Ronnie's body and looked up at Eddie and me. "Hey, Fitz. How's tricks?" he asked like we'd run in-to each other at the supermarket.

"Morning, Busby. Long time, no see," I answered and let the lead tech get back to work.

"Look familiar?" Eddie asked.

I didn't answer but noted how Ronnie had been tied spread-ea-gle to the bed. Her face had been beaten. The corpse was naked, though I noted pajamas piled on the floor by the bed. The sheets had been saturated in blood.

"Familiar," I said, "and some pretty big differences."

"Want a closer look?"

"No, I'm liable to throw up."

"You? You used to be able to get close to cadavers in the worst shape possible and then go chow down on a platter of raw oysters."

"It's been a while. One *small* difference I notice is no cuffs," I pointed out.

"Scarves for all four limbs."

"And the big difference is that the killer cut her throat."

"Yeah," Eddie said. "Maybe the killer is escalating."

"The killer being Mack?"

"Sure looks like it."

"From suffocation to slitting a throat—that's a big difference." I burped and tasted bile. "Where's the knife he used?"

"Haven't found it. He either hid it or threw it away somewhere."

I nodded. "Let's see what the coach has to say."

Eddie and I went to the kitchen, where he nodded to a couple of uniforms, who went to the living room to give us some privacy. Coach Thorpe was sitting with his face in shaking hands. He was crying and once again carried that sour odor of a man who'd drunk heavily the night before. Sweat shone on Mack's flesh.

"Mack," I said.

He started and looked up suddenly. His red eyes were wide and glassy with black circles underneath. His mouth was slightly open, his lips trembled, and a thin line of saliva went from the corner of his mouth to his chin.

"Fitz?" He closed his mouth and swallowed. "Fitz, you have to help me. Ronnie... Ronnie..."

I considered patting Mack's hand, but I didn't want to touch him, didn't really want to be in the room with him. I felt an odd mixture of revulsion and pity for the guy. But if Mack had killed his wife, cut her throat, would he be as upset as he appeared? Well, yeah—maybe what he'd done sickened him.

"Mack, what happened?"

"I didn't... didn't kill Ronnie. I was down... downstairs. I went up to... and she was..." Mack worked at putting together a cogent sentence. "I didn't kill Ronnie."

My eyes went from Mack to Eddie and back toward Mack. "This is getting old, Mack. This is just like McGovern. You look guilty as hell but claim innocence."

"I'll pay you, Fitz, give you all I got. Just prove I didn't do it." Mack looked down and reached out and grabbed my wrist. "Find out who killed Ronnie, and fuck the cops—I'll kill him myself."

I pulled my wrist away, and Eddie spoke up. "Your priority should be proving your innocence, Mack, and not killing anyone."

"I didn't kill Ronnie or McGovern."

"You need to call Ross, get him over here," I said.

"David Ross?" Eddie asked.

I said, "Mack's lawyer."

"He's useless," Mack said. "But I'll call him. I want to talk to you first."

"Privately?" I asked. "Do you want Detective Schmitt to leave?"

"I don't care if he's here or not because I didn't kill her." Mack put his face back into his hands.

Eddie threw out a hand, giving me an *after you* gesture.

I pulled out a chair and sat across the kitchen table from Mack. "All right, might as well give us the lowdown."

Mack took a few deep breaths and, keeping his face buried, said, "It started when you came over."

"Me?"

"I didn't want to hear anything Ronnie said about being with someone else. So I left."

"Where'd you go?" Eddie asked.

"Started at one bar, moved on to another, another after that, you know."

Eddie said, "We'll need a list of the places you went."

"Sure."

"After that?" I asked.

Mack dropped his hands and looked at me with tired eyes. "I got a bottle of Jack, can't remember where. Somewhere between Cheatems and here."

Cheatems was a strip club outside the city limits.

I said, "Catch some flesh before coming home?"

"Yeah, why not? But then, as I'm watching them, I got to thinking how the woman I'm married to is more of a slut than any of those girls twirling around the poles."

"Make you mad?" Eddie asked.

"And depressed."

"What time did you get here?" I asked.

"I don't know. I..." Mack paused. "It was a little after nine. I remember Ronnie saying something about the time."

"Why'd she bring up the time?" Eddie asked.

"I don't know. I can't remember."

"Was she mad because you'd been gone all day?" I asked.

"No. Maybe. I don't remember. Maybe we argued for a little bit, but then, she went upstairs."

Eddie asked, "What'd you argue about?"

"I can't remember—doesn't matter. We always argued."

"She went to bed and..." I led him.

"And I turned on the ball game, drank my Jack, and went to sleep in my recliner."

Eddie asked, "Did you kill your wife?"

"No, I told you that."

"But you found her?"

"Yes."

"What happened, Mack?" I asked.

Mack held up a shaking finger. "Just shut up and let me tell you, okay? Let me get through it before you start asking me stuff."

"Fine," Eddie said. "Go ahead."

"I woke up in my chair. The TV was on, and I had to piss something fierce. I peed in the bathroom down here and went up to our bedroom. It was just after five, and I didn't want to wake her, so I left the light off. I got undressed and into bed. Something didn't feel right."

I leaned forward and put my elbows on the table. "What didn't feel right?"

"Well, for one thing, she wouldn't move her arm. I mean, it was in the way, and I couldn't move it. I asked her... and... and nothing. And then, I realized the bed was wet. I turned on the light, and she was..." Mack started to cry.

He was deconstructing before our eyes. Between his drinking and anger issues, the man had been going in a downward spiral for years. I wondered why Mack had been blind to his own behavior but then realized the same could be said about me. I'd used drunkenness to stave off memories of my wife, to hold back depression. *Fuck it. This isn't about me.*

"Nothing you've told us is getting you out of the hot seat, Mack," I told him.

"I know." He sniffed and wiped his nose with a forearm. "Maybe it has something to do with the texts."

"What texts?" Eddie asked.

"She's been getting texts. Her phone is on her bedside table. Get it, and I'll show you."

Eddie called for one of the uniforms and told him, "Go upstairs and ask Busby if we can look at the victim's phone. Should be on the nightstand."

While we waited, Eddie said, "Tell us about these texts."

Mack licked his lips and said, "Ronnie thought I sent the first one, started bitching at me until she figured out I didn't know what she was talking about. They started coming in after McGovern got killed. Whoever wrote them was trying really hard to be mysterious, but I thought they were juvenile, like maybe one of my students was sending them as a prank."

The uniform returned, holding an evidence bag with a pink cell phone in it.

Eddie took it and passed it to Mack. "Keep it in the bag, but bring up the texts."

That took him a minute, then he said, "Here," and passed the bagged phone to Eddie.

I scooted my chair next to him and read out loud, "'You shouldn't have done what you did.'"

Eddie passed me the phone and took out his notebook.

"Want the number it was sent from?" I held the phone out to Eddie, who copied down the number. Then I looked for the next text from that number. "'I know what you did.'"

"See what I mean?" Mack said. "They read like some teenage slasher film. 'I know what you did, and I know who you are'—that kind of thing."

"'I'll kill you,'" I read from the next.

"Whoa," Eddie said and took the phone. "There's one more from that number. It says, 'You're dead, slut.'"

"When are you tracking the number?" I asked.

"Right now. I'll see you soon." Eddie got up and went to talk to the uniforms in the living room, taking the phone with him.

A moment later, the two policemen came in and made Mack stand. They put handcuffs on him and led him out.

Chapter 18

I thought about using one of the photos I took of Ronnie in the throes of passion with the fitness trainer, but that would've been too much like mocking the dead. So I went online and found a photo of Ronnie Thorpe with her husband at a football jamboree picnic. I cropped the coach out and zoomed in. Though it was fuzzy, I printed it out and put it up on the blackboard then added what I'd learned. My head started to spin as I went over everything again. The damn case was so confusing that I would need to flip the board over and work on that side too.

I glanced up at my living room clock. Hand-painted, it depicted a Florida beach scene with a palm tree. The time was a little after five. I went and took a shower and put on a clean T-shirt, a pair of jeans, and Teva flip-flops. I took ten minutes to walk up the Intracoastal to Doone's Fish Camp. Since it was Friday, happy hour was more crowded than usual.

"Skipper!" I called out over the noise of the crowd as I stepped up to the bar in the main room. My favorite bartender in the world looked up, winked, and whipped up what I believed was the perfect Cuba libre. "How you doing, Fitz?" Skipper growled.

"Great. Love the shirt," I replied, indicating Skipper's black Hawaiian shirt with Day-Glo hula girls.

"Thanks. No fights with Rick, okay?"

"Crap, he's not here, is he?"

"Not that I know of. Just in case."

I held up a hand. "On my honor."

I worked my way through the crowd, talking to those I knew and flirting with attractive ladies. I stepped out onto the first deck just as everyone broke into the Electric Slide.

I shook my head and muttered to myself, "They should let that dinosaur die a peaceful death." Then I jumped between two college-age girls and went through the moves without spilling a drop of my drink.

I wasn't sure if the girls were laughing with me or at me as I left that deck and made my way to the one closer to the docks, which was always quieter and more laid back. A dozen people were there, shaded from the sun by live oak limbs overhead. Since the day was fairly hot, the river breeze felt nice, and I didn't regret wearing long pants. I spotted long red hair on a woman on one of the barstools lining the deck railing. Then a young stud made a beeline for the empty stool next to her. I ran over and got there two steps before him. The fellow looked a little miffed but gave me a nod that said, *"Well played."*

"Hello, Fitz," Mattie Castro said, holding a half-empty martini glass up in a salute.

I raised my Cuba libre in return. "To you, Mattie Castro."

She sipped and turned her gaze out toward the Intracoastal. She wore a short white skirt, and I vowed I wouldn't be mesmerized by her legs, but my eyes betrayed me. Her legs were well formed, smooth as alabaster, and had perfect muscle tone. Her cotton half-blouse was denim blue with spaghetti straps and could have passed as a sexy piece of lingerie. It revealed Mattie's tight belly below and freckled cleavage above. *Oh crap,* I thought, *I'm smitten.*

I cleared my throat and asked, "What brings you to my home away from home?"

"A long day. And I'm bummed about Ronnie Thorpe."

"You were friends?"

Mattie stirred her martini with a toothpick-speared olive. "More like friendly acquaintances. We bumped into each other over the years, and recently, we served on a board together."

"So I hear. You mind if I ask you—"

"Fitz! I'm still waiting for your call." Seri, in short cutoffs, inserted herself between Mattie and me. She cast a quick glance at Mattie then pushed against me like an affectionate cat. "I was worried you weren't coming today." Seri put her arms around my neck and whispered in my ear, "I get off at nine tonight."

I had a hot flash that would impress a woman in the throes of menopause. "Well, hey there, Seri. Yeah, about that—"

Someone caught Seri's eye and held up an empty glass.

She said, "Hold that thought, Fitz. Back in a flash."

"Well, well," Mattie said with a smile. "What's the male version of a cougar?"

"Used to be sugar daddy, but I don't have enough money to qualify." I looked from Seri to Mattie. "It's not what you think."

"I bet it is."

"I've known her since she started working here. A couple of weeks ago, she asked if she could flirt with me because she was trying to cool things with an ex-boyfriend who wouldn't take no for an answer."

Mattie looked around at the crowd. "Is he here?"

"I haven't seen him today. It seems the mock flirting has turned into serious flirting."

"I can help if you want."

"How?"

"A little mock flirting of our own," Mattie said.

"You'd help me out of a jam?" I asked.

"Blame the booze."

What to do? I watched Seri, twenty-plus years younger, move to the bar. I turned toward Mattie and sighed. "Yeah, that's probably for the best."

"Probably? If you don't know who Dua Lipa and Marshmello are, you won't have a thing in common."

"Who?"

"Exactly."

"Thanks." I sipped my Cuba libre and then made a show of looking around the deck. "Where's your shadow?"

"What?"

"You know." I held my hand out at the height of a young child. "Sky. Your daughter. She's adorable, you know?"

Mattie gave me a warm smile. "Thanks. She's at my sister's house."

"Thanks for bringing her by yesterday. She made my day."

Mattie sat up straight and cocked her head. "Is that a compliment, Fitz?"

"Complimenting your daughter, not you." I paused then said, "Yeah, I guess it's a compliment on being a good mother."

She gave me a smile that warmed my body a couple of degrees.

A horn sounded on the Carroll Street Drawbridge, signaling that it was going up. In a Doone's Fish Camp tradition, everyone cheered, held up a drink in salute, and took a sip, swallow, or gulp, including Mattie and me.

Mattie and I grew quiet and stared out toward the river. When the bridge was fully raised, three sailboats, masts furled, powered through the open gap. Two kept going while one turned in and prepared to dock at Doone's.

"So, what have you heard about Ronnie?" I asked.

"That her psycho husband killed her. I'm guessing it's because of her and Mitch."

"Mitch?"

"McGovern, the senator, Mitch McGovern."

"Sorry. It just seemed so casual—Mitch."

"Well, I knew him. You know, because of being a journalist and all," Mattie said. "What do you care?"

"You still hoping for the reward for solving his murder?"

Mattie looked left then right. "Yes. Why?"

"You offered to work together and split the reward. I'll agree, but only if we're working on it together at the time it is solved."

"Meaning what?"

"If we solve it together, we split it. If you have to cover the flower show on the day I solve it, the money is mine. If you solve it on a day I'm bedridden with a hangover, the reward is yours. What do you say?"

The sun dropped closer to the horizon, and we were no longer shaded by tree limbs. Mattie dug a pair of bug-eye sunglasses out of her purse and put them on. Since she was going espionage, I did, too, and took the aviator shades from my neckline and slid them on.

"Okay," Mattie said. "Deal. Twelve thousand five hundred a piece."

I motioned her closer and whispered, "Ronnie was found nude and tied to her bed just like the senator."

"What? Oh my God. Mack's such a nutcase."

I glanced down then back at her eyes. "I'm not so sure Mack did it."

She gazed at me with a half smile that fell when she saw I was serious.

"He claims he was passed-out drunk downstairs. I saw him this morning, and he was still mostly drunk."

"Maybe he killed her in a blackout."

"She'd gotten four anonymous threatening texts since McGovern's murder."

"You think the same killer is responsible for both murders, and it's not Mack?"

I finished my drink and put it on the railing. "Look, if it turns out to be Mack, he probably did both crimes but worked out a good alibi for the senator's murder. The police will figure that out, and we won't see a cent of the reward. But if someone else is responsible—and believe me when I say that Mack isn't smart enough to lie convincingly—then the reward is still up for grabs."

"Okay. What can I do to help?"

"Tell me about the senator's homeless initiative board."

Mattie seemed thrown by the change in topic, and she needed a few seconds to answer. "There are several of us on the board. I mainly handle publicity. Why?"

"At some point during the senator's murder, the killer went downstairs to his beach home office, picked up a framed photo of the homeless initiative board, took it back up to the sex room, and smashed it across his face."

"What?"

"You do know that Ronnie and the senator got it on the night before his murder?"

"I heard."

"Well, Ronnie is in the photo, and she said that while it sounded like something a jealous wife would do with a photo of her husband's lover, Lucinda Combs-McGovern wasn't the kind of person who'd do that."

"It would be out of character," Mattie said.

"What if there was someone else?" I put my idea out there.

"What do you mean?"

"Ronnie confided in me that she was the senator's only mistress." I nibbled my lip in thought. "But what if there was another woman who thought she was the senator's only other woman?"

"So you're saying that she finds out there's another other woman, and even though the senator was married and she was the other woman, she felt betrayed by the, uh... other, other woman."

"I'm confused." I paused to use my index finger to try diagramming it in the air. I gave up and said, "You're in that photo."

"Yes."

"So does the murderer breaking it on the senator mean anything to you?"

"No. Are you sure the picture wasn't just handy and the killer grabbed it in the heat of the moment?"

"That's what I initially thought," I admitted. "Now, I don't think so. Ronnie didn't remember seeing it in that room."

All of a sudden, Mattie threw her arms around my neck and pulled me close.

"What are you doing?" I asked.

Mattie whispered in my ear, "Your little waitress is coming, and I'm mock staking out my turf." Even though what she said was not at all sexy, the warm breeze of Mattie's whispered breath made goose-flesh rise.

Seri slowed her approach, casting a questioning glance at Mattie. She picked up another Cuba libre from the tray she carried. "I brought you another drink..." She paused then emphasized, "On me."

Mattie pulled my face next to hers so that we both faced Seri. "Oh, lover," Mattie said, "is this the hot young waitress you want to bring into our bed?"

Though Mattie held me tightly, my eyes flicked from her to Seri, back and forth. "I... uh... well... that is..."

Seri slammed the drink on the railing so that half spilled onto my pants leg. "Here!" She turned and stormed off.

Mattie pushed me away. "There you go. Problem solved."

I used a bar napkin to wipe at my wet jeans and watched Seri's awesome legs carry her through the crowd. "Thanks. I'm not sure my willpower was up to the task."

A few minutes later, I went to the bar to get another martini for Mattie and a rum neat for me, with a Duke's Brown Ale chaser.

When I set the martini down in front of Mattie, I said, "I have a question for you."

"I'm going to be interrogated by the hard-boiled private eye? Fire away."

The martinis were having an effect on her, and I hoped she was a happy drunk. "Promise not to get mad, because I don't want any more alcohol soaking my clothes."

"Okay." She held up her hand in a Commander Spock Vulcan greeting. "Scout's honor."

"I asked Ronnie if it was possible that the senator slept with any of the other women on the board, and she said she wouldn't be surprised."

Mattie blinked at me.

"Well?"

"Well what?"

"Did you and the senator, you know, shake the sheets?"

Amusement left her face, replaced by a stern look. "Are you implying that I'm the other, other woman?"

I thought a moment. "No, in this theory, Ronnie is the other, other woman, so wouldn't that make you the other, other, other woman?" I shook my head and quickly added, "I'm not being nosy. I'm just trying to wrap my head around that photo and its significance."

Mattie sat up straight, sniffed, took a drink, and said, "No, I didn't screw the senator."

"Okay."

"Okay."

"Sorry."

"No, I understand why you asked." Mattie tapped her lips. "You know, you may be on to something. We should talk to all the women in the photo."

"You think?"

"It's a direction."

"You want to see my blackboard?" I blurted out.

She looked at me. "Is that a euphemism? Because I don't get it at all. Unless it's like inviting me to your place to see your etchings."

"It's my crime blackboard. I used it when I was a cop working hard cases with lots of twists and turns. I broke it out for this one."

"Then I definitely want to see your blackboard."

I settled the tab and escorted Mattie to her car. Since she'd had a few martinis, I put her in the passenger seat. As I rounded the car to the driver's side, something struck me in the head. An olive hit the ground a couple of feet away. I looked back toward Doone's just in time to see Seri push through the crowd.

Driving to my house from Doone's took all of three minutes. As we got out, I pulled out my cell and punched Eddie's name on my contact list.

"Who are you calling?" Mattie asked.

"Eddie. Hang on."

Just when I thought the call would go to voicemail, Eddie answered, "Hey, Fitz."

"Hi, Eddie. Was calling about those texts. Did you trace the phone they're from?"

Without a pause, Eddie said, "Not only that, but also learned about the Goldens up at the Lodge and Club."

"Awesome. Can you *please* tell me what you've learned? You'll have my deepest respect and gratitude."

"I like this new Fitz," Eddie said. "First off, the computer showed Glenn using his key card about nine thirty that night. Stuart went to his room a little after ten thirty and Ginny around eleven. None of their key cards were used again until the following morning. They had a breakfast meeting that started at eight a.m., plenty of witnesses, and the next time they all used their key cards was after nine thirty a.m. Doesn't mean one of them couldn't have done it, but they had to have left the room, driven to San Marco, killed the senator, driven back up to Ponte Vedra, sat in on the breakfast meeting, and waited until after nine thirty a.m. to return to their room."

I shook my head. "It's feasible, but I'm not feeling it."

"Me neither. As for your other inquiry, those four texts to Ronnie came from a burner phone," Eddie said.

"You think Mack got a burner and sent them?"

"I didn't get that impression, but I haven't had a chance to press him on that. We didn't find another phone at their house."

"Well, when you do find out, can you let me know?"

"I'll think about it," Eddie said and ended the call.

"What'd he say?" Mattie asked.

"The texts came from a burner, and the alibis for Glenn, Stuart, and Ginny Golden are pretty good but not rock solid." I turned toward the Intracoastal. "Want me to make you a martini? We can watch the sunset from the dock."

"I thought you were showing me the blackboard."

"Priorities. Ever had Rain vodka? Makes a great 'tini."

"Fix me up."

While I mixed drinks—since both were basically straight alcohol, not much mixing was going on—Mattie phoned someone and stepped out onto the deck. I finished as she ended her call. She carried our drinks to the end of the dock while I dragged out two Adirondack chairs. We sipped and watched an encore-worthy sunset. After that, somewhere between the end of the dock and the house, we kissed.

"You know who I called?" Mattie asked me, her voice soft.

"Haven't a clue."

"My sister. She's going to keep Sky all night."

If anyone had wanted to find us after that, they could've followed the random pieces of clothing that trailed from the dock to my bed.

Chapter 19

We sat close to one another on the porch swing hanging from the limb of a tree near my front door. Mattie leaned against me with her legs pulled up beside her. She wore one of my bathrobes, and I was in sweatpants and a sleeveless T-shirt. The time was late at night or early in the morning—neither of us wanted to check because the moment seemed mystical and dreamlike. We sat in darkness as the nearest lights were on the Carroll Street Drawbridge. A low fog blanketed the Intracoastal Waterway, and the stars stippled the sky.

"It's on occasions like this that alcohol comes in handy," Mattie said.

"You want a drink?"

"No. It's just that tomorrow, in the full light of day, I can blame this on martinis."

"And I can blame rum."

"But you know what?"

"What?"

"I'm stone sober now and still plan to jump your bones before the sun comes up," Mattie whispered.

"At least we're on the same page." I thought about the past couple of hours and who I was with. Without intending to say it, words came from my mouth. "You know, I hated you with a passion."

Mattie looked at me without surprise. "I know. And I told myself that you were a bum and that I hated you, which I didn't. It just made me feel better about those stories I wrote."

The swing went gently back and forth. We both knew we were on precarious ground, that the magic of the evening could be broken if we didn't proceed carefully. But it was a road that needed traveling.

"I didn't mind that you wrote about me," I said. "I hated that you brought Molly into it, along with all the ways you twisted tragedy and threw everything into one big innuendo so all your readers could pick and choose which to believe, like some depraved buffet of half-truths and lies."

"Fitz, I—"

"Most people, to this day, probably believe that she was drunk and because I was a cop, I covered it up with a bogus coroner's report."

Mattie sat up and leaned away from me. "I didn't say she was responsible or you covered it up or that you lied."

My temper clicked to a low boil. "No? But insinuation in a newspaper is as good as condemnation in the public's mind."

Out of reflex, Mattie started to protest but stopped. "In this case, I agree."

I began to further my argument when I realized what she'd just said. I shifted on the swing to face her. "Really?"

"I didn't want to include all that implication in the articles, but my editor thought it belonged."

"Barry Golden," I mumbled.

"Yeah."

"His nickname was Golden Boy in high school."

"You went to school with him?" Mattie asked.

"He never told you?"

"No."

"He was a righteous prick, editor of the school newspaper. Me and Rick Forester and our friends often found ourselves butting heads with Barry and his bunch. He even wrote a couple of editorials in the school newspaper about the wrong element among the student body. He didn't use names, but it was obvious he was referring to us." I kicked against the ground to get the swing moving. "Even back then, he was good at implication without facts."

"He never said anything about that. When the accident happened, there was liquor spilled inside the car—the highway patrol went out of the way to make mention of it. So I included it in the initial piece. When the postmortem pronounced there was no alcohol in her system, I wanted to drop that from future stories. But Barry insisted that I include what the highway patrol had reported, and I could follow up with the autopsy results."

"And it ended up sounding like I had covered up the real results, that my wife was intoxicated and caused the wreck that took her life."

"I'm sorry," Mattie said.

"And then, when I got in trouble, when I quit the force, your stories always circled back to those innuendos." My voice shook with anger. "Each new story meant I had to relive it all."

Mattie's voice was tremulous when she said, "Barry made me include all that, but knowing that doesn't help, does it?"

I took her hand and squeezed. In a rasping voice I said, "Actually, it does." We sat quietly, both of us in our heads, then I said, "Sometimes, I have dreams about the accident."

"But you weren't there."

"I am in my dreams, standing on the side of the road in the rain. I see a car coming and know it's her, and I have to stop her before she rounds the curve. If I can't, I know she'll lose control and drive into that big fuckin' live oak."

"Do you ever stop her?"

"No."

Mattie stared down at her hands and interlaced her fingers. "I've talked to people about you—I mean out of curiosity, not having to do with the paper."

"Yeah? Like who?"

"Like people who really know you, not just your reputation. If you were the loser some people think you are, then I wouldn't feel so bad about those stories. But damn it, those who know you, those you worked with say that yeah, you're colorful, you're a character, but you were good at the job, damn good. You took your work seriously. You had heartfelt compassion for victims. They all say that your truly eccentric behavior was a result of your wife's death and, as they put it, my hit pieces. A couple of people, in not-so-nice terms, let me know how you were doing actual good and fighting for justice, while I'm a poseur who pretends I make a difference through my reporting."

"That's a bit extreme."

"Well, you have people who respect and love you, and they're not fond of what was written about you. So, for all of that, let me say again, I'm sorry."

"You don't have to—"

"Fitz, please. Just tell me you forgive me." She turned away, but not before I saw a tear on her cheek.

Wow. All those years, I'd never even considered in the least that Mattie would want my forgiveness. Now, here she was next to me, asking just that. Not long ago, I would have answered that by spitting in her eye, maybe even literally. But not now.

"Mattie, yeah, I forgive you."

Mattie wiped her cheek and leaned against me. I put an arm over her shoulders and pulled her tight. While the spell of the evening had been tested, it hadn't been broken.

A little while later, Mattie said, "I have to go to the little girls' room. Can I bring you anything?"

"Yeah, bring me some water, in a tall glass with a lot of ice cubes."

Mattie got up. "Will do. I'll even pretend I'm your little waitress friend, and when I bring it back, I'll make a bad double entendre."

"You're my kind of gal, Mattie Castro," I said. She laughed and walked up the dock. I muttered in amazement, "Who'd have thought?"

While she was gone, I thought about how lucky I was that Mattie had come home with me. As Ronnie had said when she and I were looking at the photo of the senator's board, Mattie had sexual potency. Close to my age, she was experienced and forward and eager under the sheets. I didn't know where this would lead, if anywhere at all, but this night would remain as a favorite memory.

The screen door squeaked open, and Mattie spoke in a concerned voice, "Fitz?"

"Yeah?"

She stepped out, holding her phone and looking at the screen. Without saying another word, she handed me the phone.

I read aloud a text that she'd received. "'You shouldn't have done what you did.'"

Trying to sound unconcerned, Mattie said, "Since Mack's locked up, I guess we can safely say he's not sending the texts."

I gazed out toward the waterway. "Then who is?"

Chapter 20

"Wake up."

I grunted and rolled over, and I was pretty sure I farted.

"Fitz, wake up. We have to go talk to the women of the board."

I opened an eye to a beautiful sight: Mattie Castro in the buff, red hair askew, smiling down at me as morning light flooded the windows. I scootched up to take her in. My two surfboards, a longboard and a short, leaned against the corner behind her, making her look like a model for some sexy-ass surfboard advertisement.

"I called my sister. She's planning a picnic with her kids and Sky. I have the morning free and think we should interview Mitchell's Angels."

"Yeah, sure." I moved about and sat against the headboard. "I hope you're not feeling like you screwed up last night."

Mattie moved next to me. "Actually, I feel pretty good about it. How about you?"

I crossed my arms and brought a finger to my lips. "Surprisingly, I feel good too. And frankly, some of what happened deserves repeating."

Kissing, we slid back down on the bed, and I pulled the sheet up over our heads.

Sometime later, I said, "Yeah, still feeling good about it."

Breathing heavy, Mattie said, "Yeah, good."

"Normally, I'd suggest a leisurely bath in my claw-foot tub, but we've blown enough time, so... Mattie fuckin' Castro—"

"Mattie Nora Castro."

"Would you do me the honor of taking a shower with me?"

After the shower, we dressed, ate a breakfast of Captain Crunch, and sat in front of my blackboard as we finished our coffee.

"It really is a nice blackboard," Mattie said.

"Yes, it is."

"What's the strategy for our interviews?" she asked.

I got up and stood by the board, pointing out the appropriate entries. "The person who murdered the senator broke a framed photograph of the homeless initiative board across his face. Whoever did that had to go downstairs to McGovern's home office, find that picture from among all the ones on the wall, and carry it up to the sex room. So let's make the educated assumption that the photograph has significance."

Mattie took up the explanation. "A photo featuring the seven members of Senator McGovern's Homeless Initiative board, also known as Mitchell's Angels."

"Might be tied into our other-other-woman theory, or it might not." I pointed at Ronnie's photo taped to the blackboard. "But we do know at least one, not including his wife, was sleeping with the senator. After his death, she received a series of anonymous and threatening texts, and then she was murdered." I looked at Mattie and noted that she appeared a bit pale. "Are you all right?"

"Just thinking about how I got that text last night. That means I'm on the killer's radar, right? And why? Just because I'm on the board?"

"That's what we have to find out with the other members. Has anyone else received these texts? And I think we need to ask if they slept with the senator as well. You didn't, but maybe someone besides Ronnie did."

"Well," Mattie said, drawing out the word.

"What?"

"In the interest of full disclosure—"

"You slept with the senator?"

"Let's just say that he came on to me," Mattie said. "A few times. Left it dangling out there that if I was interested, I only had to say the word."

I chuckled. "Left it dangling."

"A little maturity, please."

"Sorry. Well, even if it wasn't consummated, that leaves us with a sexual component, right?" I asked.

"I suppose."

"Let's go talk to Mitchell's Angels."

We rushed outside but paused by our vehicles to argue about who was driving. "Come on, Fitz. If we show up in your truck, they'll think we're there to cut the lawn."

I said, "Fine, you drive. But I get to man the radio."

We got in Mattie's sedan and headed for the mainland. She handed her phone to me and said, "Everyone on the board is in my contacts. Who's first?"

Going through her list, I said, "Let's go see Dhalia Duchess Blackmoor. She's a crazy-good singer." I pressed the connect button and handed the phone back to Mattie.

"Hello, Dhalia. It's Mattie. How are you?" Mattie turned onto the Carroll Street Drawbridge. "I know. It's awful, isn't it? That's why I'm calling. I have some board business to discuss, and I'm hoping to drop in on everybody today." She paused while Dhalia talked. "Okay, see you in an hour." She hung up and passed her phone back. "She had a late gig and is sitting around in her jams. No one sees the duchess until she's had time to dress and put on her face. Try Margaret Stone."

I found her name, hit the call button, and put the phone to my ear, figuring I'd take this one.

Margaret answered, "Hi, Mattie. What's up?"

"Mrs. Stone. Hi. My name is Geronimo Fitzgerald. Mattie's driving, so I'm calling for her."

"What can I do for you, Mr. Fitzgerald?"

"Call me Fitz. Mattie is dropping in on all the board members today, a little business to cover. She was wondering when would be good for you?"

"I'm at the church right now if she wants to swing by," Margaret Stone said.

"We'll be there in ten minutes," I said and hung up.

Grinning, we looked at each other. I didn't know how she felt, but I had that wonderful feeling one got the first time they woke up next to someone they really liked. I tuned in an oldies FM station, and we sang along with Cyndi Lauper's "Time After Time."

Mattie turned into the parking lot of San Marco Baptist, a sprawling behemoth of a modern church that had traded in the fire and brimstone for Kumbaya pop sing-alongs. It had one service on Saturday and three on Sunday, and the parking lot was usually full for each. Made of yellow brick and coquina, the building, along with the spreading parking lot, covered at least five acres.

"She didn't say where we should meet. I guess park by the front door," I said.

"You a churchgoer, Fitz?"

"Worried about a lightning strike when we cross the threshold?"

"Seems a legitimate concern."

As Mattie parked, I got out my clergyman credentials, a black plastic card with gold lettering. She shut off the ignition, and I passed it to her.

She looked it over and said, "You're kidding. You're a minister?"

"With the Universal Life Church."

Passing the card back to me, Mattie asked, "Why?"

"I conduct weddings, and it was either minister, ship captain, or notary. Minister was cheapest and easiest."

"You make much money at it?"

"Not really, but I do attend some awesome receptions."

"I don't know, Fitz. That makes it seem a lightning strike is even more likely."

"Don't worry, I'm a believer. Though I don't think a church is necessary for a relationship with the big kahuna. Though sometimes my father's Irish Catholic upbringing takes over, and the next thing you know, I'm scaring a priest while confessing my sins in painstaking detail. How about you?"

"A lifelong member of St. Andrews, choir member, and cantor."

"You go every week?" I asked.

"Eight a.m. Mass."

"Eight in the morning? Wow. Think you could put in a good word for me? I need all the help I can get."

Mattie turned toward me with a raised eyebrow. "So, on that next rare occasion you go to the priest, will you take last night to the confessional?"

"Last night seemed more blessing than sin."

"Awww." Mattie pulled me over for a kiss.

"Yep, still a smooth talker," I said to myself while opening the door.

Several cars were parked near the front, and I figured a church that big probably had people present all the time, from worshippers to employees to volunteers.

"Over this way," Mattie said, pointing away from the four large double doors that undoubtedly opened to the worship area at a single glass door that had Offices printed on it.

We went in, and a woman working at a copy machine behind the counter directed us down a hallway with classrooms for Sunday school and religious education on either side. We pushed out a double door into sunshine and saw a trim brunette on her knees, working in a garden.

As we approached her, Mattie whispered, "I'm a little reluctant to ask if she fooled around with the senator."

"Let me take it. I have years of experience asking hard questions," I said.

"Me, too, but I'll gladly let you ask this one." As we got close, Mattie called, "Margaret."

The woman looked up and smiled. She'd been beautiful in the photo, but in real life, she was even more so. She wore knee-length denim shorts and a white sleeveless button-down blouse.

"Mattie, hi." She stood, taking off gardening gloves, and gave Mattie a hug. Holding out a hand to me, she said, "And you are Mr. Fitzgerald?"

"Fitz," I said, shaking her hand and wishing I'd gotten a hug too.

"These are our memorial gardens," she said, brushing dirt from her knees. "In memory of the deceased. Members of the congregation can tend their own gardens. This is in honor of my mother."

The gardens were eight-by-ten plots that ran along the back side of the building, where they would get a lot of morning and early-midday sun. They all featured different types of flowers and bushes and even small trees, but the variety added to the appeal. A rock in her garden had been smoothed with chiseled words added: "in memory of Susan Bowen." She pointed out various flowers and plants, telling us what they were, though none of it stuck with me. However, I did get a kick when she pointed out the right-hand corner by the building, where a dozen or so thick green and yellow leaf-like stalks stood straight up from the ground.

"That's called mother-in-law's tongue. My husband, Bob, thought it would be funny to include it. My mom would agree." She wiped at her brow and pointed toward a picnic table next to a tree and shaded by its limbs. "It's going to be a hot one. Let's talk over there." As we walked over, she told me, "You look familiar. Have you been to services here?"

"No. I need bingo and booze, so I stick with the Catholics."

That got a laugh from Margaret. She got to the table and sat. "It's so sad and confusing about Mitch and Ronnie. What's going to happen with the homeless initiative?"

Mattie sat next to her. "Most everything has been put in place and is moving along. Hopefully, we can continue the work."

I leaned against the tree trunk, moving up and down to scratch my back. "Go ahead and tell her about Ronnie."

Margaret looked at Mattie. "I've heard. Mack killed her."

Mattie shook her head. "Details haven't been released, so keep it to yourself for now, but she was killed in a way that mimicked how Mitch died."

"What?"

"She was stripped, tied to her bed, and beaten."

"Oh dear God. Beaten to death?"

"There were differences," I said. "A knife, or a sharp blade of some kind, was used, and she bled out."

"It was Mack, wasn't it?" Margaret asked, almost seeming to hope.

"Fitz is a private investigator, and he and I are looking into the crimes. For now, everything points to Mack for his wife's murder. And while he had an alibi for the senator's murder, it could have been faked."

"However," I picked up, "Mattie and I think he may be innocent."

She looked at me like I'd just spoken in Mandarin. "Innocent?"

"Okay, innocent and an asshole. There's reason to believe that the board of the senator's homeless initiative has something to do with all this."

"The board?"

Mattie said, "That publicity photo of the group was found at the first crime scene. There's something else."

"What?"

I said, "Shortly after the senator's death, Ronnie started to get anonymous and threatening texts."

Margaret's jaw dropped. "Texts?"

"I got one last night," Mattie said. "Have you received any?"

Margaret got her phone out of her pocket, worked the screen, and passed it to Mattie.

"'I know what you did,'" Mattie read from the text.

"I got that this morning and received another almost like it the night before last. Weird and all, but not threatening. Or is it?" Margaret looked at them in confusion. "And Ronnie got texts?"

"The first two Ronnie got were the same as these," I told her. "The third mentioned killing her, and the fourth was, and I quote, 'You're dead, slut.'"

"That makes three of us on the board who have gotten these texts," Mattie said. "If they're from the killer, then it couldn't be Mack because he's locked up."

"Am I in danger?" Margaret asked.

"Better safe than sorry," I said. "Until this thing is solved, I wouldn't go anywhere alone, even here in your garden."

Margaret nodded, concern evident in her eyes. Mattie looked at me and gave me a go-ahead gesture with her head.

"Huh?" I said. "Oh, yeah." I cleared my throat and moved closer to Margaret. "Mrs. Stone, sometimes, in investigations like this, we have to ask..." I stalled, searching for a good word. "Uncomfortable questions, difficult questions."

"Okay," Margaret said.

"Because of what's happened so far and because it appears that Ronnie and McGovern were having a bit of an affair, and not to mention the way the bodies were found, I have to ask you something. And please don't take it personal."

Margaret looked at me blankly.

"Okay, well then. Mrs. Stone, did you sleep with the senator?" I gave Mattie a quick nod, having gotten the question out.

Margaret looked at me, turned her head one way and then the other. She slowly stood from the picnic table, and quick as a snake, she slapped me. It sounded like a whip crack, and in the next second, pain hit. Margaret pushed past and walked briskly to the church.

Once she got inside, I put a hand to my burning cheek and said, "I'll take that as a no."

"Fitz, Fitz, Fitz..." Mattie shook her head and smiled. "Take that as a definite yes."

Chapter 21

"Y'all come on in and make yourselves comfy." Dhalia Duchess Blackmoor led Mattie and me into her condo. We ended up in the living room, overlooking the Cushman Marsh, which, after two or three miles, connected to the Intracoastal Waterway. "I'll be right back. I'm fixing us a pot of hot ginger tea."

"You don't have to do that, Dhalia," Mattie said.

"Oh, honey, I drink a pot every morning after a performance. Keeps my throat healthy."

Her living room reminded me of something out of a home in New Orleans's Garden District. The furnishings, though meticulous, were all antiques reminiscent of a day when Billie Holiday was the queen of jazz. Mattie and I sat on a plush dark-purple sofa. There were several lamps with exotic shades, a Victrola sat on a table in the corner, and a white baby grand piano sat in the center of the room. Painted portraits of jazz giants hung on the walls, including, appropriately, one of Billie Holiday. Nina Simone was represented, as well as Miles Davis and Duke Ellington.

Putting a hand to my still hurting cheek, I said, "You ask her if she screwed the senator."

"I thought you were expert at handling those tough questions."

"Look, Dhalia weighs a good hundred pounds more than me—"

"Be nice," Mattie warned.

"I'm not insulting her. Hell, she's gorgeous. I'm just saying that if she slapped me like the good preacher's wife, she's liable to take off my head."

"Here we go, my lovely guests," Dhalia said, entering the room carrying a large oriental tray that held a matching tea service. She put it down on the coffee table, and I was happy to see the tea was accompanied by warm cinnamon buns.

The jazz singer's hair was perfectly styled, and her makeup looked as if it had been applied by a professional. Her silk dressing gown highlighted her beautiful dark complexion. She might have been a single woman, but she had four large diamond rings on her fingers, and I would have bet none of them were fakes. Her gown made a V as it joined across her voluptuous cleavage and opened in an upside-down V just above her knees. She wore pink-and-purple leopard-print slippers.

After settling on a love seat that matched the sofa, Dhalia prepared the tea and handed a cup to each of us. "Oh, Mattie, what are we going to do without Mitch?"

"We go on, I hope. That's certainly a question we'll have to address as a board."

"I thought that's why you came over this morning."

I piped up. "First, I want to tell you I'm a big fan. I've seen you a few times, and that Nina Simone song you do, 'Feeling Good'..." I could almost hear her singing in my head.

"Anthony Newley wrote that," Dhalia said, smiling as if she'd heard it all before and still enjoyed hearing it.

"I find myself singing it days afterward."

"It's one that gets in your brain—that's for sure."

I nodded. "I have one of your CDs. I wish I'd brought it so you could autograph it."

"Perhaps another time."

"And," Mattie jumped in, "if you're done being a fanboy, we can tell Dhalia what's going on."

Basically, we shared what we'd told Margaret Stone, but when I explained about the texts and Mattie asked her if she'd slept with McGovern, Dhalia laughed.

"That man had an appetite. You didn't learn that, Mattie?"

Mattie blinked at the question then looked at me and back at Dhalia. "What? No, I mean, the senator said that if I ever..." She took a breath. "Basically, no."

An amused look in place, Dhalia looked from Mattie to me. "Oh, I see how it is."

Mattie gazed down, and I grinned sheepishly.

"Well, good for you. But yeah, Mitch had a long pecker—long in that he liked to reach it out to many different women. When I got those texts, I thought maybe they were from Lucinda. Wouldn't be the first time I heard from a wife. I can't help it if women can't keep their husbands under control, now can I?"

"Can I see your texts?" I asked.

Dhalia got her phone and brought up her messages and handed it to me. I scrolled through and asked, "You got three?"

"Yes."

I told Mattie, "Same messages Ronnie got. Like Margaret Stone, the last Dhalia got was when Mack was in custody."

Mattie thought a moment and said, "The texts Ronnie, Margaret, and I received all came in after the senator was killed."

"Mm-hmm, mine too. I thought that maybe in her grief, Lucinda was working out some issues, dealing with the man's pleasure seeking."

"Have you spoken to Lucinda since Mitch's death?" Mattie asked.

"Yes, I called to offer my condolences. She seemed happy to hear from me, considering the circumstances. So now that I think about it, maybe I shouldn't have assumed the texts were from her."

I said, "With all that's happened, be extra careful. If Mack isn't responsible, then there's a killer out there who may have an issue with the board."

"Oh, I can take care of myself," Dhalia said. From the folds of her dressing gown, she produced a pearl-handled derringer. "The duchess has been taking care of herself for a long, long time."

We ended our visit, and Dhalia showed us to the door. As we crossed the condo parking lot to Mattie's car, I said, "That was awesome."

"You were starstruck," Mattie said.

"I know. I can't believe she laughed when you asked about senatorial shtupping. I ask, and I get slapped." Though the sting was finally gone, I touched my cheek. Looking over the top of her car, I said, "Speaking of which, why did she seem so surprised that you hadn't made bacon with McGovern?"

Mattie looked at me, pursed her lips, and said, "How should I know?" She opened her door and got in.

We attempted to phone Elizabeth Melrose, but her voicemail said she was out of the country and provided the date she'd left. She'd been overseas for over a week.

Mattie scrolled through her contacts. "Should we talk to the senator's daughter, Jillian?"

"I think so," I said. "We'll temper the questions, just find out if she got any texts."

"I wonder where she was when her father was killed?" Mattie asked.

I reclined the passenger seat and sat back, thinking what Mattie was considering. "You're thinking that maybe she killed her father?"

"Anything's possible."

"I suppose. Hmm, so maybe she happened over to the beach bungalow, found her father, bound and gagged."

Mattie added, "Maybe she's heard rumors about her father for years, and that anger has been percolating all that time."

"And finding him like that would have enraged her enough at what she considered his betrayal of her mother and, to some degree, her."

"And in that rage, she killed him. Later, still furious, she killed the woman her father had been cheating with," Mattie finished. She turned to me. "What do you think?"

"It doesn't excite me," I admitted. "Though I suppose we could at least ask her about what she was up to when her father was killed, subtly find out if she has an alibi."

Mattie pushed the call button and spoke with Jillian, who gave directions to her dorm room at San Marco University.

We found her dormitory easily enough, but we had to park at a distance and hike across the parking lot.

Jillian opened the door at our knock. "Hi, come in."

Mattie introduced me as we entered the dorm room. Jillian and her roommate had decorated the small space nicely so that it seemed like a tiny apartment. Jillian sat on her bed, and Mattie joined her there. I sat on a rolling office chair in front of one of two small built-in desks. Jillian was beautiful, taking after her mother, but without being marred by the cynicism Lucinda displayed. Still, she had dark circles under her eyes and seemed to lack energy, and the fact that she clutched a Kleenex tissue indicated she'd been crying.

Placing a hand on Jillian's knee, Mattie said, "I'm so sorry, Jillian. It must be terribly hard to lose both your father and your mother's cousin under these horrible circumstances."

"Thank you. It is hard."

"We just have a couple of questions, and then we'll get out of your hair."

"Is this about the homeless initiative?"

I leaned forward, elbows on knees. "Kinda, sorta. I'm a private detective, and I've been working with the police, as well as Mattie, to try and learn who is responsible."

"Oh?"

"When you heard the tragic news about your father, did anyone come to mind as possibly being responsible?" I asked.

Jillian thought a moment and then shook her head. "I'm sorry, no."

"You don't have a thing to be sorry for," Mattie said. She took Jillian's hand and asked, "Have you received any strange texts lately?"

Jillian knitted her brow. "What do you mean? What strange texts?"

"I take it you haven't gotten any?" I asked.

"No. Texts from who?"

"It doesn't matter. Just working a long shot," Mattie said.

Mattie looked up at me, and I knew she wanted me to go fishing for an alibi.

"Um, Jillian," I said, "it must have been awful when you received the news about your father."

She nodded. "I couldn't believe it when Mom called."

"She called you here, at the dorm?"

"No." Jillian dabbed her eyes with a tissue. "I was with friends in Key West. We'd gone down for a long weekend."

So much for the killer-daughter theory. Neither Mattie nor I liked it anyway. We said our goodbyes, and Mattie promised to call.

In the parking lot, as we made for Mattie's VW, a black Jaguar with heavily tinted windows pulled up next to us. We didn't recognize the driver until the window lowered.

"Lucinda," Mattie said. "I'm so sorry to hear about Mitch and Ronnie."

Lucinda looked as regal as she had when I first met her at the senator's offices. She wore large sunglasses, though I could feel the heat of her gaze as she tried to understand why Mattie and I were there together. "I certainly hope you aren't here to bother my daughter. She's had a hard time as it is without a visit from a private investigator and a reporter."

Mattie knelt by the open window. "We're visiting all the board members, Lucinda. It seems Ronnie received threatening texts before she was killed. I got one last night. Margaret has received a couple, and Dhalia got three."

Her gaze traveled back and forth several times from Mattie to me. "I'm sorry. I'm confused as to what you're getting at. Isn't Mack responsible for Ronnie's murder?"

I bent down beside Mattie. "Possibly. It sure looks like it. But it's also possible that someone else is. We think that maybe these texts are being sent to members of the homeless initiative board who have... uh..."

"Who have what?" Lucinda asked.

"Who have something to do with the case, though we don't know what," Mattie quickly said.

"Has my daughter gotten a text?"

"Thankfully not," I answered.

"And neither have I," Lucinda said. "If you'll excuse me..." She rolled up the window and parked.

Mattie and I watched her walk to the entrance of the dormitory. I turned to Mattie and said, "She most definitely slept with the senator, yet she hasn't received a text."

"Meaning what?" Mattie asked.

"Meaning I don't know. Maybe she's acting out, sending texts to everyone she thinks slept with her husband. Except not everyone did. You didn't, right?"

"Would you quit asking me that?"

"Sorry, it just doesn't fit with what we've learned."

"It does if the killer *thinks* I slept with him." She stopped and said, "Look, maybe there was a little innocent flirting between us, okay? And maybe we kissed a little bit, once, but that's it."

Kissed? I chewed on that as we got into the car. Mattie seemed ill at ease and nibbled at her upper lip as she turned the ignition.

"Okay," I said, thinking, "maybe the killer thinks you two hooked up, and that's why you're on their text list."

"And maybe the texts don't have anything to do with Mitch's hookups."

"Maybe. I need to go stare at my blackboard again."

"You want me to drop you at home?"

"Yeah." I checked her dashboard clock. "And then I have to go see a friend."

I felt as awkward as a schoolboy on a first date when I got out of Mattie's car. I didn't know whether to kiss her, shake hands, or give her a fist bump. She, however, had no qualms about pulling me into a soulful kiss followed by "I'll see if I can get in touch with Elizabeth Melrose. Oh, and Fitz?"

"Yeah?"

"Let's do last night again, real soon."

"The sooner the better."

As much as I enjoyed spending time with Mattie, I was glad to go solo. She was too much of a distraction.

Chapter 22

I got in my truck and headed for the mainland and Buddy Reid Security Systems. I'd known my boss, Buddy, from when I was a cop and he was a suspect. A dozen or so years earlier, Buddy had moved to San Marco and opened his security business. Then a string of burglaries took place in the more upscale neighborhoods. As a homicide detective, I got involved when a homeowner surprised the burglar and was murdered. My investigation led to Buddy Reid. Buddy was that rare breed of thief, a cat burglar. More artisan than criminal, Buddy had plied his skills in New York, San Francisco, and Milwaukee, for which the FBI had a file on him. Still, he was too good and was never caught in the commission of a crime or in possession of stolen goods.

The third time I brought Buddy in for questioning, he'd said, "Let's speak hypothetically, Detective Fitzgerald."

"Okay. Hypothetically."

"Three things—hypothetically. First off, if in my past, I had engaged in criminal pursuits, I am no longer engaged in such activities. Second, I would never put myself in a situation that would result in murder. And third, Detective Fitzgerald, I can help you catch this burglar."

I took him up on his offer and let Buddy look at the files and took him to several crime scenes. Buddy digested all this information then told me with certainty which neighborhood the burglar was likely to strike next, as well as a time frame for when it would happen. Thanks to that info, I nabbed the guilty party. When I left the force, Buddy offered me a commissioned position as a consultant whose main job was to look over a potential client's home or business and advise them on what kind of security would be beneficial.

I knew Buddy spent Saturdays at the office, doing paperwork, and I saw the company truck in its usual spot by his building, a cinder-block construction with a small office up front and the entire property surrounded by chain-link fencing. I went through the glass front door, passed through the lobby, and knocked on the doorjamb of Buddy's office. With hair so blond as to look white, he sat at his desk, computing numbers in his head and writing the answers on a sheet of paper. Finally, he looked at me with a grave expression. That was the thing with Buddy—he was a serious guy.

"Hi, Fitz," Buddy said, standing and moving to a filing cabinet with deliberate grace. "What's up?"

"I want to see if you're interested in a job."

Buddy cocked an eye and said, "Maybe. Let's take a walk."

Because of the FBI's past interest in him, Buddy was paranoid about his business being bugged. He swept the property regularly, and though he'd never found a listening device, old habits died hard. We stepped out into the afternoon sun and meandered around the property.

"What kind of job?" Buddy asked.

"I need to help a friend."

"A hush-hush job?"

"A mum's-the-word-until-your-dying-day kind of job," I said.

"Dangerous?"

"Would you expect anything less from me?"

Buddy pondered that and asked, "More dangerous than that last thing I did for you?"

"Yep, probably."

"What's the fee?" Buddy asked.

"Let's just say there's a chance at a high fee. All depends how things shake out."

One of the few things that could make Buddy smile was the prospect of a high-risk job. Without expression, he said, "Sounds like my kind of employment. Tell me about it."

And I laid out my plan to help Rick.

Happy hour was close to over, and I sat at the end of the bar, drinking beer and eating fish tacos made with off-the-boat mahi. They were so good I damn near moaned after each bite.

"Skipper!" I yelled down the bar. "These tacos are amazing. God bless you, sir."

Laughing, Skipper came over and said, "'God bless you'?"

I shrugged. "I went into a church today. I guess it stuck."

"Save room for dessert."

"Oh?"

"Homemade key lime pie."

My eyebrows shot up. "That's the sexiest thing anybody has said to me all day."

Skipper said, "I doubt that. A little birdy told me you woke up with Mattie Castro."

I slapped both hands on the bar. "Really? The San Marco rumor mill is already running with it?"

"Small-town living."

"*Hola, muchacho,*" Eddie said and sat on the barstool next to me. He watched me take a finishing bite. "That looks good. Snapper?"

"Mahi," I told him.

"Oh man." Eddie turned his attention to the bartender. "Let me get an order of those, Skipper. And pour me an Intuition IPA."

I looked at Eddie in his shirtsleeves, his tie firmly in place. "Drinking on the job?"

"Off the clock."

"Top me off," I said, pushing my empty pint glass toward Skipper.

When we got our beers and Skipper wandered off, Eddie leaned close and said, "How's the quest for twenty-five grand?"

I used an index finger smeared with a little sour cream to write imaginary digits in the air. "It's a quest for twelve thousand five hundred dollars."

"Since when?"

"Since I told Mattie we could work together and split the reward."

"That was one expensive hookup."

I had a taco to my lips but stopped midbite. "What? You heard about it too?" I put on a show of being perturbed, but a little pride was mixed in.

The ringtone on Eddie's cell sounded. He looked at it and said, "Hang on a second. It's Carl."

"Your son?" I asked.

He nodded as he answered. He listened for half a minute and said, "If it's okay with your mother. Be home for dinner, and be careful on the road." He ended the call and turned to me. "Where was I?"

"Wait a minute. Carl's driving now?"

"Boy's seventeen, Fitz. You gotta come over for dinner, get reacquainted with everyone."

I'd almost been part of Eddie's family when we were partners. My stupid pride had ended that. "I'd like that, Eddie. I really would."

"Me too." Eddie patted my shoulder. "Anyway, I was looking for you to see if you'd be interested in—"

A firm, tanned, young body pushed between us. Seri smiled brightly and said, "Hi, Detective Schmitt. How are you today?"

"Hi, Seri. What's up?"

"Same ol'. I just wanted to say it's always a pleasure to see you in here." She turned to give me the stink-eye of death and left.

Eddie laughed out loud. "I'm not the only one who's heard about you and Mattie. That right there was damn entertaining."

"You were saying?"

"Oh, yeah. I have a little primo information I'd be happy to share if you'd return the favor with anything I might not yet know."

I took a swig. "I might know a thing or two that I haven't shared with you."

Eddie nodded. "What I have concerns the senator's widow. Tell me what you got, and I'll go into detail."

"Hold on. Don't count your chickens before they killed the cat."

Poor Eddie tried to hide his reaction.

I told him, "Look, I know some interesting things about Lucinda as well."

"I probably already know what you know, while I'm pretty darn sure that you don't know what I know." Eddie paused a few beats. "You know?"

I looked up at the ceiling and shook my head. "Fine. Here's what I got. There were seven women on the senator's homeless initiative board. Apparently, McGovern made whoopee with more than just Ronnie. There was his wife, of course, and Dhalia Duchess Black-moor."

"Really?"

"She told Mattie and me like it was no big deal. And it appears that the right Reverend Stone's wife, Margaret, also tasted of the fruit of lust."

"Hmm. That is new."

"And Mattie was propositioned by the senator, though they only kissed a little." Oddly, I felt a little pang of jealousy in my belly.

"Yeah," Eddie said in a skeptical tone. "Let me guess—Mattie told you that."

"Yes, she did. Why?"

Eddie held up a hand. "No reason. Let's see—one of the others was his daughter, and then there's Elizabeth Melrose, who's approaching her seventies or eighties."

I leaned into him. "Here's a little more to consider. Ronnie wasn't the only one to get threatening texts."

"What?"

"Everyone who dallied with the senator has gotten texts. Even Mattie. In fact, the only one who has bedded the senator and not gotten threatening texts is the widow, Lucinda Combs-McGovern."

"Interesting," Eddie said, "especially on the heels of what I've found out."

"Which is?"

Eddie drained his beer, held up the glass for Skipper to see, and spun on his stool to face me. When we were partners, he'd get this excited when we were close to solving a case. He had that same kind of elation as he said, "Okay. How did the killer undress and tie Ronnie to the bed?"

"Hmm. Damn, I hadn't thought about that. Ronnie's a sound sleeper? Nah, that wouldn't wash unless she drank like her husband and passed out. So the killer was strong enough to overpower her. Very strong to undress her and tie her up."

Eddie said, "Diazepam."

"Gesundheit."

"The coroner found a hypodermic needle mark on Ronnie's neck. She was injected with enough diazepam to render her unconscious."

"Diazepam? Rings a bell," I said.

"Maybe you'd be more familiar with another of its names, Valium."

"Ohhh."

"Now, guess who suffered from anxiety attacks his whole life and regularly took diazepam both orally and by injection?"

"Who?"

"Senator Mitch McGovern."

"No shit?"

"Lou found it in a locked cabinet in his office bathroom as well as his medicine chest at home and the beach house. She found out he had a prescription and had been taking it for years." Eddie checked to make sure no one was too close before continuing. "And for the game-winning question, who had ready access to the senator's supply of diazepam?"

"Lucinda Combs-McGovern."

Eddie smiled and tapped the end of his nose. "Now, let's move on to the topic of the handcuffs. Two sets of prints were found on the handcuffs, and the wise man would say they belonged to..." He paused, waiting for me to answer.

"Ronnie and McGovern."

Eddie made a buzzer sound effect. "The two sets of prints we got off of them were Ronnie's and Lucinda's. All over the cuffs. We did get the senator's middle finger prints, but only on the quick-release mechanisms and nowhere else. So we know he tried using those releases, but they'd been tampered with."

"But if he'd used them recently with Ronnie, as she said, why weren't his prints all over the cuffs?" I asked.

"Maybe that was because he or Ronnie or Lucinda cleaned them or polished them after he'd last handled them. We know Ronnie's prints were on them because she got them out of the wardrobe and cuffed up McGovern, but if Lucinda hadn't used them in a long time, as she said the first time we talked to her, why were her prints on them?"

"Because she tampered with them, putting superglue on the cuff releases," I said. "Wait a minute. She has an alibi for the murder. Her mother was visiting."

"Come on, Fitz. How much effort would it take to sneak out of their mansion to do the deed while a senior citizen snoozed away?"

"Good point. How about servants? Any see her leave or could swear she was at home all night?"

"Nope. They have a few day servants but no one who stays after dinnertime."

"This could turn out interesting." My cell phone rang. Checking the caller ID, I said, "Hang on, it's Mattie." I answered, "What's up, buttercup?"

"I got another text," she said.

"Whoa." I told Eddie, "Mattie got another text."

"What's it say?" Eddie asked.

"What's it say?" I echoed into the phone.

"'I know what you did,'" Mattie said.

"That's the same second message Ronnie got," I said.

"And Margaret and Dhalia," Mattie added. "Look, Fitz, I'm a little worried about Sky and me being alone at my place. You mind if we stay at the Folly tonight?"

Covering the phone mouthpiece, I said to Eddie, "She can't get enough of me." Then I said to Mattie, "Yeah, that'd be great. We can—wait—hang on." I asked Eddie, "Are you bringing Lucinda in tonight?"

"You bet I am, and you can join in the fun."

Back into the phone, I said, "We've learned some things about Lucinda Combs-McGovern, and Eddie's bringing her in to question. You want to drop Sky at your sister's and come watch on CCTV?"

"Can't. My sister has plans. I think we'll just go over to your place and wait for you. You can fill me in later."

"Okay. One of the top bricks on the fire pit is loose. The spare key is under it. Make yourselves comfy. You can fold out the sofa into a bed for Sky. And after she goes to sleep, you can wait for me in my bed."

"Keep dreamin', lover boy, and thanks."

"She didn't say no," I said to myself as I pocketed my phone.

Skipper set down two full beers.

I lifted my glass to Eddie. "To Lucinda Combs-McGovern."

Eddie lifted his glass and said, "To Lucinda and what promises to be an interesting evening."

Chapter 23

"Ready?" Eddie asked.

I straightened my shirt and ran my fingers through my hair. "It's important to make a good first impression when interrogating upper-class muckety-mucks."

Lou said, "Have fun, boys. I'll watch on the closed circuit."

Eddie and I stepped into the interview room.

"You have some nerve." Lucinda Combs-McGovern looked amazingly out of place as she sat at the interview table, her posture rigid and her chin held high. "Dragging me down here is your first of many mistakes."

"No one dragged you," Eddie said, "though I'm sure the police officers sternly recommended you come with them."

I sat across from her and said, "Some things have come up, Lucinda, which make you a..." I looked at Eddie.

Eddie didn't say anything but held his hand flat and wobbled it back and forth.

I turned back toward Lucinda. "A person of interest."

She crossed her arms. "I'm a suspect?"

"That depends on how this interview goes," Eddie replied. "First off, let's talk about your cousin's murder."

Lucinda stared at him. "I'm waiting for my lawyer, and I'm not saying a thing until he gets here."

"And you called him?" Eddie asked.

"When I was asked to come down to the station, I attempted but couldn't get through. So I called my husband's personal assistant and told her to find my lawyer as soon as possible and to tell him I was to be interrogated by the police and the maladroit private detective, Mr. Fitz-something or other."

"Buttering me up will get you nowhere," I said.

Eddie asked, "Your husband's assistant? That would be Caroline Ortiz?"

"Yes."

"Why don't you call her and see if she got in touch with him and how long he'll be?" Eddie suggested.

"Very well." Lucinda put on a show of retrieving her phone from her handbag and searching through her contacts list. Finally, she called and spoke with her for a minute. "I see," she added and pressed the end button. "He was at a function in Jacksonville and is on his way back as we speak."

"An hour and a half at best, probably two," I said. "You sure you don't want to talk to us? The sooner you do, the sooner you get out of here."

"I'm not talking without my lawyer present."

I turned my chair so that it faced Eddie. "'I'm not talking without my lawyer present.' That's what guilty people always say."

"In my experience, pretty much."

"Guilty? What do you mean guilty?" Lucinda said.

"I always found it a sure sign that I was fishing in the right watering hole," I said.

"What are you talking about?" Lucinda asked, her voice raised.

Without looking at her, I used my thumb to gesture at Lucinda. "So how long can you hold her?"

"We can't hold her, Fitz. You know that. She's free to leave anytime she wants."

"Hmm," I said, "an uncooperative person of interest, bordering on suspect, in two murders?"

"You have a point. If I consider there's a flight risk, it might be prudent to arrest her. And seeing as it's taking her lawyer so long to get here, I'd think I could hold her a good while. With her money and position, though, her lawyer can get her sprung by tomorrow morning."

"Tomorrow morning?" Lucinda echoed.

"Geez, if it takes that long, then the media is going to be all over this," I said.

"No doubt."

"Okay, I'll talk with you," Lucinda nearly shouted. "But when my lawyer arrives, I want him brought here immediately."

"We can do that," Eddie said and turned toward the CCTV camera. "Got that, Lou? Bring her lawyer in as soon as he gets here."

Lucinda looked up as if seeing the camera for the first time. "Oh lord, is this being recorded?"

"Standard operating procedure," Eddie said. "No one will see it but us cops."

"Unless they break it out for the trial," I said.

"Trial?"

"Diazepam, Lucinda," I said.

She blinked several times before asking, "What?"

"Tell us about your husband's medication," Eddie said. "The diazepam."

"Well, Mitch suffered from severe anxiety attacks. Regular injections of diazepam prevented them. As a politician, you don't want to show any signs of weakness, including things beyond your control like panic attacks."

"No doubt," I said, my voice dripping with condescension. "However, your cousin was incapacitated by an overdose of diazepam on the night she was murdered."

She looked from me to Eddie. "What?"

Neither Eddie nor I spoke right away. Instead, we watched Lucinda's reaction. Her lower lip quivered, and she struggled for words as her eyes filled. "I thought that Mack—he was mad about Mitch—I thought he killed her."

"Yes, he is a suspect," Eddie said. "But the fact that your husband was treated with diazepam and you had access to it certainly raises red flags."

Lucinda regained her composure and looked at Eddie. "Yes, I suppose it does."

I said, "When we talked earlier about your husband's toys, you said that you didn't care for those handcuffs."

"So?"

"It's just interesting because if you didn't use them, then why were your fingerprints on them?"

She looked around the room while answering. "As I said, we did use them once, but it's been a while."

Eddie sat on the corner of the table. "See, that doesn't wash. Your prints and your cousin's were all over them. If yours were still on there from long ago, your husband's prints would be there as well." Eddie left out the part where the senator's prints were found on the quick-release mechanisms. "But at some point since the last time your husband used them—"

"Which was the time before last with Ronnie," I interjected.

"The cuffs were wiped down or polished. So you handled them recently."

Lucinda gave us an unpleasant look and lifted her chin defiantly.

"Does that mean"—I lifted my chin as well—"that you don't want to talk about the handcuffs?"

She didn't respond.

"Hoo-boy. Once again with the silent treatment," I said, standing. "I get that a lot from women." I grabbed Eddie's upper arm and pulled him across the room like we were going to have a hushed conference, though I spoke loudly enough for Lucinda to hear. "So how do you think it played out?"

Eddie looked at Lucinda then turned his back to her as he answered. Like me, he made sure she could hear him. "I think she learned about her husband and cousin having an affair and didn't like it."

"I know what you're trying to do," Lucinda said.

Eddie ignored her and went on, "Knowing they'd get to the handcuffs sooner or later, she booby-trapped them."

"Ha. *Booby-trapped* is funny when talking about sex."

"I know you men are trying to play mind games," Lucinda called.

"A little superglue on the safety releases, and they turned into real handcuffs. After Ronnie left, her husband showed up and beat the crap out of him. Then at some point late at night, Lucinda snuck out of their mansion without waking her mother, came over to the beach house, saw her husband trussed up, and lost it."

I tapped my lips with a finger and said, "Yeah, that makes sense. Lucinda found out that Ronnie, her cousin, was banging her husband like a screen door in a hurricane. She killed her husband while she had the opportunity, and then she killed her cousin."

"No!" Lucinda screamed. "I didn't kill anyone. And I wanted Ronnie to fuck Mitch. I told her to!"

Silence enveloped the interview room. After half a minute, I made my way back to my chair and said, "I was not expecting that."

"Can you please tell us about your last statement?" Eddie asked.

Lucinda took a breath and leaned against the table. "Mitch was not a good husband. I'm not saying he was a bad man. In fact, he was a good man and a good father to Jillian. But he was not a good husband. And it goes beyond all the hanky-panky. His job demanded all his time, and I'm sure many senators' wives would agree that it's more like their husbands are married to the job while we wives are more along the lines of window-dressing." She stopped then asked, "Can I smoke in here?"

"Let me see your cigarettes," Eddie said.

Lucinda pulled a pack and a lighter out of her voluminous hand bag and handed them to Eddie.

Eddie shook a cigarette out of the pack and held it out to Lucinda. As she took it, he said, "This is a no-smoking building." He flicked the lighter and held it up to the end of the cigarette as she inhaled. When the cigarette was lit, he went on, "So I'm sorry, you can't smoke in here."

Eddie left the room and came back a moment later with an empty soda can for her to use as an ashtray.

She smiled at his consideration and continued. "The sex did play a part of it. Before we married, when we were dating, well, I never had a man who was so passionate and creative and, well, crazy about sex. It was wonderful. After we were married, the sexual intensity increased, and we experimented with many things I won't go into, and then he had that sex room put in. By that time, Jillian was born, and Mitch was into his political career as a state representative. At some point, I realized that I was having sex just to satisfy him. Over the years, things cooled down, and though I suspected him of fooling around, I really didn't care so much. By this point, I no longer loved Mitch, and I knew he'd be careful because of his career. He was smart enough to choose women who wouldn't gain anything if the news came out. And each coupling with someone else was one I didn't have to endure." She gathered her thoughts. "I guess it sounds awful when put into words, but it was a situation that came into being over years and years."

"Tell us about Ronnie," Eddie said.

Lucinda nodded. "We grew up between here and Gainesville in Welaka. Our mothers were sisters. Her parents and mine only lived a couple of blocks apart, and both houses were on the St. Johns River. We were like sisters who lived in two different homes. We spent all our time together. Both our bedrooms had twin beds, and more nights than not, we slept over at each other's house. After high school, we came to San Marco together and enrolled in the university. Neither of us finished. I met Mitch, and we married after a year. I think that inspired Ronnie to find a man for herself. Unfortunately, she found Mack Thorpe. And admittedly, he wasn't so terrible at first. But she could have done much better."

"Okay, the background's been laid. I'm dying to know why you would tell your cousin to peel your husband's banana," I said.

Lucinda said, "An interesting vocabulary, Fitz, but your charm is wearing thin."

"Yeah, I get that a lot. You were saying?"

Lucinda sighed and sucked on her cigarette. "I got the idea when Mitch started on his homeless initiative and chose seven women to serve on his board. Four of those women were attractive and in Mitch's age range. It's safe to say he slept with them all."

"Not Mattie Castro," I said.

Lucinda smiled sympathetically at me and reached over the table to pat my hand. "Bless your heart." She sat back and said, "Anyway, Ronnie would never have slept with him, and when he made a move on her, she told me. I no longer loved Mitch, and Ronnie was in an atrocious marriage. We both wanted out."

"There's this little legal thing," I said, "called divorce."

"Yes, but Mitch's father insisted I sign a prenuptial agreement. I'd get nothing in a divorce. Same for Ronnie, but that's just because Mack has no money. However, the prenuptial agreement would be null if I could prove Mitch was committing adultery."

"So you told Ronnie to go ahead and sleep with him," Eddie said.

"Yes. And it wasn't anything terrible for Ronnie, sexwise—the opposite, really. Mitch was handsome, well endowed, well skilled, and Ronnie liked to fool around. We came up with different possibilities for exposing the affair—everything from photos to me accidentally on purpose catching them in the act. Maybe I'm a little paranoid, but I know the McGovern family lawyers are like pit bulls and would pull out all the stops to see that the adultery charge wouldn't hold up. I'd be penniless."

She looked from Eddie to me, seeing if we understood the gravity of her situation. When she saw no sympathy, her gaze fell to the tabletop, and she continued at a softer volume, "Mitch had that homeless initiative press conference Tuesday morning, so Ronnie arranged a tryst for Monday night at the beach house. Before that happened, I put superglue in the release latches of the handcuffs. After Ronnie and Mitch fooled around, she pretended like it was a joke that she left him cuffed, because, at least to his way of thinking, he could easily work the releases. She also left the front door open."

Lucinda took a deep drag and slowly released the smoke. "The plan was that all the journalists would show up for the press conference Tuesday morning and find Mitch tied and gagged in his silly room. No way Mitch's lawyers could disprove their testimony."

"You'd ruin him as a senator," Eddie said.

"I don't think so. It seems that some politicians get a boost from sex scandals. But frankly, by that point, I didn't care. The only thing I worried about was how it would embarrass our daughter, Jillian, though it wouldn't come as a surprise. She's aware of her father's predilections. We've spoken of it." She took a last hard drag on her cigarette and dropped the butt into the can. "We had no way of knowing that Mack would follow her there. Or that someone would kill Mitch." She started to cry but quickly pulled herself together. "Ronnie also planned to get a divorce, and we'd leave San Marco."

All in all, a respectable bit of chicanery. I asked, "What were you going to do after all that?"

"We hadn't decided on anything specific, though we talked about moving to the Caribbean or to Italy or to California wine country and starting a business of sorts." As tears started again, she looked at me. "We had different parents, but we really were sisters. I'll miss her as long as I live."

"Why didn't you tell us any of this earlier?" Eddie asked.

Lucinda shook her head and sighed. "Ronnie and I thought we were in control of everything, but then it all spiraled into chaos. We talked about it, about telling the police what really happened, but we decided to wait and see if we could weather the storm. And then Ronnie was... Oh, Ronnie."

Eddie said, "Mrs. Combs-McGovern, please tell us the truth. Did you send those threatening texts to the members of the board?"

"No, Detective Schmitt, I did not." She pulled a monogrammed handkerchief from her pocketbook and dabbed at her eyes.

"Anything else, Fitz?"

I shook my head.

Eddie said, "You're free to go, Mrs. Combs-McGovern. Tell your lawyer we're sorry he had to come down for nothing."

"Don't worry about that, Detective. He'll bill me."

"Detective Peters will drive you home."

Chapter 24

Eddie walked down the hall while I found a number in my phone contacts and pushed Call. "Didn't see that one coming."

"Yeah. I'll keep Lucinda on the list, but I believe her," Eddie said.

"Which leads us back to square one," I said. "At least I can bill Mack for all my hours even if the reward doesn't pan out."

"Don't count on getting paid."

I held up a finger and listened. The call went to voicemail, and I hung up. "What do you mean about not getting paid?"

"Mack is a mess, like he's having a breakdown. They moved him into the jail infirmary."

"Shit. This whole thing has been a fuster-cluck since the get-go. And with the texts, especially the ones coming in after he was locked up, Mack's not our man." Frustrated, I jabbed Redial and put the phone to my ear.

"Who are you calling?"

Eddie opened the door that led to the parking lot. Long after dark, the numerous streetlights were keeping it well lit.

I stepped through and said, "Trying to get Mattie."

"I thought she was staying at the Folly tonight?"

"She's supposed to, but I can't reach her."

"You worried?"

"Not really. But she was."

"I have paperwork courtesy of our interview," Eddie said. "But if you want, I can have a car cruise by your place."

"Nah, that's not necessary. I'm heading home right now."

"Tell you what," Eddie said. "I'll swing by on my way home and make sure all is shipshape at the Folly."

I threw him a salute and walked across the lot to my truck. I started the engine, turned off the radio, and hit Redial on my phone—again, five rings and voicemail. I'd told Eddie I wasn't worried, but that wasn't true. I was, if only a little. I nearly hit a squad car backing up then turned out of the lot. As I made my way toward US 1, I thought about what Lucinda had revealed. She'd set up that whole sex-room bondage thing in the hopes of collecting half of McGovern's money in a divorce. And now, courtesy of a killer, she'd be getting it all, or so I assumed. I wondered if the money would take the sting out of two members of her family being horribly murdered. And then my thoughts turned to Mattie and how serious she'd sounded when asking to stay at the Folly. I couldn't blame her—two dead, those texts seemingly involved. And I wondered what those texts meant, other than the obvious. They demonstrated someone was carrying around a great deal of rage. These were crimes of passion, fury, hate. *But who and why? And is Mattie really a target? And can I afford to assume she isn't?* No, I could not, especially since her four-year-old daughter was with her.

I turned too fast onto US 1 and got the old truck up to sixty miles per hour, fifteen over the speed limit. If a cop tried to pull me over, I decided I'd keep going until we both got to the Folly. At that point, the cop could do whatever the hell he wanted with me. I gave the truck more gas. Dodging cars and good sense, I once again hit Redial. When it went to voicemail, I hit End and tossed the phone to the passenger side and turned onto the Carroll Street Drawbridge. I sped over it to turn onto A1A. I raced past Doone's and, a minute later, slowed and turned onto Dos Casas Lane.

The truck chassis squeaked and bounced as I continued driving too fast on the dirt road. When I passed Consuela's, I got a sinking feeling in my gut. All the lights at her house were blazing, and her front door stood wide open. A few more bumps and I hit the brakes, the truck sliding to a stop just past Mattie's VW. Not one light was on at the Folly, inside or out, so I left the truck headlights on. Thinking that calling Eddie before I went in might be safer, I reached for the phone but then saw, like at Consuela's house, my front door was open.

"Shit," I said and jumped from the truck.

As I crossed the threshold into my little living room, I reached for the light switch and flipped it up. The house remained dark.

"Mattie?" I heard no answer. Adrenaline flushed through my system, firing up the tempo of my heart. "Mattie?" I called louder.

Leaving my headlights on provided some illumination that came in through the kitchen window. I headed that way first. After two steps, I could make out a body lying on the floor.

"Oh no."

At once, I saw that it was too small for Mattie and too big to be Sky. I knelt by the body, turned it over, and recognized Consuela's still form.

"Oh God. Consuela, are you all right? Wake up, you old crone." I patted her cheeks, but she didn't respond. Scattered around her were a number of crusty fruit-filled pastries and broken pieces of a plate. "Please, oh please." I reached a trembling hand to her neck, hoping for a pulse.

Consuela exhaled then drew in a long chainsaw snore.

"Oh yeah, atta girl. Throw in a belch and you'll be back to normal."

Something thumped, followed by three soft knocks. It came from the far side of the living room, maybe from within my bedroom, where little from the beams of the headlights pierced. I stood slowly, wishing I was one of those private eyes who always packed a gun. I did have two. One was a Glock 17, shut up in a gun safe in the closet of my bedroom, and it probably had more dust on it than gun oil. The other was the unregistered .38 hidden in my truck tool-box. I entered the living room and stared into shadows and darkness. I made it across the room and stood at the threshold of my bedroom. The night before, I'd enjoyed glorious sex in that room. Tonight, I seriously wondered if I had the balls to enter. Swallowing, I could just make out my bed. Moving closer, I saw something on it.

"What the hell?" I realized it was a small backpack sitting right in the middle of my bed. *Is it Mattie's? Sky's?*

Reaching out, I upended it. Scarves, a length of rope, a flathead screwdriver, and a wicked-looking folding knife fell onto the bed. I scanned the room, but nothing stood out in the darkness. *Fuck this,* I thought. I would go to the truck, get my phone, and call Eddie. Then I would get my .38 and keep watch over Consuela until the cavalry arrived.

Sensing movement behind me, I turned. A wasp sting pierced my neck, and I was instantly drunker than I could ever remember. As if blundering around in the dark wasn't bad enough, what little I could see kept blurring and turning into double and triple vision. The floor rocked back and forth, and the mahi taco I'd eaten earlier was in danger of returning. Then I saw someone, a silhouetted figure. My vision was too blurry to make distinctions like size or identity. Feeling malice emanating from the person, I took a swing and missed. My body turned with my punch. Whoever it was pushed me so that I staggered a few steps. The intruder grabbed something from the bed then turned toward me.

"Who are you?" I meant to yell, but it came out slurred and mumbly.

The figure charged, and I instinctively raised my arms. Through the dullness of my senses, a sharp pain opened across my right forearm. I went down.

Struggling, rising, climbing, swimming to the surface, I gasped. I was on my back at a roadside in the rain. Though I couldn't see, I knew a car was fast approaching, and I had to stop it before it rounded the curve. I struggled, but my eyelids were held shut by heavy weights. I groaned with effort, which turned into a grunt and finally a roar. My lids opened, and I screamed as I took in figures over me.

Mattie knelt at my side, her hands at my cheeks. "Oh, Fitz."

Next to Mattie, eyes wide and clutching tightly at her mother, Sky echoed, "Oh, Fitz."

Chapter 25

I was sitting next to Consuela's hospital bed. Mattie came into the room and pulled a chair close to me and put her hand on my good arm. Having come from church, she was dressed in a conservative gray dress.

She gave me a sympathetic smile and asked, "How you doing, lover?"

"I'm still foggy in the brain, and my arm hurts." I reached and took her hand. "And I'm scared."

"Scared? You survived the attack, Fitz. You'll be okay."

I couldn't explain what I felt, but I gave it a try. "This case has taken on a whole new level of significance," I explained, which prompted an unreadable expression from Mattie. "I'm serious, Mattie."

"Serious? You? Serious? Is that even a possibility?"

"Don't you get it? It wasn't me they were—"

"Well, well, well. Aren't you the picture of the wrong end of an ass-kicking." Eddie leaned against the door frame in a T-shirt and jeans, his arms crossed.

Before I could respond, Consuela cried out, *"Besarme en mi lugar secreto!"*

"What'd she say?" Eddie asked.

I shook my head. "Hell if I know. She's drugged, and every now and then, something pops out."

With an amused expression, Mattie translated, "She just said, 'Kiss me in my secret spot.'"

"Hmm," I mused, "I wonder if she means locale or on her body."

"Don't want to know the answer," Eddie said. "How are you feeling?"

"Like I'm in a dream. My head feels like it's stuffed with cotton, and I could sleep for a week."

"Maybe you should," Eddie said. He looked over at Consuela and said, "What's her doctor say?"

"Consuela has a skull fracture—calls it a simple fracture—and a spinal sprain. Normally not something considered life threatening, but he is concerned because of her age. She's in a lot of pain, so they're drugging her. The doc thinks the intruder tackled her from behind, which caused the sprain, and she suffered her fracture when she fell."

Eddie shook his head. "Who'd attack an old lady?"

"Someone who'd commit murder," Mattie said.

I said, "It looks like she walked into the Folly—"

"She was probably looking for me," Mattie said. "I'd stopped by her place on the way, to let her know Sky and I'd be there. She said she'd pop in later and bring us some mango pastelitos. After Sky and I got settled, we went for a walk and stopped by Doone's."

"Next time, take your phone with you," I said in a stern tone.

"Sorry," Mattie said. "I should have stuck around."

"Hell no," I blurted out. "That's what I was talking about. If you'd stuck around, you may have ended up tied to my bed and dead."

"That walk and drink at Doone's probably saved your life," Eddie said.

"What? You think..." The light bulb over Mattie's head clicked on to a full one-hundred- watt brightness. "Oh my God, what would have happened to Sky?" Mattie visibly shivered and crossed her arms. "Wait. Who's to say I was the target? It happened in your home—makes more sense that the killer was after you."

I reached out with my right arm, with its large bandage on the forearm, and placed it comfortingly on Mattie's leg. "If that were the case, they'd have finished the job after I went down."

"I agree," Eddie said. "With the texts and all, I'd say the killer was after you."

"But how'd the killer know I'd be at Fitz's?"

"Did you tell anyone where you'd be?" Eddie asked.

"No, just Fitz." Mattie thought a moment. "Wait a minute. In case my sister came by, I left a note on my kitchen table saying where I'd be. You don't think—"

"Yeah, I think the killer might have been in your home," Eddie said. "Maybe you and I should go over there after our visit with the infirm. Anyway, we think Consuela came to the Folly and went inside."

"See why you should knock, you crazy old lady?" I said to Consuela's sleeping form.

"Mattie, if the killer knew that was your car parked there, then they knew you weren't far. They shut off the main breaker switch and then waited in the dark for you to return, but Fitz got there first and received the diazepam overdose that was meant for you."

I patted her knee. "I'm glad it was me and not you."

Mattie lifted my hand to her mouth and kissed it.

Consuela cackled and said, "*Mira toda la pelusa me sacó de mi ombligo.*"

I turned to Mattie, who said, "Look at all the lint I pulled from my belly button."

"Now you're just making stuff up," I said.

Mattie traced an invisible X on her chest. "Cross my heart."

"I arrived just after Mattie and Sky found you," Eddie said. "You lost a lot of blood, even with the improvised bandage Mattie gave you, but the ambulances got there quick."

"Thanks," I said to Mattie. "And I'm sorry Sky had to see that."

"Once she got over the shock, Sky helped me with the bandage and didn't seem bothered at all by the blood. I might have a future doctor on my hands."

"Tell Sky I said thanks."

Eddie said, "Anyway, the killer was gone by that time. Must have left just after attacking you."

"I didn't see any cars other than Mattie's," I said.

"They could have parked at Doone's and walked over, along either the river or A1A. You didn't see anyone going or coming from Doone's on foot, did you?" Eddie asked Mattie.

"No."

"Hell, they could have parked on A1A, for that matter, or along one of the streets in the neighborhood south of you."

"*Uno mas margarita, por favor,*" Consuela blurted out.

"I know that one," I said.

Eddie stretched and asked, "When do you get out of here?"

"I may just walk out of here today."

"No, you won't," Mattie said and turned to Eddie. "They want to keep him for now." Looking back at me, she counted off my injuries on her fingers. "You suffered an overdose, blood loss, and a concussion from bouncing your head on the floor."

"A mild concussion," I added.

"Only because you're hardheaded."

"You need to warn Margaret Stone and Dhalia Duchess Blackmoor," I said.

"Already done. Patrol cars are making regular passes by their residences."

"Could either of them be the killer?" Mattie asked.

"I'm not ruling anything out," Eddie said.

"And Lucinda Combs-McGovern was with us at the station," I said.

"She could have hired help," Eddie said.

"These aren't the type of crimes you hire muscle for. This is fueled by rage. It's personal," I said.

"Quit looking at the women he loved, and look at the women who loved him."

Neither Mattie, Eddie, nor I had spoken, and we all turned toward Consuela, who gazed at us with clear eyes.

"Consuela, you're awake. How are you?" I asked.

"My *cabeza* hurts. My *espalda* hurts. You are all talking too loudly. But as I said, quit looking at the women the senator loved, and look at the women who loved him."

I considered that a moment. "Okay. Anything else?"

"*Sí*, everybody knows the only thing the senator needed in a señorita was a heartbeat between her breasts and hot fire between her legs." Consuela closed her eyes and snored.

"They should put that on a Hallmark card." I looked at Eddie. "But there's a lot to what she said about—"

"Mr. Fitzgerald." A large nurse pushed past Eddie and stood with her hands on her hips.

"Nurse Ratched."

"What are you doing out of your room?"

"Visiting my landlady."

"And the visit is over. Back to your room and in your bed," the nurse ordered.

"Fine," I said, getting up.

The nurse crossed her arms and stared holes in me.

"He's one of *those* patients, isn't he?" Mattie said to her.

"A textbook example."

We moved into the hall, and I leaned against Mattie and said, "Come keep me company."

"Mattie's coming with me," Eddie said as we walked down the hall. "I want to check out her house, see if that note is how the killer found out she was at the Folly. Might dust for prints. And if it's all right, Mattie, I was thinking I might sneak back later and spend the night, see if the killer makes another go at you."

"That would be great," Mattie said. "I was a little nervous about Sky and me being on our own."

We stopped at my room, and Mattie gave me a quick kiss. "Be nice to the nurses."

Eddie clapped my shoulder. "We'll let you know how things go."

I watched them disappear around a corner and felt melancholy set in. "I want to go too."

Chapter 26

"Hey, roomie," a man called from within the hospital room. "Lord, give me strength," I muttered.

I'd awoken that morning to meet the man in the other bed, Bernie Tantorre, a retired contractor from Long Island. In that short time, I'd already learned intimate details about Bernie's diverticulitis, his wife, and what she'd been in the hospital for on three separate occasions. I knew about each of his kids and their interests, including that bum, Stanley King, who dated his daughter, Bunny.

"We got us a big decision to make, Fitzie."

"We do, huh? What's that?"

"NFL action kicks off in a couple of hours. Which game you wantin' to see?"

I lay back and answered to the ceiling, "Whatever game I can watch on my own TV, in my own house, with my own bathroom a few steps that way and my own refrigerator a few steps that way."

Bernie got up on an elbow and looked at me a moment. "The Jets it is."

Before the game started, I put a bathrobe over my gown and sneaked down to the gift shop, where I purchased a whodunnit novel. On the way to the elevator, I heard a quiet voice from behind me.

"Mr. Fitzgerald?"

I turned to find Senator McGovern's personal assistant. "Ms. Ortiz? Caroline. Hi."

She looked at me shyly.

I grabbed the lapel of my bathrobe and said, "Pardon my formal wear."

She smiled.

"What are you doing here? Visiting someone?"

"Yes." Her eyes went to the floor. "You."

That was the last response I expected. "Oh? How did you know I was here?"

"What happened last night is in the news," she said.

"Really?"

"In this morning's *Ledger*."

"Ohhh." *Of course.* I knew Mattie couldn't pass up that good a story. "There's an atrium just past the elevators, Caroline. Let's go relax there."

The atrium was small, a little corner for people to get into if they needed privacy. It had been built so that it extended into the courtyard and had glassed-in walls. A sofa and several stuffed chairs sat there with the mandatory ficus tree in a big planter.

"Are you in pain, Fitz?" Caroline asked.

"Not too bad. To what do I owe the honor of this visit?" I asked as I sat on the sofa.

Caroline dropped next to me. She looked away then back. "Coach Thorpe isn't the killer, is he?"

"No. Sure looked like it, though. For a while."

"Do you have any suspects now?" Caroline asked.

"To be honest, it's plodding along too slow to suit me. It's damn frustrating."

Caroline cleared her throat. "I'd like to help if I could."

I resituated on the sofa so that I faced her. "Excuse me?"

She thought a moment and said, "Do you mind if I tell you why I thought so much of Senator McGovern?"

"Of course not," I said and settled back on the sofa.

Caroline shifted a few times as if trying to get comfortable in her chair. "It's probably not a surprise that I'm a shy person."

"It kind of comes across."

"Which makes it odd that I'd want to get into politics. Senator McGovern told me it was a lot like someone with terrible eyesight wanting to fly fighter jets."

"Good analogy."

"He hired me right out of school. Political science at University of Florida. He'd come to speak to one of my classes. My professor had me stay after class to speak with him. I think the professor was hoping that I'd freeze up and recognize that frontline political warfare wasn't for me. And I nearly did freeze up, but Senator McGovern was so nice and open. We spoke a little, and then he took me to a coffee shop, and we talked for an hour, mainly about politics and about his job. But he asked about my history, and I told him."

Caroline stopped and waited for me to say something. I decided to play dumb. "What'd you tell him?"

Caroline looked at the floor and told me about her sad childhood and philandering father.

I leaned close. "I'm sorry you had to go through all that."

"I believed my father when he said the devil made him do bad things. And then I went on to believe my father when he turned the blame onto the women he'd preyed upon, saying they were doing the devil's work, trying to bring him down. One morning when he left the house, my mother packed a bag for her and a bag for me, and we went to stay with an aunt in Palatka. She eventually divorced my father, but by then, he had fled San Marco, and I never saw him again.

"But see, in a strange way, it worked out for me. I withdrew socially and focused all my energy on schoolwork. I was always first in my class, high school valedictorian. I got a full scholarship to University of Florida, and that's where I ended up meeting Senator McGovern."

"You must have impressed him."

"He told me he appreciated my intelligence and how I thought. He said I'd be a strong member of any political machine, that my only drawback was my shyness. He made me an offer, said he was in need of a new personal assistant. He said he'd hire me and help me with my shyness if I promised to work hard at overcoming it."

"No wonder you were fond of him."

"I learned a lot from him, and he respected my work."

"Thanks for opening up to me."

She looked me in the eyes, which I could tell was difficult for her. "Mr. Fitzgerald—Fitz—please let me help you." Her volume increased as she spoke passionately. "I'm still working at the senator's office, but there's really not much for me to do. I can visit people, ask questions, make phone calls, act as your secretary, research online. Whatever. I want to be a part of bringing down the monster who killed the senator."

I felt sorry for her. She'd been taken on as a personal assistant to a powerful man, a senator, a man she idolized. Now, she didn't know what she could do. Maybe nobody besides McGovern would see her worth and take her on. The poor kid must've felt like she was adrift at sea on a flimsy raft.

"Sure, Caroline, I'd welcome your help. Let me run down what we've found so far. Promise me you won't get mad at me, because some of it doesn't paint the senator in a good light."

"I understand," she said, her smile and her eyes reflecting her gratitude.

I listed the basics of the case, omitting a detail here and there, and finished with "I'd like to know who had access to the senator's diazepam."

"It's locked in a cabinet in his office bathroom."

"Who else besides the senator had access?" I asked.

"Only the senator, I think. Well, Mrs. Combs-McGovern at home. And she had a key for the cabinet at the office as well."

"Eddie is keeping an eye on her, but even though she and her cousin were up to no good, I don't see how it could be her," I said.

Caroline's face darkened. "I don't understand how she could do such a thing to Mitch—to try and humiliate him, all for money."

"Oh, people will do all kinds of things for money. I tell you what, Caroline, if you really want to help me, poke around and see if anyone else at the office had access to the senator's medication."

"I will. And thank you, Fitz."

Angry Nurse Ratchet met me as I got off the elevator. She escorted me back to my room, letting me know that the doctor had come to check on me when I was gone. Apparently, that was an unforgivable offense in her eyes. I settled on my bed, ignored Bernie, and opened my book. Twenty pages in, I figured out who did it and why and wanted to throw the book away. But it was either conversation with Bernie or reading, so I read to see why it was taking so long for the dimwitted private eye to solve the crime. Then I wondered if I were in a book, whether the readers would think I was a dimwit for not solving the senator's case yet.

After halftime, I feigned an interest in the game, joining Bernie when it came time to cheer. When the Jets lost, Bernie pouted, said he was taking a nap, and called the nurse to pull the privacy curtain around his bed. I turned off the TV and turned onto my side. I figured my frustration at being stuck in the hospital was actually a reflection of my frustration with the case. Almost a week had passed, and I didn't have anyone I could call a suspect. I wondered if I'd lost my mojo since leaving the San Marco PD, but maybe I was just feeling the aftermath of the diazepam.

The nurse stopped in the room and asked, "How are you feeling, Mr. Fitzgerald?"

"Nurse Ratched, can I ask you something?" I asked.

"It's Nurse Sanger, Mr. Fitzgerald."

I rolled onto my back and gazed up at the ceiling. "What would you do if you realized you were no good at your job?"

Without missing a beat, she responded, "I'd find another profession."

I asked for a pen and paper and spent some time listing other jobs I could pursue. The things I came up with didn't follow any logic: butcher, working full-time for Buddy Reid, pizza delivery, surf shop sales, bartender, Carroll Street Drawbridge tender, bait-shop sales, and if I really sucked up to Rick Forester, maybe my old friend would take me on as a hand on the *Titanic II*.

I looked over the list and groaned, "I suck," and threw the paper and pen onto the floor.

I tried to sleep, but I got Molly instead. The memory of her was more potent than any lingering effects of Valium. She was in my head like a close-up in a movie: her dark complexion, the almost Asian cast to her eyes. In my mental movie, she pushed her dark hair behind an ear and spoke. I couldn't hear what she said, but it didn't matter. I could stare at her mouth for hours. Her full lips moved sensually when she talked, erotically when she smiled, and they stopped my heart when they were open in the heat of passion.

I'd met my first wife when I was fresh out of school and wearing my new police uniform and Molly had been a business major at San Marco University.

A stalker had been plaguing female students in rental houses around the university, and she woke one night to find the man standing by her bed. She screamed, and he fled. My partner and I responded to her call, and besides her evident beauty, I could tell right away that she had an amazing intellect. The stalker was caught soon after, and I made it a point to go by and tell her myself. That turned into a date and then another, and by the third, it was a full-blown relationship.

We had nine years of marriage, nine of the happiest years of my life, and then she was gone—completely, utterly gone.

"Damn it." I turned over in my hospital bed and tried to think of anything else, but my thoughts kept returning to Molly: how she'd stopped at the liquor store to get me a bottle of rum; how her car had been in the shop and she'd borrowed my Mustang; how it was raining, and the storm picked up as she headed home. We'd lived a couple of miles southwest of San Marco, out in the country, and on a lonely stretch of road, she rounded a curve, lost control, and drove straight into a live oak. A couple of nights later, Eddie found me out there drunkenly wielding a chain saw as I tried to cut down the three-hundred-year-old tree.

"Come on, let me sleep," I whispered to God or Morpheus or even the sandman, whoever would bring me slumbering relief.

Instead, I cried on my hospital bed and blamed it on the di-azepam. Anger ignited in my breast as I recalled how the *San Marco Ledger* had gone on the warpath against me, and their first printed insinuations were that Molly had been drunk, causing her fatal one-car crash. That bottle of rum had broken, and the smell of liquor permeated the car. Once the coroner's report came out showing that Molly had no alcohol in her system, Mattie's stories in the *Ledger* began to hint at a police cover-up via the coroner's report. That was when my hatred of Mattie Castro started, but now, I knew Barry Golden was the one who'd been pulling the strings on those stories.

A new guilt merged with my old anger, guilt that I'd forgiven an enemy, Mattie Castro. "Am I betraying you, Molly? God, I hope not."

Chapter 27

I felt pretty damn good when I woke up. I lay awhile with my eyes closed and wondered how Consuela was doing. After reviewing the case in my brain, I opened my eyes, stretched, and sat up. I saw they'd put a fresh dressing on my wound while I'd slept.

"Hey there, roomie."

"Morning, Bernie."

"Man, you slept a good twelve hours. No football today. I hope you're a soap opera fan."

"Actually, I'm bequeathing the room to you." I got up, paused until a slight bit of light-headedness passed, and then opened the closet.

"They're discharging you?" Bernie asked.

"I'm discharging myself," I said, grabbing clothes and throwing them on my bed.

"You can't do that," Bernie said.

"Watch me." I started to take off my hospital gown but paused. "Watch me leave, but don't watch me strip down."

"Gotcha," Bernie said and looked out the window. "Why the big rush? You oughta kick back, enjoy it. Get to lounge around in bed, eat in bed, watch the tube in bed."

"I have to help a friend tonight." I slid on my boxers just as Nurse Sanger walked in.

"Nurse Ratched," I said in greeting.

"He's checking himself out," Bernie said. "Can he do that?"

"He can," she said through thin lips, "though it's my job to talk him out of it." While I stepped into my pants, she said, "No, don't.

Stop. You can't leave. Please wait until the doctor says you can go," with a total lack of inflection. "There, that should cover it." She picked up my T-shirt and helped me put it on.

I almost called a cab but then had a better idea and punched in a number on my phone.

"Morning, Fitz," Mattie answered. "I stopped by on my way to work, and you were sleeping like a baby, as in drooling on your pillow."

"Must have been dreaming of you. I was going to call a taxi, but I have this urge to kiss the next person who gives me a ride, and I'd rather it be you than some fat guy named Sal the cab driver."

"I'm sorry, Fitz. I'm about to go into a long, boring meeting. Anyone else you can call?"

"I can try Eddie, but do I really want to kiss him?" I had an idea. "Wait, I'll call Caroline Ortiz."

"The senator's assistant? You want to kiss her?"

"No. Not kiss her," I explained, "get a ride. She came by the hospital yesterday, said she wanted to help me with the case."

"That shy little thing? What'd you say?"

"I told her she could help. I mean, she sounded so desperate to do something. I figure I can have her chase down things that'd probably end up wasting our time."

"Still, that's very sweet of you," Mattie said.

"She'd probably feel like she was helping if she drove me to the Folly."

"Look at the time," Mattie said. "Gotta go."

I didn't have Caroline's number, so I called the senator's office, and she was in. I asked if she would come get me, and she sounded happy to do so.

"Thanks. I'm sitting out front, soaking up the rays."

When she pulled up, I got in the passenger seat of her Toyota. Checking out the car as she pulled away, I noticed that she kept it meticulous.

"Thanks again for coming to get me."

"I'm glad to. Let me give you my cell number in case you need me for anything else."

I got out my phone and programmed her in. "Got it."

She looked at me then back at the road. "I haven't found anyone who had access to the senator's diazepam."

"How are you approaching it?"

"Asking everyone if they know who might have a key."

I scratched my ear. That wasn't exactly how I would go about it, but then, I couldn't very well advise her to check everyone's key chains and try any suspect keys. "Well, keep plugging away."

We discussed the case, and I gave her a little make-work to create a file on every member of the senator's homeless initiative from what we've learned of them, what she could find about them from news archives, and from Google. Finally, she turned onto Dos Casas Lane.

"Pull up to that house, will you?" I asked, pointing at Consuela's. "It's my landlady's."

"I heard she got hurt too."

"Yeah, she's still in the hospital. I need to pick something up."

Caroline stopped in front of the house. I got out and ran around the back to Consuela's shed. I hoped she wouldn't mind if I helped myself. I got back to Caroline's car carrying a couple of gallon jugs.

Caroline asked, "What's in those?"

"My landlady's homemade rum."

We pulled up to the Folly, and I saw a welcome sight: Mattie's car parked by my truck. A second later, Mattie walked around the corner of the house.

"Mattie Castro?" Caroline said her name like a question.

"Yeah, and don't bother with making a file on her. I'll handle that one," I said.

"Why?"

I grinned at her. "I think she's my girlfriend."

We got out, the women greeted one another, and I said, "I thought you had a meeting."

"I do, but it got pushed back. I had just enough time to drive over and give you this." She handed me a folded piece of paper. "Sky made it for you."

I opened it to a crayon beach scene with a big sun, crashing waves, palm trees, and flying dolphins. Over the picture, a childish scrawl read, "GET WELL SOON."

I stared at it and felt a swell of emotion.

"Why, Mr. Fitzgerald, are you tearing up?" Mattie asked.

"Huh? No. I've got something in my eye."

"Both of them?"

I swiped at my eyes. "Allergies."

She kissed me on a cheek and said, "You're sweet."

"Thank you," I said. "Sky's only four, and she can write?"

"Not exactly. She knows some letters, and some I showed her." Mattie kissed me on the lips and said, "I have to get back." She took my hand and pulled me away from Caroline. "Excuse us a moment."

"Of course," Caroline said.

After a dozen or so feet, Mattie asked, "Want me to come over tonight? I can show you the latest from the Lingerie of the Month Club."

I wanted desperately to say yes. *Damn responsibilities.* "Aw, man, you make it hard to say no."

Mattie gaped at me like I'd just confessed to the murders. "No?"

"I'm helping out a buddy tonight," I grumbled. "I don't know how long it'll take."

"Sigh." She said the word. Then her expression turned serious. She looked back at Caroline and said, "Look, Fitz. I haven't been exactly honest about me and the senator."

I felt something like a stab of resentment. "Oh really?"

"I never got all sex-room crazy with him, but..." Mattie turned away. "We made out, okay? Maybe a little petting." She thought a moment and chuckled. "Heavy petting."

"Made out? Heavy petting? You said you guys just kissed a little."

She turned back to me. "I wasn't myself."

"And who says *heavy petting* anymore?"

"We'd been flirting, innocent flirting, after a meeting. Everyone was gone, and he did this ear thing, and the next thing I know—"

"Ear thing? What ear thing?"

"An ear-tongue thing."

My voice got shrill. "An ear-tongue thing?" I noticed Caroline turn toward us and repeated in a forced whisper, "What ear-tongue thing?"

"Wait, I'm not saying this right. See, I turned to leave, and he stepped behind me and put his arms around my waist. I was about to tell him to keep his mitts to himself when he did something with his tongue behind my left ear. The sensation was, well, amazing, and I felt like I was melting into a puddle on the floor."

"What'd he do exactly?"

"I'm not sure. He was behind me, so I only felt it. It wasn't like he licked me all slimy, but my best guess is he was flicking the tip of his tongue up and down, applying the perfect amount of pressure to the back of my ear, and the next thing you know, we're pressed together tighter than two teenagers dry humping."

"Thanks for that image," I mumbled.

"Why, Fitz, are you jealous?" Mattie asked with a wicked little smile.

"No. Maybe. Yes. It's just that at first, you said nothing happened between the two of you, then you said you only kissed, and now, we're up to this humpy grope-a-rama."

"While he was an excellent kisser and knew how to use his hands, the effect from the ear-tongue thing receded, and I insisted we stop."

"Good," I said, and after she gave me a quick kiss, I thought of something. "Hey, next time you stay over, maybe we should see if we can figure out that ear-tongue thingy."

"Mmm, it's a date," she said and started toward her car.

"Be careful. Our maniac is still out there."

"I know. My sister is letting us stay with her family until this thing is over," Mattie called to me. She waved at the senator's personal assistant. "Bye, Caroline. Good to see you."

When I walked back to Caroline, she asked, "You're a couple?"

"A couple of crazies, but yeah." I saw something in her expression that caused me to ask, "Why? Don't you like her?"

"Oh sure, it's just a surprise, the two of you in love."

"Whoa, hold the fort," I said, wagging a finger at her. "Love is a powerful word and a declaration neither of us has made."

"Sorry."

"Wait a minute." A memory came to me. "My landlady, Consuela, said something yesterday."

"What?"

"Well, she babbled a lot of nonsense, but there was one thing that made sense, something along the lines of 'Quit looking at who the senator loved, and look at who loved the senator.'"

"Meaning what?" Caroline asked.

"Well, while there was a whole lot of lusting going on, I don't think there was much in the love department."

"You mean more than physical love?"

"Yeah, I mean, from what I'd seen, none of the senator's playmates seemed to love him. Hell, even the senator's wife had fallen out of love with the guy, and considering what she and her cousin attempted, there was some hate thrown in there. No doubt, the senator was a well-respected man, but did anyone love him with a passion twisted enough to do these things?"

"I don't know," Caroline said.

"Well, that's what I want to find out."

"How?"

"I'm going to approach it like you did with your fellow employees when you asked them if they had access to the senator's drugs," I said.

"You think they'll admit it?"

"Maybe. I'll ask them flat out if they loved him and see what their reactions are, though I should wear protective head gear when I ask Margaret Stone."

"I better get to work on those files," Caroline said.

Caroline left. I showered and ate and decided to make what would probably be the most difficult visit of the day my starting point. I drove over to the church and was directed to a small office. I peeked in at Margaret Stone and seriously considered chickening out. Instead, I tapped on the door.

"Hi, Mrs. Stone."

"Geronimo Fitzgerald," she said like my name tasted bad. A few seconds of silence ticked by. "I suppose I should apologize for striking you the other day."

"No apologies necessary, though I'm sorry to say that I have something else on the sensitive side to ask you."

"I see," she said, her words icy. "Come in, then, and have a seat."

"I'll just stand here in the doorway."

She stared at me expressionlessly.

"Out of reach." I looked up and down the hall to make sure no one would hear then asked, "Mrs. Stone, did you love Senator Mc-Govern?"

If the question caught her by surprise, she hid it well. "We are taught by the Bible to love our neighbors."

"I'm not speaking of neighborly love, Mrs. Stone."

As she stared at me, I thought how Stone was a fitting name. Her eyes were hard.

"No, Mr. Fitzgerald, that kind of love did not come into our relationship. Please close the door before you leave."

I did as she asked, grateful that I wasn't leaving like I did last time, with her handprint on my cheek. I next drove to Dhalia Duchess Blackmoor's condo and put the question of love to her. She gave a joyous laugh as she told me no.

Back in my truck, I called the senator's widow to see if she knew of anyone who might have had a crush on her husband. In a clipped tone, she said she didn't. Between the iciness of her response and Margaret Stone's, I hoped I wouldn't get frostbite.

On a whim, I looked up Elizabeth Melrose's number and called. Expecting voicemail, I gave a little fist pump when she answered. I explained who I was and how I was working with Mattie. She said she was back in town and would be happy to chat, but she had a full schedule until the following night. So we agreed to meet up at her condo at eight thirty.

Chapter 28

Right hand on the steering wheel, left elbow out the open window, I navigated my truck back to Fitz's Folly. I spent the day going over my ludicrous plan to help Rick. I would have to call Eddie and arrange for backup, but I had to do it in a way that wouldn't get Rick into trouble. I thought it best to wait until the last minute before getting Eddie involved.

At twilight, I arrived at the San Marco Municipal Docks. After parking, I walked through the dock building, which included a small store, offices for the various charters and boat tours, and showers and restrooms for boaters. The door to Forester Fishing Charters was closed and locked, so I headed out to the docks. The *Titanic II* was tied up between an ecocruise pontoon boat and a steel monstrosity called the *Kraken*, a cheesy faux pirate ship that took families on cruises around the harbor while men and women in pirate costumes said things like "arghhh" and "matey," sang sea chanties, and pissed off the locals every time the Carroll Street Drawbridge had to be raised for the ship to pass through.

As I walked down the floating dock, the dock lights clicked on with a buzz. I caught sight of Rick spraying the deck with a water hose, meaning he'd been out chasing fish. His lips were pursed and his eyes narrowed, a clear indication he was in a foul mood.

"Ahoy, Captain Rick," I called, making him jump. "Permission to come aboard?"

Rick scowled as he looked at me. "What do you want, Fitz?"

"Like I told you the other afternoon at Doone's, I want to help."

"I don't want your help."

"That may be, but I'm the man to give it." I waited for permission to get on the boat then, when it didn't come, climbed aboard anyway. "Why the hell did you do a run for the Bennett brothers?"

Rick's mouth moved like he was ready to say something, but instead, he hopped off the boat, turned off the water hose, and coiled it on the dock. "I wish to hell that Ivy hadn't told you."

I shrugged.

Rick said, "I needed money fast, and it seemed easy enough."

"And now?"

"They had me run some pot." Rick sounded like he'd been exhausted by stress. "Now, they want me to run fifty pounds of meth upriver." He spat as if the words had left a bad taste on his tongue.

"Can't say I'm surprised they're cooking that poison," I said.

"Yeah."

"There could be a silver lining to this. They're so stupid they may just blow up Bennett Town."

"From your lips to God's ear," Rick said.

"Cleaning the gene pool, " I said then asked, "Who's on the receiving end of the delivery?"

Rick sighed. "The Rage."

I didn't think I could be surprised any more than Rick running drugs for the Bennett brothers, but he'd just proven me wrong. "Let me get this straight. You're tied up with the Bennett brothers running drugs to the Road Rage Motorcycle Club?"

"That's about it."

"You're not just in the shit—you're neck deep. When are the Bennetts supposed to show up?"

"Soon."

"You can't do it, Rick."

Rick got back on the boat. "I don't want to. I told them one and done. They came back a couple of weeks ago and said that they wanted me to do the meth run, and dammit, Fitz, they won't take no for an answer."

"Meaning?"

"They said they'll kill me if I don't make this run, and that includes more runs in the future."

I thought a minute and asked, "Do you remember that time in high school when we got caught using fake IDs to get into the Pagoda Lounge?"

"First time in a strip club—how could I forget?"

"Remember right before they kicked us out, they said they were turning the IDs over to the police?"

"Yeah, had our school pictures pasted on 'em. We'd have been busted for sure."

"Remember how we handled that problem?"

Rick grinned and said, "The gator."

We'd gone driving out in the country after getting the boot at the Pagoda, resigned to the fact that we would get in trouble when they handed the fake driver's licenses over to the police. The headlights on Rick's car illuminated two glowing orbs on the road in front of us that turned out to be the eyes of a four-foot alligator crossing from a retention pond to a creek. Rick got in front of it and distracted it while I jumped on its back and held its mouth shut so that Rick could wind duct tape around it. Then we wrestled it into the back seat of Rick's 1981 Chevy Malibu. The alligator tore up the seat, but we thought it was worth it when we sneaked the gator through the back door of the Pagoda, cut the tape, and released it on the dance floor. In the ensuing hubbub, we'd found our fake IDs in a box behind a counter near the front door.

Ah, good times.

"We need a creative solution like that," I said, a wide grin in place.

For the first time, Rick looked hopeful. "Agreed. Got one?"

I shrugged. "Just that we need to leave right now."

"Leave? Run away? That's your plan?"

"I know—not as sexy as the gator solution. But, Rick, you can't use your father's boat."

"It's my boat now," Rick grumbled.

I raised my voice. "That used to belong to your father and your grandfather before that. The *Titanic II* is a third-generation Forester vessel. You don't want to sully its reputation by running meth, do you?"

"Of course not," Rick said. "But they'll come after me."

"We'll handle that when the time comes. Running, however, is the first step."

Rick looked down at his worn deck shoes, thinking. Looking up at me, he nodded and started the engine while I untied the boat from the dock.

As we headed away from his rendezvous spot with the Bennett brothers, Rick asked, "Where to?"

"Let's go tie up at my dock," I said. "You can spend the night, and we'll call Eddie in the morning."

"I'm a dead man," Rick said, adding more speed.

Half an hour later, Rick sat at the blazing firepit in front of Fitz's Folly.

The night was cloudless, the stars dotted the sky, and the moon was just showing itself in the east. The smell of the river, salty and organic, filled the air, as did the sound of insects. I could also hear an outboard motor in the distance.

Rick looked miserable, so I said, "You're safe here. The *Titanic II* is tied off on my dock, and you are *not* in the company of the Bennett brothers. I'd say things are going well for you this evening."

"This evening. It's the rest of my life that I'm worried about."

I poured rum into a short glass and passed it to Rick before pouring one for myself. The drone of the boat motor got louder, and I looked over at an approaching boat, barely visible on the dark water.

"Were the Bennet brothers driving to the dock to meet you?" I asked.

Rick looked out to the water. "No, they were coming in their—oh shit."

When the boat got close enough, I asked, "How many were you expecting?"

Rick muttered, "The ones not in prison."

A voice called from the boat in a Southern drawl, "We knew this is where you'd run to, Forester. You think we're stupid or something?"

"Actually, we do!" I yelled back.

"You're not helping," Rick whispered.

"Shut up and run to the house. I'm right behind you."

Rick didn't need any coaxing and ran for the house like Usain Bolt fleeing from a hungry bear.

I pulled out my phone and called Eddie. As luck would have it, it went to voicemail. I had to wait through Eddie's message, which I judged way too long. At the sound of the beep, I launched into our predicament, speaking rapidly. "I don't have much time, buddy, but Rick and I are about to get carjacked—wait, make that boat-jacked—by the Bennett brothers. They're kidnapping us and using the *Titanic II* to run drugs up the Intracoastal. I've enabled the GPS on my phone. You can track that. You can pick us up anywhere along the river until Jacksonville. But if you wait until we make our drop, you can bust a bunch of the Road Rage as well. Gotta go." I ended the call, muted the phone, and put it somewhere warm and safe.

Their boat bumped against the dock, and I ran for the front door of the Folly, muttering, "You better check your damn voicemail, Eddie."

Once inside, I shut and locked the door. I knelt down and looked out the small window by the door.

"This is what happens whenever I put my trust in you," Rick whispered behind me.

"They've tied off and are heading this way."

"Now what?"

I stood and smiled. "While they're at the front door, we'll go out the back, get in my truck, and depart." I led Rick through the Folly, got to the back door, and held a finger to my lips as one of the brothers banged on the front door. I whispered, "You'll see. There's nothing to worry about."

I opened the back door to the business end of a sawed-off shotgun shoved into my face. "Howdy, shithead."

"Now, you can worry." I backstepped as Jermaine Bennett followed, gripping the gun in shaky hands.

Chapter 29

Tito Bennett, the eldest of the trio, held a black .45 in his hand as he followed Rick and me aboard the *Titanic II*.

"Ready to make some scratch, Rick?" Tito said, speaking in fluent redneck. He was smiling, which accentuated angular features including a hawk-beak nose. The tallest and biggest of all present, Tito was a weightlifter who undoubtedly fueled his muscle growth with steroids. He'd tied his long, greasy dark hair into a ponytail, but much of it had pulled free and hung in tangles to his shoulders. Massive arms decorated with homemade blue-ink tattoos were exposed by the sleeveless sweatshirt he wore over cutoff jeans and ratty construction boots. "Oh wait, you tried to back out of the run." He laughed, though the levity did not make it to his black eyes. "That means you don't get shit for this trip."

"Why do you need Rick?" I asked. "You have plenty of boats over in Bennett town."

Tito looked at me in such a way that I wondered if he was weighing whether to answer me or punch me. I gave a sigh of relief when Tito spoke.

"The authorities know our boats. They see us making a long-distance nighttime run, they're likely to investigate." As he spoke, Tito looked around the deck, in the wheelhouse, and went a couple of steps belowdecks to check it out. "And Mama always taught us the importance of making a good impression. Ain't none of ours this big. And though this is a floating shit pile, it makes a better impression on our buyers." Tito went to the railing and called down to his two brothers, "Bring it on up." He turned around and grinned, stuffing the pistol in the front of his pants. "And best of all, if we see a Fish and Wildlife boat heading our way or one of the sheriff's boats, we can slip over the side and swim away and let our buddy Rick handle the cops."

The other Bennetts came on board, one on each side of a large cooler. They hoisted it on deck and followed.

Jermaine was rail thin and carried the sawed-off in his other hand. "You should have seen your face when I pointed this cut-down in your face, Fitz."

"Didn't your mama ever teach you that it's not polite to point?" I asked.

The second oldest of the trio, Jermaine was twitchy, his eyes alight, and I figured he'd been tasting the product they'd cooked up. He had a white-supremacist buzz cut and prominent cheekbones that gave him a living-skull appearance. Barefoot, he wore overalls held up with one strap, with a soiled white T-shirt underneath.

"Mama taught us a lot, but not that," Jermaine answered in an accent so thick that his brother Tito sounded like Ian McKellen in comparison.

"Hello, Fitz," the third brother said in a soft voice, dropping his end of the cooler on the deck.

"Hi, Little Michael. How's it hangin'?"

"Oh, you know."

"And how's your sister?"

"Billie Jean's fine." All in all, Little Michael was a sweet kid. He probably wouldn't have ever gotten in trouble were it not for the influence of his older brothers as well as every other Bennett in Bennett town. And though he might not instigate trouble, he was dangerous because he would do anything his brothers instructed him to do, and without a thought. If Tito told Little Michael to shoot me, I had no doubt he would, but he would probably apologize first. Thin, but not as severely as Jermaine, he had an androgynous body and face, dark complexion, and black hair that shot off in all directions. He wore straight-legged jeans rolled into cuffs at his calves, high-top sneakers, and a faded black Michael Jackson concert T-shirt. And frankly, as I compared Little Michael with the Michael on the T-shirt, there was a bit of a resemblance with the famous one, somewhere at the tail end of all his facial deconstruction.

Using a booted foot, Tito opened the oversized cooler, displaying ten squares wrapped in black plastic and crisscrossed with silver duct tape and stuffed in a row. "Each of those bundles is five pounds of fresh-from-the-kitchen meth. Didn't hardly cost squat to make, and the Road Rage MC is paying eight grand a pound for uncut. We're gonna be entrepreneurs, Rick, so you better damn well get your act straight." He kicked the lid closed and told his brothers, "Take it below." He shoved Rick toward the wheelhouse. "Start 'er up. We got some miles to cover."

As Little Michael and Jermaine carried the cooler to the hatch, I clapped Tito on the shoulder and said, "Well, I know you guys have places to go and people to see, so I'll catch you on the go 'round."

I started for the dock, but Tito grabbed me by the back of the neck and squeezed.

"Ouch!"

"Fitz, I ain't decided what to do with the two of you when we're done. Keep being a smartass, and I might just feed you to the gators."

Rick warmed up the engines, and Jermaine untied the *Titanic II* from my dock.

"Let's go," Tito ordered. "Take it north at a good clip, but not too fast. Running lights and everything, all legal and aboveboard."

"Same place as last time?" Rick asked.

"Nope. The Rage don't use the same place twice in a row. You just go, and I'll tell you when to change course."

After a couple of hours skipping over the water, slowing as we cruised past more populated areas like St. Augustine, we passed a couple of closed fish camps. The night was dark, even with the moon and stars overhead.

Tito stayed mostly in the wheelhouse with Rick. He would come out now and again to stand at the bow, looking like Billy Bob Blackbeard on *Queen Annie's Revenge*. For much of the trip, Little Michael sat at the bow, his feet over the side, staring vacantly ahead. Jermaine kept making trips belowdecks and would come up again more fucked up than before. I don't know whether he was sampling from the sale merchandise or had his own, but I was getting apprehensive about such a methed-up Bennett in possession of a cut-down shotgun.

Tito went to the deck in front of the wheelhouse and pointed toward the west side of the river. "Cut in over there."

"Over where?" Rick asked.

"West side of the bank. When we get close, you'll see a creek." Tito pronounced it *crick*. "That creek widens to a river that leads to a little boat ramp. We'll tie off on a dock there."

I looked up and down the river as we crossed it. Not a single light was shining except the ones on Rick's craft. I was planning strategies in case things spiraled out of control, and the best I could come up with was to jump overboard and swim for it. Rick slowed the *Titanic II* and entered the creek. At that point, it was only wide enough for two lanes of boat traffic. It opened up into a proper river as we cruised it. Tito climbed into the wheelhouse next to Rick and turned on the spotlight and shone it off the starboard side. Up ahead was a small dock that would fit only one other smaller vessel once the *Titanic II* was tied off. A concrete boat ramp left the water toward a parking area that could accommodate only a dozen vehicles. Rick expertly cruised up, putting the engines in idle so they thrummed rhythmically. A few seconds later, the *Titanic II* gently thumped alongside the dock.

"Shut 'er down and go tie us off," Tito ordered Rick.

"I'll get it," I said and leapt to the dock. While fussing with the lines, I called up to Rick as he left the wheelhouse. "You know, Rick, as I'm tying these ropes, I can't help but think what a class act the Bennett brothers are."

"What they hell are you talking about?" Rick asked in a hushed tone, crossing the deck toward me.

Making sure I was plenty loud, I went on, "What I mean is, we aren't willing participants on this trip, right? And now they're about to enter into the most delicate part of their deal, the transaction, and here we stand free to move about."

"Shut up," Rick said in a loud whisper. "Just shut up."

I kept going. "I know what you mean, Rick. If it was me doing a deal worth hundreds of thousands, I'd tie up anyone I didn't trust until it all was over."

Tito, in the door of the wheelhouse, looked down at us. "Jermaine, find some rope and tie up these two dinguses."

A minute later, off the boat and on the dock, Jermaine was tying Rick's hands behind his back while Little Michael worked on mine.

"You're a nutjob, you know that?" Rick growled at me. "I don't know why I was ever friends with you."

"I don't know why I was friends with you. You're cranky, unforgiving, and have a temper," I said.

Jermaine cackled a lunatic laugh.

"Shut up, Jermaine," Rick and I said in unison.

Jermaine answered by slapping us both on the back of our heads, and he jumped back on the boat to huddle with his brothers. They talked among themselves for a couple of minutes, and I was unable to make out what they were saying.

"Probably talking about where to dump our bodies after this is all done," Rick said, sounding defeated.

"Aren't you little Mary Sunshine?"

From the boat, Jermaine said a little louder, "Aw, come on, I only want a little to keep me razor-sharp."

I snickered and leaned in to Rick. "Jermaine, sharp? That'll be the day."

"Don't talk to me," Rick said.

"You ain't smokin' anymore until the deal's done. You're fried enough as it is," Tito yelled. "Get down on the dock, both of you." He jumped off the boat and shoved Rick and me to the gravel parking area. "You two princesses stand here and keep your mouths shut." He turned to his brothers. "Hold your guns, but don't aim them unless they start firing first."

"I didn't bring a gun," Little Michael said. "No one told me to bring a gun."

Tito sighed and shook his head. Jermaine cackled again, the sawed-off cradled to his chest.

A loud engine filled the night air, followed by another. Light exploded from across the parking lot. Two vehicles raced in from the entrance road. One was a giant pickup truck with a light rack blazing on the roof. It braked with a crunch of gravel, its lights aimed just to the left of me, Rick, and the Bennett brothers. The other vehicle looked to be a classic Impala, mid to late sixties, and it parked so that its high beams shone just to the right of us. I looked from one vehicle to the next, noting both were painted flat black. Their powerful engines purred low and slow, like giant jungle cats. For a full minute, no one moved.

Finally, the passenger door on the Impala opened, and a man got out. He, like Tito, was barrel chested with a weight lifter's physique. To say that he was ugly was putting it kindly. Luckily, much of his face was hidden behind a beard and long hair, both gray. I guessed two things about the man: one was that he was in his fifties, and two, that he was the Jacksonville chapter president of the Rage, Billy Blade. Not his real name, but according to rumor, one well earned.

He was in full biker regalia, a do-rag on his head, a cutoff and faded jean jacket with patches all over the front and undoubtedly the club colors on the back, grease-stained jeans, and Frankenstein-like engineer boots.

"Tito," Billy called in a hoarse voice.

"Billy," Tito answered.

The driver's-side door opened, and a small biker got out, seriously small, definitely under five feet. His club brothers probably called him something like Pee Wee or Tiny or the ever- ironic Big Jim. When the little biker reached into the car and retrieved an AR-15, I vowed to make no short jokes. Two more bikers got out of the big pickup, each with an automatic pistol tucked in their waistbands.

"You bring the stuff?" Billy asked.

Tito looked at Jermaine and Little Michael and gestured with his head for the boat. They jumped on board.

"You bring the money?" Tito asked.

Billy snapped his fingers, and one of the bikers from the truck ran to the back of the Impala.

"This is awesome, like some sixties-era drive-in biker movie," I whispered.

"Shut up," Rick answered, "and maybe we'll get out of this alive."

Our whispered conversation caught Billy's attention. He looked us over and asked, "What's up with those two?"

"That one's the owner of the boat, the other's a friend of his," Tito said, pointing at us. "They got a little squirrely about making the trip."

Billy spit while eyeing us. "We'll take care of 'em if you want. For an extra pound of product next buy."

Tito seemed to consider it but ended up saying, "Nah, the captain just needs a little attitude adjustment is all. We can handle that."

The biker who went to the Impala's trunk retrieved a large black sports bag. A second later, Jermaine and Little Michael walked past

Rick and me with the large cooler. They stopped next to Tito. Billy snapped his fingers, and the biker with the sports bag unzipped it, angling it to show Tito the banded stacks of bills. Tito nodded and snapped his fingers. After a moment, he looked at Little Michael and snapped again.

Under Tito's glare, Little Michael took a step toward his big brother. "What?"

In a forceful whisper, Tito said, "Show 'em the meth, numbnuts."

"Oh," Little Michael said. He opened the lid of the cooler and leaned it forward, displaying the ten plastic and taped bundles.

Billy snapped his fingers again, and the biker passed the sports bag to Billy and took out a knife, unfolded a wicked blade, and approached the meth. Tito snapped and looked at Little Michael.

In a panicked voice, Little Michael said, "I don't know what you want."

Tito growled, "Go count the money!"

Little Michael didn't move. "But you know I ain't good at math."

"Holy fuck, am I the only one born with any smarts in this family?" Tito snarled. "Jermaine! Are you too fried to count the money?"

Jermaine used the barrel of the sawed-off to scratch the side of his head. "Well—"

"Go count the damn money!" Tito roared.

Jermaine handed the shotgun to Little Michael and started for Billy and the sports bag. The biker at the cooler knelt in front of it, using the knife to count the parcels of meth. Randomly selecting one, he made a small cut in the plastic. Jermaine, in the meantime, put the sports bag on the ground and counted banded stacks. The biker took out a little product and rubbed it between his thumb and index finger. He pulled a small glass pipe from his vest, loaded a little meth into it, and lit it. He inhaled deeply and held his breath. Exhaling, he paused a few seconds and then turned to the others with a smile and held up a thumb.

Jermaine worked at the money a couple of minutes more, stood, and said, "Looks good." He followed that with a mumbled, "I think."

The sampler spread his arms wide and grabbed both cooler handles. He lifted it like it weighed nothing and carried it to Billy Blade and put it at his feet, saying, "It's good shit."

Jermaine brought the sports bag to Tito, who gestured over his shoulder to the *Titanic II*. I watched Jermaine toss the money onto the deck, and then he went and collected his sawed-off from Little Michael.

Billy scratched at his beard and asked, "When can we get another fifty?"

"Give us a couple of weeks," Tito said. "We can have—"

Like an audio replay of the Rage's arrival, engines roared all around us. More vehicles raced into the boat ramp parking lot. The itsy-bitsy biker tossed the AR-15 over the roof of the Impala to Billy Blade, who pulled back the bolt and turned to the approaching vehicles. Like a magician, Pee Wee produced an enormous hand cannon from out of nowhere and sighted in on the new arrivals. The night was lit with the dancing headlights of several large black SUVs bouncing up the dirt road. Behind them, several squad cars raced in, light bars flashing. I wasn't sure who fired first, though I suspected Billy.

As a gunfight ensued, Tito yelled to his brothers, "Get to the boat!"

I kicked Rick's feet out from under him, and he fell. "Stay down," I told him.

The gunfire was deafening. All the muzzle flash added a strobe-light quality. SUVs and cop cars were in a semicircle facing the drug deal. Black Kevlar–covered cops fired from the cover of open doors and behind vehicles. Tito and Jermaine made for the dock. Billy Blade hunched down by the grill of the Impala. He rose and let off a burst with the AR-15. Return fire struck him, and the multiple rounds spun him like he was dancing ballet. The AR-15 flew from his grasp, and he landed face-first in the parking lot.

Little Michael ran in a circle, fully panicked. There was one tree growing out of the hard-packed dirt of the parking lot, a live oak twisted by years of wind. Little Michael ran smack into it. Instead of falling, he hugged the tree in terror.

"Shit," I mumbled, and, hands still bound behind my back, I ran toward Little Michael. I hit him in full charge, and he squealed just like the real Michael. We both went down. A second later, a number of rounds slammed into the tree, sending up a spray of splinters. Staying flat on top of Little Michael, I turned my head and saw the other two Bennett brothers looking out at the *Titanic II*. No longer tied up at the dock, it drifted twenty yards out in the river.

Little Michael started to cry, his sobs muffled under me.

"Don't worry, Little Michael," I told him. "Stay down. You'll be safe."

The gunfire died out, and I lifted my head to watch Tito drop his .45 to the dock, and Jermaine bent over to put down the sawed-off. Three officers aimed their semi-automatic rifles at them, and they raised their hands over their heads.

"In the heat of things as usual." I looked up as Eddie approached, and I rolled off of Little Michael.

"How about a little help?" I asked. As Eddie hauled me to my feet, I added, "Perfect timing."

Eddie pointed to Little Michael, and a uniform in Kevlar came and cuffed him. Eddie took out a pocket knife and started sawing at my rope. We went over and freed Rick as a detective in a bulletproof vest approached.

When the ropes were cut, Rick and I rubbed our wrists as Eddie introduced us. "This is Captain Walter Baines of Jacksonville vice. Walt, this is Rick Forester, the boat owner. The Bennetts forced him to captain the run. And this is Fitz, the gentleman who alerted me as to what was going on."

Baines shook both our hands. "A pleasure, gentlemen. We've been after the Rage for some time. This will give us all we need for a citywide raid on the club."

"You cut off the head of the snake," I said, nodding toward Billy Blade's prone form.

"Yeah, sorry he didn't live so we could nail his ass, but your guys will be icing on the cake," Baines said, indicating the Bennett brothers, who were in the process of getting cuffed. "Give me the Cliffs-Notes version of what happened."

Rick started to answer, but I put a hand to his chest and said, "I got this." I cleared my throat and said, "We've known the Bennetts for years. A bunch of criminals—we never got along with them. Anyway, they kidnapped us at my place on the Intracoastal, stole the boat, and tied us up." I looked at Rick and winked. Getting tied up should go a long way in court if they tried to say we were in on it or if they ratted out Rick for that one pot run he did.

Eddie said, "Fitz called me as the Bennett brothers were getting set to abduct them. I called you, and luckily, that far a cruise upriver took time so that you could get everything arranged on your end. Fitz kept his phone turned on so we could follow him via GPS to the site of the deal."

"Yeah, I stuffed it down the front of my pants in case they searched us," I said. "The vibrate setting can be very pleasant."

"Remind me to never borrow your phone," Eddie said.

"Good job." Baines clapped my shoulder. "We drove US 1 and A1A while following your signal."

"This is bullshit," we heard Tito yell as he and his brothers were being led to the squad cars. "Me and my brothers was just fishin'. We didn't know there was a drug deal going on when we pulled up.

Those two"—he used his chin to indicate Rick and me—"were the ones selling meth."

"Fishing with a sawed-off?" I called. "And how'd you know it was meth?"

Tito's lips moved a moment without sound, and then he shouted, "We ain't done nothing."

"Tell it to the judge," I called.

"Put those boys in the cars," Baines ordered his men. He turned to me and asked, "So where's the money for the buy?"

I pointed out to the *Titanic II* where it had drifted further into the middle of the river. "Safely stowed on that boat."

A second later, the *Titanic II* blew up with an explosive *WHOOOMPH*, accompanied by a fireball that looked like a giant orange flower reflecting on the surface of the river. Ten seconds later, pieces rained down.

Chapter 30

We hung out at the boat ramp until Baines told us, "You guys can head on back. Thanks for your statements, but I'll need you to drive up and make them official." He handed me his card.

"No problem," I said.

"Sorry about your boat," Baines said to Rick.

"My boat," Rick groaned.

"Only thing I can figure is bullets hit the fuel line or fuel pump or something, somehow started a fire, and when it reached the tank, she blew."

"I guess," Rick said.

"How much money was in play?" Baines asked.

"Tito Bennett said eight grand per pound, and they had fifty pounds, you do the math," I said. Turning to Eddie, I said, "Rick and I are worn out. How about a ride home?"

"Yeah, I'll meet you at the car in a minute."

I took Rick's arm and said, "Come on, buddy, this way."

"I can't believe the *Titanic II* is gone."

"That's oh for two for *Titanic*s. Name your next boat something else," I said.

"Next boat?"

"The *Titanic II* was insured, wasn't it?"

"Yeah, but it was over seventy years old. I could only afford to cover its actual worth. I won't get enough to buy another charter, nothing in half-ass shape, anyway."

We got to Eddie's car, and I opened the back door. Rick climbed in, moving like he was a hundred years old.

"File your claim. Maybe the city of Jacksonville is liable for some recompense seeing as your boat blew up during a police operation."

The slightest of hopes showed in Rick's eyes when he looked up at me. "You think so?"

"Not really. At least we got the Bennett brothers off your ass," I said and closed the door. I got in the front seat. "Man, I'm exhausted. How are you doing?"

When I got no response, I looked back to see Rick had fallen asleep. And no wonder. The stress leading up to tonight had built over a couple of weeks. Rick probably hadn't had a decent night's sleep since he'd heard from the Bennett brothers. I got comfortable, took a deep breath, and closed my eyes. I wanted to rest for just a minute, until Eddie got to the car.

When I woke, we were on I-95 and passing the St. Augustine Outlet Mall, meaning we were halfway home. "Sorry, I didn't mean to fall asleep."

Eddie looked over, his face lit from the dashboard. "No problem. A lot of excitement will take it out of a man."

"What time is it?" I asked.

"Almost two."

I nodded off again and woke as Eddie pulled onto Dos Casas Lane. Consuela always kept a couple of lights on overnight, a welcoming beacon on those nights I returned home late. Tonight, all her lights were out. Hopefully, she'd be discharged from the hospital soon.

Eddie pulled next to my truck. "Here you go. I'll take Rick home."

As if in answer, Rick said something in his sleep.

I looked Eddie directly in the eyes. "Thanks, Eddie. I'm not sure we'd have survived the night without your help."

Eddie grinned. "Anytime, my friend."

I got out, and he drove off. I went inside, fell on my bed, and slept deeply.

I woke just after noon to the wonderful feeling of Mattie's lips on mine.

"Am I dreaming?" I mumbled.

"Sweet dreams, baby." Mattie lay beside me. She smiled warmly, then sniffed, then wrinkled her nose. "I was just about to get frisky, but you smell."

I sniffed under my arms. "Whoa, you're right. Things got pretty intense last night."

"You can tell me about it after you shower."

I hopped out of bed and started for my bathroom. "I'll tell you about it after the friskiness."

A bit later, we lay tangled in sheets and breathed hard. I gave her a detailed rundown of the previous night's events, making sure I highlighted any heroics on my part, real or imagined.

Head propped up on her hand, Mattie said, "I can't believe you two made it out unscathed."

I stared up at the ceiling. "Frankly, I'm a little surprised too."

Mattie sat up and scooted back to sit against my headboard. "Now that that's out of the way, are you ready to focus on finding the senator's killer?"

I wiggled up to sit next to her. "Hell yeah. In fact, I've arranged to meet with the one member of the homeless initiative we haven't talked with yet."

"Elizabeth Melrose?"

"Yep. Want to join me for a visit to her condo tonight? Eight thirty?" I asked.

"Sky's preschool has an open house this evening, but yeah, I could probably drop her off at my sister's and then meet you."

"Cool." I cuddled up to her.

"Start without me if I'm late. If I can't make it, I'll call and let you know." She returned my cuddle with her own, and we were soon into round two of blissful friskiness.

Chapter 31

I gave Mattie an extra several minutes as I sat in my truck in the condominium parking lot. At 8:36, I got out and went to knock on Elizabeth Melrose's door.

"Thanks for seeing me," I said as she invited me into her first-floor, beachfront condo.

"Thank you for trying to find the person responsible for the deaths of Mitch and Ronnie." She may have been elderly, but her speech was precise and energetic. She was a small woman, ninety pounds max, I thought. But inner strength was evident in her bright, cognizant eyes. She had the short gray-haired poodle-do that many her age sported, and though her face and hands exhibited the wrinkles one expected of a person her age, I also saw youthful vitality in the way she moved.

I looked around her condo that was located in the Brisas del Mar complex, probably the most luxurious and expensive in San Marco. "Nice digs, Ms. Melrose." And they were. It may have been a condo, but it was expansive and furnished with items she'd picked up in her round-the-world journeys.

"Thank you, Mr. Fitzgerald." She guided me to a sofa, and it felt like I was sitting on a cloud. "I used to live in a home near the McGoverns, but I found it was better to downsize the older I got. I'll turn ninety years old in six weeks, and believe me, I'm so much happier without having to deal with stairs."

"If you don't mind my saying, you don't seem eighty-nine."

"I attribute that to genetics. My parents and their parents all lived into their nineties, and my grandmother made it to one hundred and six. I also practice yoga, though a tamer version." She sat next to me and added, "And I credit one Jameson's whiskey and bitters every evening before bedtime. Speaking of which, can I interest you in one?"

"If it wouldn't be too much trouble."

"Two shakes of a lamb's tail," she said and went into the kitchen.

A few minutes later, she emerged with two whiskey glasses with two fingers of Jameson in each. She handed me one and then settled on the other end of the sofa.

"I understand you've been traveling," I said.

"Yes, I was in Scotland as part of the homeless initiative. BAE Systems Maritime expressed an interest in placing a shipbuilding plant in San Marco."

I looked at the clock on the opposite wall. Mattie was almost a quarter-hour late. As if on cue, my cell phone's ringtone chirped. "Excuse me." I pulled the phone to see it was Mattie calling, no doubt to let me know she couldn't make it. I hit the ignore button. I'd get back to her once I was done speaking with Ms. Melrose. "I heard Northrup Grumman and Hyundai are considering putting a plant here too."

She nodded her head slowly. "It would be a shame if Mitch's initiative ended before it got started." She turned to me, and I could see a firm resolve in her eyes. "I don't plan on letting that happen." She took a sip of Jameson, and I noticed a slight tremble in her hand. She turned to face me more directly. "What can I do for you, Mr. Fitzgerald?"

I started to tell her to call me Fitz, but it just didn't seem right with her. "I am approaching the case from a direction that has to do with the senator's homeless initiative."

"I personally don't see how that could come into play, but then, I'm not an investigator. How does it link to two murders?"

"I've found a connection. The first thing I learned was that a photograph of the board was used to assault the senator as he was tied up."

"That photo?" Elizabeth pointed to a nearby wall. She had the same photo hung amid other photographs.

"That's the one. Further investigations revealed that some on the board had been fooling around with the senator."

"I suspected as much. As one ages, one gets more observant."

"And it seems that everyone on the board who engaged in a little senatorial philandering has received threatening texts, including Ronnie Thorpe, who got four before she was murdered."

Elizabeth shook her head before saying, "I understand her husband is in custody for the crime."

"That's right, but it's doubtful he's the culprit. Those texts are still being sent even though he's locked up. You haven't received any, have you?"

"No, I haven't, but then I'm past the age for hanky-panky."

"Here's the thing. Both murders seemed to be fueled by rage and passion. I know McGovern was fooling around, but it doesn't seem anyone he messed with had enough emotional baggage to account for these crimes." I got up and stood in front of the photo. "I really felt the homeless initiative board was key."

"Perhaps the board isn't the place to look," she said.

"You're probably right." I stared at the photo and spoke more to myself than to her. "Though I was sure one of you in this picture would lead me to the reward."

"Is that why you're investigating, Mr. Fitzgerald? The reward?"

"Well, I'm also doing it for the senator and for justice. But, yeah, mainly the reward."

She laughed at my honesty and looked back to the picture. "I should point out that that's not the entire board in that photo."

I quickly returned to the sofa and sat.

She went on. "There's one more member, but she was taking the photograph, so she's not in the picture."

I almost heard the clacking and clunking as things started to click into place. "Caroline?"

"Yes. Senator McGovern's personal assistant."

"She was a member of the homeless initiative board?"

"I assumed so. She was at each meeting and acted as secretary, recording the minutes of the meetings, that kind of thing." She stopped to think and said, "On the other hand, she may have just been there as Mitch's assistant."

I took a moment to digest this information. Trying not to sound excited, I asked, "As an observer, would you say that she and the senator...?"

"Oh no, I seriously don't think so. I imagine Mitch's dalliances were with women who could keep it hush-hush. When you start seducing young members of your staff, you're opening yourself to trouble that could kill a career."

"A lot of politicians aren't that smart," I said.

"Mitch was. Plus, I think he liked a challenge. Caroline would be like shooting fish in a barrel."

Okay, maybe no sex, but I thought there could be another plausible angle. "She had him perched high on a pedestal, didn't she?"

"Well, she admired him greatly." She smiled at a memory. "She followed him around like a puppy."

I stared to see her reaction. "Or like a daddy's girl?"

She blinked twice and then returned my gaze. "Yes, very much so."

Chapter 32

I sat in my truck in the parking lot for a good ten minutes, thinking about whether Caroline could have committed both crimes. As the senator's personal assistant, I'd bet dollars to donuts that she had access to his diazepam. To suffocate the senator in that fashion would require so much violence, not to mention rage. Having witnessed her anger when someone spoke ill of the senator, she certainly had the passion evident in the murder. Ronnie had been drugged, stripped, beaten, and killed. There was that intense anger again. Why the texts? Had she somehow seen herself or the senator as being wronged by these women? I was no psychiatrist, but even I could see how it all might fit in with her tormented childhood. What emotional and psychological damage had her father's scandal caused to an impressionable young girl?

I nodded as I sat in the dark. I felt that I had the answer.

I started the truck and then noticed that it had been drizzling while I'd been thinking. I remembered I needed to call Mattie and pulled out my phone. There was a voicemail from the aforementioned beauty, and I hit play.

She sounded excited. "I was on my way to our meet when I got a call. Lucinda wants us to swing by. She thinks she may know who the killer is, and if she's right, it's someone on the staff. I'm heading over there now. Come by when you've finished with Elizabeth. That reward is almost ours, loverboy."

The message ended, and I grinned stupidly at my loverboy nickname. I put the truck in drive and started for the McGovern mansion. That was where old-money homes were located, as part of Flagler Plantations. It wasn't a long drive, but I had to slow considerably when an explosive flash of lightning kicked off a raging storm.

"I need new wipers," I mumbled as I leaned forward to peer through the storm-battered windshield.

My thoughts turned to the case and Lucinda. *Why hadn't she called the police?* Maybe it was because she knew Mattie fairly well. Maybe she wanted to get our opinion first. Whatever, it was a stroke of luck that she reached out to us first.

Another fifteen minutes of slow going in the raging storm and I turned in next to Mattie's car parked at the end of the driveway. I pulled in a little farther and saw the driveway gate was closed, but a pedestrian gate next to it was open. Not very welcoming, Lucinda. I'd be drenched before I got five steps. Oh well, that was why I got paid the mediocre bucks plus expenses and, hopefully, half a reward.

I opened the truck door and jumped into the deluge. As I jogged for the gate, I mentally told myself that when I finally got around to new wipers for the truck, I'd also invest in a good umbrella. Initially, I thought I couldn't see much because of the rain, but as I approached the mansion and still couldn't see it, I realized that no lights were on, which probably meant they lost power in the storm. Two successive lightning strikes illuminated the mansion, which was closer than I thought. It could have made a good joke: *A man runs into a mansion. I'll bet that hurt.* At the steps leading up to the front door, the thunder rolled. I looked up at the entrance, which was the size of a castle portcullis. The door was made of heavy oak, stained dark.

I reached to the doorbell, an ornate gold fixture that protruded and ended with an ivory button. There was no sound when I pressed it.

"Oh yeah, power outage."

I squeezed my hand into a tight fist and banged on the door. I'd intended to do so repeatedly, but on the first strike, the door swung open a couple of inches.

I pushed it open far enough that I could lean in. "Hello?"

The inside of the home was impenetrable darkness. Another blast of lightning gave me a quick glimpse of the foyer. Not as furnished as the foyer of their beachfront residence, it resembled a room from *Downton Abbey*. Twin staircases from the second-floor landing curved down on either side to the foyer floor.

I stepped fully inside. "Lucinda?" I called loudly. "Mattie? It's Fitz."

I tried a light switch, and as expected, it didn't work. I envisioned Mattie and Lucinda sitting in a candlelit room in the depths of the house, reviewing whatever Lucinda had found that pointed to the killer being a member of the senator's staff, i.e., Caroline Ortiz.

I shivered in my wet clothes. Though the power was out, it hadn't been for long because it was still cool enough to know the air conditioning had recently been running. When I found the women, I'd ask Lucinda if I could borrow some dry clothes, but for now, I'd have to slog through the house, leaving puddles wherever I went.

I walked to the base of the twin stairs and called, "Mattie? Lucinda? Hello?" I'd expected an echo in a house that big, but my voice was muted the moment it left my mouth. This was getting creepy. "Mattie!" I shouted louder, but it garnered the same empty results.

I pulled out my phone and hit the flashlight function. I held it out to the stairs and then to the hallway past them, trying to decide which way to go. I figured upstairs was mainly bedrooms, while downstairs, there would be a parlor, living room, den, dining room, kitchen, and the like. So it seemed probable they'd be in one of the downstairs rooms. I'd taken a few steps down the hall when I heard a noise from above: a thump and three soft taps. Fresh waves of a chill that had nothing to do with wet clothes ran across my flesh, from the top of my head to the pit of my stomach. The night I'd been attacked at the Folly, before I'd been drugged, I'd heard the same thing.

I didn't expect an answer, but I called, "Hello?" I waited a few heartbeats and added, "Fuck this," and started upstairs.

I took the right-side staircase, my shoes squishing with each step. As I approached the next level of gloom, my instincts chimed in and told me to turn tail and run. But that wasn't going to happen. Mattie had received those threatening texts, and she was somewhere in this mansion.

My heart pounded as I ran up the remaining few stairs. "Mattie!" My voice quivered.

On the landing, I held the phone out to the right and saw the start of a hallway. There was another in front of me and another to the left. Three hallways leading from the landing—the house was too damn big.

From the center hallway, I heard something that caused goose bumps to rise on my flesh. It repeated, sounding like a high-pitched moan, or maybe a cry from behind a gag. Thinking the worst, I hurried to the hallway, traversed it only ten feet, and saw something cowering against a wall.

"Monty?" I got on my knees. "Here, boy, c'mere, Monty. You remember me, don't you?"

Lucinda's dog crept toward me, tail tucked, avoiding a direct gaze. He was terrified. When he got within smelling range, he perked up at my scent, wagged his tail twice, and ran up and leaped into my arms.

"Hey, buddy, what's..." I shined my light on him. Some of his fur had blood on it. "Are you hurt, Monty?" I looked him over. The blood wasn't his. I went to a nearby room and opened the door to a guest room. "Don't worry, I'll come back for you." I put Monty down and shut the door.

I started back the way I'd come. There was a scream, fierce and feral. A dark form rushed past me and turned right at the second-floor landing.

"What the hell?"

A second later, a line of fire burned my right arm. I took the phone in my left hand, held it over the pain, and saw a deep slash above the bandage on my already damaged arm. When the blood started to flow, I realized this was an even worse cut than the one I'd received at the Folly.

Fear turned to panic, and I wanted to flee. Then the fact that I'd just got cut again transformed that panic into anger. Gritting my teeth, I charged to the landing and into the dark hallway after my attacker, phone held out in front.

I came to a closed door and slowed, but Caroline wouldn't have had enough time to open a door, go in, and close it again before I got there, so I continued to run and passed another closed door on the opposite wall and then another. When I came to an open door, I stopped. I had to fight the urge to charge in. I chewed on my lips as I made myself wait ten seconds, thirty, a full minute while listening. I took a moment to scan my wounded arm. There was too much blood. I held up the phone to the door and used my other hand to push it fully open. The inadequate light on my phone failed to illuminate anything other than a cavernous room. I cautiously entered, sweeping the phone back and forth, and when I felt a moment's vulnerability at my back, I whipped around. No one was there.

Following along a wall, I came to a dresser that seemed as long as the main bar at Doone's Fish Camp. I selected a drawer at random and opened it. It figured that I'd go right to the panty drawer, stocked with silk and cotton and lace. I shined the phone light along the top of the dresser, past perfumes and lotions, and stopped at a large jewelry box. Reflections glittered when I opened it. I took a piece of jewelry out and then another. The real deal, it was Lucinda's stuff, which would put me in the master bedroom.

I turned and swept the phone back and forth. I took a couple of steps forward. A couple of more steps and I found the bed. I had an idea, and focusing my attention on sound, listening for the slightest movement, I followed the right side of the bed to a bedside table. I pulled the drawer open, producing a squeak that made me jump.

I shined my light in and whispered, "Bingo," and pulled out a small metallic flashlight.

When I turned it on, it seemed a high-powered spotlight compared to what I'd been using. I pocketed my cell phone and moved the flashlight beam to the right, taking in a lamp, a painting, and a door that opened into the master bath. An open closet door was on the next wall and a settee next to it. I continued my circuitous route with the flashlight, ending up back at the bed.

"Oh shit!" I'd been standing next to Lucinda and hadn't known it. She was naked, beaten, tied to the bed, and dead.

Chapter 33

Like her cousin's, Lucinda's throat had been cut, leaving a gaping wound. Blood had flowed from her neck to soak the pillow and sheets under her. I did my best to ignore the nausea in my belly. I inspected Lucinda's body; rigor mortis had set in, and she was room temperature. I pushed her up enough to note the lividity in her back. All that and the tackiness of her blood indicated Lucinda had been dead for hours. I thought back to Mattie's message. She said she'd gotten a call that Lucinda found something. But Lucinda was already dead by that time.

I brought up voicemail and listened to Mattie's message again, "I was on my way to our meet when I got a call. Lucinda wants us to swing by." Mattie hadn't said who'd called but that she'd received a call and Lucinda wanted to meet with us. Had Caroline called, saying she was calling for Lucinda?

A stinging pain pierced my lower back. I instinctively spun, sweeping my arm, and I connected with something solid. There was a grunt of pain. A shadowed figure ran to the bedroom door, stopping to look back just as I lifted my flashlight. Caroline Ortiz glared back at me. Her lips pulled from her teeth like a junkyard dog's. And then she disappeared into the hallway.

I shouted after her, "I knew it was you!" I twisted around and shined the light on a hypodermic needle stuck in my flesh just above my right kidney. "Really? Again?" I pulled at the syringe, snapping the needle so that half of it remained in my back. "Son of a bitch."

I held the hypodermic in front of the flashlight, seeing a good bit of diazepam in the barrel. So I didn't get the whole dose. But how much did I get? I heard Caroline knock something over in the distance and lifted the flashlight. The beam split into twin shafts of light. Instantly dizzy, I dropped the needle.

"Aw man," I said with a yawn and stumbled to the left and fell back, sitting on the bed. That was better. Once I was off my feet, my head stopped listing. I took several deep breaths, trying to fight the desire to lie back and close my eyes. I noticed something in my peripheral vision, looked down, and recognized Lucinda's arm next to me as it stretched to a bedpost. My scream came out like a gargle, and I leapt off the bed. The momentum carried me across the room and straight through the open door, into the closet, and finally into a wall. I tried shaking the cobwebs from my head, and saw that I was sitting on the floor, the flashlight by my hand. Tangled in clothes and clothes hangers, I took some time to work myself free. The idea was to stand and go after Caroline, but I noticed how comfortable I was sitting on the floor amid a chaos of high-priced fashion. Maybe if I fell asleep in here, Caroline wouldn't find me. I was so damn sleepy that it seemed a risk worth taking.

Mattie.

Her name shone in my mind like it was on a freshly polished brass plaque out in the noonday sun. Mattie was here too. I'd seen her car, had heard her voicemail. I had to get my ass up and find Mattie before she ended up like Lucinda—if I wasn't already too late. Grabbing the flashlight with my left hand and reaching to built-in shoe shelves, I started to pull myself up but landed on my ass again. I saw blood on the shelving and the shoes I'd pulled down. I'd bled so much that my hand was covered, and I'd slipped. I stretched my wounded arm and winced. After wiping my hand on one of Lucinda's dresses, I tried again and succeeded.

Swaying slightly, I took stock of my condition. Messed up, yeah, but at least I knew where I was and the basics of what was happening, though I would win no awards for keen deductive reasoning. Basically, my head felt as if it was floating three or four feet above my shoulders. Still, when I thought about it, I wasn't much worse off than those nights when I'd consumed too much rum. And dammit, I could function admirably when drunk.

I needed to focus and figure out my objectives. First thing was to find Mattie, and the second was for us to get out of the house. Simple enough. If I was attacked again, my priority would change to defeating Caroline and then finding Mattie. But wait; there was something else to take into consideration, something that had been drummed into me in my years on the police force. If heading into danger, wait for backup. There wasn't time to wait, but that didn't mean I couldn't arrange for backup. I pulled out my phone and squinted, trying to focus long enough to find Eddie on my contacts list. When I pressed Call, I left the closet and crossed the master bedroom, exiting into the hall.

"Hello," Eddie mumbled.

I attempted to say, *I need help, buddy*, but what came out was more like, "I nee' he'p buh-ee."

"Fitz, is that you?"

I pursed my lips in and out several times and then repeatedly opened and closed my mouth, finally saying, though slowly, "I nee' you hel—help." I made sure to tack on the *p* in *help* and saw spittle fly.

"Drunk again? I'm going to sleep, Fitz."

"Wai'!" I screamed and slowed my delivery even more. "Been—drugged—again."

"What? Where are you?" He didn't sound sleepy anymore.

"McGo'ern's. Not beach – Fla'ler Plan'ation."

"I'm on my way."

I dropped the phone and started in the direction I thought that Caroline had taken. The damn flashlight felt like it weighed twenty pounds, and I had a hard time keeping it up and steady. Time and distance melted into things with no meaning. To me, it was just a matter of continuing to trek down hallways, open doors, and peer into rooms. I would keep at it until I found Mattie or Caroline or until Eddie arrived.

I turned a corner as a phantom stepped from a room and froze.

"'Ello, Car'line," I said. "Now I know wh' you so eager to he'p wi' the case."

Standing next to a large portrait in a heavy frame of one of the McGovern ancestors, Caroline breathed hard enough that her shoulders rose and fell. Her hair was down, and she wore all black. One hand gripped the knife I'd first seen the night she attacked me at the Folly.

"I figured you had the best chance of figuring it out, so I wanted to stay close to you," she said. "You've helped me quite a bit, Fitz."

"Oh?"

"That night at your little house, I'd gone by Mattie Castro's home, but she was gone. Luckily, she left a note on the kitchen table. And then when I spoke with Senator McGovern's wife when you and Detective Schmitt brought her in for questioning. You'd be out of the way, and I could kill her at your place."

I tried to deliver a skeptical "Pfffft" but just sprayed spittle. "Yeah, how'd tha' work fo' you?"

"It didn't then." Caroline, meek little personal assistant, smiled in an evil fashion that scared me. "But it will now."

"Di' the storm knock ou' power, or did you kill the breakers?"

She looked around at the surrounding darkness and giggled. "It worked so well at your place I decided to do it again here. Mattie walked right in. She didn't suspect a thing."

Trying to put all the jigsaw pieces in place, I asked, "Why sen' tex... texts? We'd pro'ly still think it ha' been Mack if you hadn't."

"Because I wanted them to suffer. When I killed Ronnie and Lucinda, when I kill the rest, they won't see it coming. They'll be drugged. The texts let them know what was coming, so they could feel the damnation of what they wrought."

"You called her, di'n't you? Sai' you were callin' for Lucinda?"

"I did."

"I's over, Car'line. The police—on their way. I called 'em."

Caroline shook her head violently. "It won't be over until I kill each and every one of those sluts. Those harlots, those strumpets are the ones responsible for everything."

"Respon'ble for wha'?"

Her voice shook with rage. "For teasing and tempting him, for making him do things that were sick and immoral, for killing him."

"Uhhh, pretty su'e you killed him."

Caroline's big eyes burned. "Not me, all those sluts on his board."

"Why kill Lu'inda? She wa' his wife."

"She let it happen. She encouraged her cousin to rut with him."

I took a step closer. "You loved him, di'n't you?"

"Yes. And he loved me too."

"Di' you sleep wi' him?"

"No," she snapped, and then her voice turned hoarse. "I told him once, when we were alone. I told him we could." She looked down, took a breath, and then her gaze snapped up to me again. "He said no. He said we were perfect the way we were. *Perfect*." She savored the word. "He said no because he loved me."

I shrugged. "Or he sai' no 'cause he knew you had a crush on him and it woul' lead to pro'lems. No, Caroline, he scratched his itch with women he knew wouldn't make trouble."

Her face contorted into a hideous mask of fury. "Lies!"

"Yeah, wha' abou' his sex room?"

"That was the bitch's," she growled, pointing past me, where Lucinda lay dead.

"Car'line, come on. He liked to screw aroun', you got juh... jealous and killed him," I said as I took another step closer.

"They made him do the things he did. The harlots, the strumpets, the sluts. He didn't want to. It made him sick, it made him angry, I knew."

"Di' he tell you tha'?"

"He didn't have to. I'd seen it before." Her free hand opened and closed into a tight fist.

"Your father? An' it ma'e you mad?"

"Yes."

"So mad tha' when it happened again with a father figure—a second father—you killed him."

Her fist slowly opened. "Out of love."

"Love? Aw, come on, Car'line. Even as drugged as I am, I know tha's fucked up."

"It's true," she shrieked and then panted heavily before going on. "When I found him that morning, when I saw him tied up and beat up and naked, when I saw that room and knew what had gone on the night before—yes, I was mad. I'd gone to help him prepare for the press conference, and then, then, I was furious. I wandered the house, trying to calm down, to make sense of everything. Without realizing it, I went into his office and saw that picture. I took it off the wall and stared at it. I knew what Ronnie wanted from him, all of them. That photograph embodies both good and evil. The good that the senator and I, along with Jillian and Elizabeth Melrose, were bringing about with the homeless initiative and the evil of the harlots and strumpets on his board. They didn't care about the initiative, they didn't care about the homeless, they only cared about getting close to the senator, to drag him into their beds, to use their bodies to pervert him." She went rigid, and her eyes snapped shut. She took a deep breath and took up where she left off. "I carried the picture upstairs with me and set it on the bed beside him. He looked at me, his eyes begging me to free him. His gaze infuriated me, so I got a blindfold from that sex wardrobe and tied it over his eyes. It didn't help, I got angrier, so I started to leave, but something made me go back and—"

"An' in a rage, you killed him."

"I hit him."

"Wi' the framed pi'ture?" I asked and took another step. I was only six feet from her.

"Yes," she sobbed. A few tears escaped her eyes. She wiped at them, and a gentle smile appeared. "But after that, I was no longer mad."

"Then why kill 'im?"

"I was on him, kneeling over him, and even though he had on a blindfold and a gag, I knew what he wanted."

"Wha' di' he want, Car'line?"

"My father wanted me to release him, to save him, to end the pain."

"Your father?"

She blinked rapidly. "I didn't say that."

"Wha' pain?"

"The pain of having to do the things the harlots made him do." Her voice turned into that of a child on the verge of tears. "Daddy wanted me to put him out of his misery."

"You can't be serious."

In that little-girl persona, she said, "And I did. I put my thumbs up Daddy's nose, and he couldn't breathe."

I opened my mouth to say something, but for the first time in probably forever, I was at a loss for words.

The child version of Caroline shifted back to scary Caroline. "I freed him."

I said, reminding her, "The police are comin.'"

"It'll take them time to get here in the storm." Her eyes shifted down, and then she smiled. "Did you tell them I was the killer?"

I blinked. Thinking back to the call, I'd been a lot groggier then, but no, I didn't think I told Eddie. "O' course," I lied.

Caroline chuckled, not believing me.

"Wha' do you have planned?"

"I'm going to kill Dhalia and Margaret and you…"

My heart sank. If Caroline hadn't included Mattie in her list, did that mean she was dead too?

Caroline pointed in the room behind her. "And that strumpet."

I stumbled forward and reached for her. She ran and vanished down the hall. I went into the room, swinging the flashlight back and forth. Mattie lay on a brass rail bed. Scarves bound her spread eagle and naked on the mattress. She'd been beaten, and one of her eyes was swelling, though both were closed.

"Please, oh please," I said and put my index and middle fingers to her neck, exhaling when I felt a pulse. I shook her. "Mattie?" She didn't respond, and I knew that she was having her own diazepam encounter.

I shined my light around. We were in a guest bedroom that was still three times the size of my bedroom at the Folly. The only other door opened to a closet. I went to check and make sure it didn't have a door at the other end, and then I went out into the hall, closed the bedroom door, and stood sentinel. Legs spread and arms crossed, I faced the direction I'd seen Caroline run. She wasn't getting past me. I'd make sure that Mattie was safe until Eddie arrived with backup.

I heard running steps. Uncrossing my arms, I bent low, preparing for the attack. When she screamed, it was too late to turn around. While I'd been in the room with Mattie, Caroline had snuck by the door and down the hall in the other direction. Her knife sliced me across my left ribcage. The force of the attack caused my drug-muddied body to spin. Equilibrium gone, I dropped to a knee. She shrieked, and I saw her coming back. I stood as she ran at me. I dropped my flashlight and threw out a fist. It connected with her face, and she twisted out of control. Her momentum carried her past me. Falling, she landed in a crouch. The beam from my fallen flashlight illuminated her as she rose into a football lineman's crouch. She still gripped the knife. She held it under her chin and pointed at me. Red trailed from her mouth, yet she smiled. Her tongue pushed past her lips and licked at the blood. And then she rushed me. I reached for her and missed. Her knife opened up a stripe of fire along my stomach. I groaned and put both hands over the wound. She flew by again, and I felt the track of her knife across my back, slashing from underneath my right shoulder blade to my left waist. I shouted in pain and fell against the wall. I grabbed at the big framed portrait and kept on my feet.

The bitch, fueled by rage, was whittling me down with each pass. Back and forth with her knife in a rhythm of insanity.

Rhythm?

I looked up at the portrait then grasped it by the frame while lifting it from its hook. The thing was heavy and solid. With my blood quickly leaking away, I wouldn't be strong enough to hold it much longer. I paused, hoping to time it perfectly. Her scream erupted, followed by charging footsteps. I swung the heavy frame like Babe Ruth. She was silenced as the picture frame smashed into her.

Ignoring my varied agonies, I scrambled for the flashlight. On hands and knees, I shined it at Caroline. She was on her back and unconscious. I'd swung in the dark but got a lucky hit, catching her square in the face. Looking closer, I saw that I'd broken her jaw.

The adrenaline pumping through me was doing its job, and I barely felt drugged, which, on the flipside, meant I felt all my wounds. Deciding to play it safe, I rolled Caroline onto her stomach without regard to further injuring her and used my belt to bind her hands behind her back.

"How about that, Caroline," I said to her unconscious body. "You hit the senator with a framed picture, and I just paid you back. Ha! Ouch!" My laugh brought on pain.

I climbed the wall to get to my feet and started to check my wounds but stopped. I didn't really want to see the damage. I used the flashlight to find her knife, went into the bedroom, and cut Mattie free. Though I wanted so badly to lie down, I first went to get Monty and returned with him in my arms. Monty and I lay on the bed beside Mattie and waited for Eddie.

Chapter 34

We sat at the bar at Doone's Fish Camp after lunch and before happy hour, so not many people were there. From left to right, it was Sky, me, Mattie, and Rick. Monty sat on the floor by Sky's stool. He had a long leash that ran up and attached to Sky's wrist. Monty's hero worship of me ended the moment he met Sky. He was now totally devoted to his new master.

"You two look like you ran into Floyd Mayweather and insulted his mother," Skipper said, addressing Mattie and me.

"No argument there," I answered. "But at least our boat didn't blow up like Rick's."

"Shut up, Fitz," Rick grumbled, staring straight ahead.

I wore an orange-and-white-striped tank top, the bandages underneath making bulges down my back, along my ribs, and across my stomach. The dressings on my arm extended from wrist to shoulder, and the doctor, wanting to restrain the arm, had me wearing a sling.

"How you like the Shirley Temple, angel?" Skipper asked Sky.

"It's good," she said.

"Want some more French fries?" Skipper asked, indicating the empty plate smeared with ketchup in front of her.

"No, thank you."

Skipper bent down until he was eye level with Sky. "Anything you want is on the house."

Sky looked up at the ceiling and pointed at it. "You mean I have to climb up there to get it?"

Skipper walked away laughing.

I took a swallow of beer and said, "You should have seen Nurse Ratched's face when she walked in and saw me in the hospital bed. Almost made the injuries worth it."

"She asked me if you were responsible for all this." Mattie pointed to her face. Her left eye sported a rainbow of black, blue, purple, and yellow, and both it and her right cheek were still swollen. "She said she'd get the police there lickety-split and have you arrested for domestic abuse. I was tempted."

"Tempted?"

"If you were out of the way long enough, I could claim the reward all to myself."

"If you'd done that, you'd have missed the big payoff," I said with a wink.

"True that," she replied.

"What the hell are you talking about?" Rick asked.

"Watch the language," I said in a sing-songy voice, tilting my head toward Sky.

"Sorry. So, what are you talking about?"

"Nothing. Just lovebird stuff." I laid my head on Mattie's shoulder. "At least we have each other."

"How's Consuela?" Mattie asked.

"She's good, but when she got home, she threw away all the painkillers they gave her."

"Tough ol' bird," Rick said.

"She's treating her pain with doses of homemade rum and runs the risk of embalming herself." I leaned past Mattie to ask Rick, "How are things going with you and your girlfriend?"

Rick glared at me. "I told you. She dumped me after the *Titanic II* blew up."

"Oh yeah. Said she needed a man who brought in a steady income."

"Shut up, Fitz."

I got up and took my beer to the stool on the other side of Rick. "If she's going to be like that, she's not worth it. Look on the bright side, Rick; the senator's killer has been caught, Mattie and I will get the reward, you no longer have to worry about the Bennett brothers, and your boat blew up."

"Shut up, Fitz."

"Seriously, though." I held up my glass. "To the *Titanic II*." We toasted the lost vessel and then had to do it again so Sky could join us. I said, "That was a crazy night."

"That was a fu..." Rick looked at Sky. "That was a messed-up night."

"Actually." I cast an eye to Rick. "Everything went according to plan."

Rick's entire body twitched. He slowly turned to me. "What do you mean by that?"

"Skipper," Mattie called. "Doubles neat of your best rum, for all of us." While the bartender filled the short glasses, Mattie said, "Let's go where we won't be heard."

"By that, she means, let's go where you won't make a scene," I told Rick.

"Skipper, can you look after Sky and Monty for a few minutes?" Mattie asked.

"Can I? It would be my honor." He bent down to Sky and said, "How would you like to learn how to make a Sazerac?"

"No, thank you," Sky answered.

"How about a Singapore sling?"

"Yes, please!"

Mattie, Rick, and I went out back to the deck overlooking the docks, Rick trailing close behind, saying, "What do you mean *fill me in* and *make a scene?*"

"Just come on," I said. "And don't spill the rum." The day was hot, and we were all in shorts and sandals. We sat at a high-top shaded by a royal palm. I took a sip. "Ahhh, the nectar of the tropical gods." There were smaller fishing boats tied to the dock, but at the very end was a large red-and-white vessel in the fifty-foot range. "Maybe with your insurance, you can get something like that." I pointed at the big charter.

"In my dreams. Even used, a nice boat like that is way outta my range." Rick drained his glass in one gulp and slammed it on the table. "Tell me what's going on."

"Fine," I said, taking another sip. "You and I weren't alone with the Bennetts on the *Titanic II*."

"What? Who else was there?"

"Buddy Reid."

"Buddy? What are you talking about? Tito looked all over the *Titanic II* when he got on."

"Knowing I could convince you to leave before the Bennetts got to the San Marco Marina and hide out at the Folly, I had Buddy wait for us there. He snuck on with a few items and hid where you keep the life vests stowed."

"Under the bench seats?"

"Yes. I can't tell you too much of his history, but before he came to San Marco, Buddy had a clandestine career getting into places that were supposed to be locked, and sometimes, that included squeezing into small spaces."

"Tell Rick what he did," Mattie said.

"Buddy stayed hidden until we got to the boat ramp. Little Michael and Jermaine brought up the cooler of meth, after which Buddy got out, put on swim fins, dive mask and snorkel, and a BCD." A BCD was a buoyancy control device, a vest that inflated and deflated, helping with a diver's buoyancy. "While the Bennetts and the Road Rage were talking, he slipped over the far side into the river. Remember how I tied off the *Titanic II*?"

Rick had dropped his head in his hands and mumbled, "Not really, but I'll take your word."

"I tied it off with a slipknot. Buddy waited until Jermaine put the money onboard, and he pulled the line, freeing the *Titanic II*, swam between the boat and the dock, and pushed it off. When his job was done, he swam out to the Intracoastal and inflated his BCD, and the current carried him down to one of the little fish camps, where he'd stashed a car earlier in the day." I went to stand by Rick and threw my left arm around Rick's shoulders. "And that's how I saved Rick Forester from running drugs for the Bennett brothers."

Rick jumped to his feet and faced me. "Which I wouldn't be able to do anyway since my boat blew up."

"But you got insurance, right?" I backed up a step. "How much did you get?"

"Sixty thousand and some change." Rick spoke through clenched teeth.

"Well, there you go." I pointed at the red and white boat at the end of the dock. "What would something like that go for used?"

Rick looked out at it and back to me. "Quarter million used, at least."

"Whoa, really? Guess I shouldn't tell you why the *Titanic II* really blew up."

Rick made a noise that I interpreted as inquisitive as he closed the distance between us.

"I forgot to mention everything that Buddy did. Among the items he brought on board were two gallons of rum that Consuela makes in her still." I backed up to the steps that led down from the deck to the dock and nimbly went down. Rick followed and then Mattie with an amused grin.

"Rum?"

"Well, that's what Consuela calls it. I prefer calling it highly combustible flammable liquid."

"Flammable?"

Rick continued a stiff yet steady walk, while I matched him as I backed up along the dock. "Buddy has some experience with explosives, getting into stubborn safes and the like. Think of the rum as detonator caps and your fuel tank as dynamite. He lit a slow fuse before he went over the side."

Rick's face turned a shade of red and then neared purple. "Slow fuse?"

"Anyway, the timing couldn't have been any better: ka-boom, right on cue."

Rick's mouth moved several seconds before he could find the words. Rick started with a choked whisper and ended with a shout, "You blew up my boat!"

I put both index fingers in front of my lips. "Shhhh, Rick, keep it down. I had to get you out of a jam, and believe me, it was all for the best."

Rick bellowed and charged. I screamed like a little girl and ran. Down near the end of the dock, Rick tackled me and forced me onto my back.

"I'm injured, I'm injured," I shouted, pointing at my slinged arm.

"You blew up my boat?" Rick straddled my chest and lifted a fist.

I marveled that this was pretty much the same location and same position we were in when this whole thing started. "Wait, look, look!" I used my good hand to point at the red-and-white boat.

Rick looked up and growled, "Look at what?"

"The name of the boat."

"Huh?" Rick said and froze.

I pushed him off, and we both got to our knees and knelt side by side.

"She's a beaut, isn't she?" I said, throwing my good arm over his shoulder.

Rick stared at the name painted on the bow. "*Titanic III?*"

"What are the odds that three vessels named *Titanic* meet a tragic end?"

"What is—I don't—What did...?"

I stood and said, "I forgot to mention that Buddy also climbed back on to the boat to get the drug money before he made his buoyant getaway."

"You blew up my boat?"

"It had to be done. A sacrifice had to be made. If the police think the money went up with the boat, they won't be looking for it."

Rick's voice dropped to a fierce whisper. "You blew up my boat?"

"On purpose." I pointed at the *Titanic III*. "So that we could get you a newer and bigger boat. This'll go a long way in fixing your charter business." I leaned into him, my hand next to my mouth as if imparting a secret. "And if the IRS gets nosy, tell them you bought it with a combination of your insurance and a loan from Buddy Reid of Buddy Reid Security Systems. He's cooked up some bogus paperwork to prove the fictional loan. You'll find your copies on board your new boat." Grinning, I added, "And don't worry about paying me for my services."

"Paying you?"

"Yeah, I deducted my fee from the leftover drug money."

"Fee?"

"And Buddy's fee."

"Buddy's fee?"

Mattie stepped beside me, and I put my good arm around her waist. "Mattie and I thought you'd want us to take what was left of the drug money and use it to help those less fortunate."

"Huh?"

"We made a donation in your name to the late senator's homeless initiative," Mattie said and then kissed Rick's cheek. "As a member of the homeless initiative board, I'd like to thank you for your generous donation."

Rick's voice reduced to a squeak. "My generous donation?" He looked back and forth between Mattie and me and then turned. He walked dazedly to the end of the dock, untied the *Titanic III*'s lines, and climbed aboard. A minute later, the engine started.

I pulled Mattie close and sighed happily as we looked at the beautiful vessel. "All's well that ends well."

"You think he likes his new boat?"

"Rick's like a kid on Christmas morning right now."

The timbre of the idling changed, and the boat began to pull away. Rick stepped from the wheelhouse, stared long and hard at me, shook his head, and went back in. The engine revved as the boat headed down the Intracoastal.

Mattie lifted her arm to check her watch. "It's been fun, but I have to take Sky to my sister's and get to a meeting."

I pulled her in for a kiss.

"Nice lip work," she said. "You are definitely a lover and not a fighter."

"What? I could have taken Rick, but I went easy on him because he's a friend."

She patted my cheek. "Uh-huh. Keep telling yourself that. Good thing I don't want a fighter."

I thought on that a second and smiled. "You're right, I'm a lover. A quality lover."

"You're a quality lover all right." She gave me a wink and started up the dock. I watched her depart. When she got to the end, she turned and said, "You're almost as good as the senator."

She was gone by the time the shock wore off.

About the Author

Andrew Nance is a writer, actor, and amateur historian. Besides writing murder mysteries for adults, he pens horror aimed at middle grade and young adult readers. Andrew lives in St. Augustine, Florida, upon which the fictional town of San Marco is based.

Scott Abrams is a writer, teacher, woodworker, and proud father and husband. After more than thirty years of acting and improv comedy, he's using his unique storytelling style to focus on writing.

He is the screenwriter of *Coffee with a Madman,* an award-winning short film presented at the Southeast Regional Film Festival. He also wrote and directed a critically acclaimed stage production based on the founding of St. Augustine, Florida, and has other works in development.

Scott lives in Western Pennsylvania with his wife and three children.

About the Publisher

Dear Reader,

We hope you enjoyed this book. Please consider leaving a review on your favorite book site.

Visit https://RedAdeptPublishing.com to see our entire catalogue.

Check out our app for short stories, articles, and interviews. You'll also be notified of future releases and special sales.